12-18

Secret Scouts and The Lost Leonardo

Watch the official

Secret Scouts book trailer

www.SecretScouts.com

secretScouts

AND
THE LOST LEONARDO
—
PART 1

Dennis Kind and Wendel Kind

Mokum Media

that the angel, unlike everything else in the painting, does not show up on the x-ray. It is completely invisible.

The Lost Leonardo

Approximately 500 years ago, Leonardo da Vinci was commissioned to create the largest artwork of his life in the Palazzo Vecchio, Florence's town hall. It was said to be the most beautiful wall mural ever painted, but today another artist's mural stands in its place. Legend has it that there is a mysterious Da Vinci masterpiece hidden behind it. This could be true, because in March 2012 professor Maurizio Seracini and a team of experts found traces of *The Lost Leonardo* hidden behind a double wall in the very same spot where Da Vinci's artwork should have been. However, further investigation has been prohibited by the Italian authorities.

The forbidden island

The plague was a horrible disease that once caused the death of millions of people. In Italy, their solution for preventing the plague from spreading from person to person was to banish the sick – or anyone who looked sick – to a small abandoned island off the coast of Venice called Poveglia. More than 160,000 victims of the plague eventually died on the island. Hundreds of years later, between 1922 and 1968, when the island housed a mental asylum, a psychopathic doctor tortured and butchered to death many of his patients. Legend has it that the spirits of the dead continue to roam the island. It has been forbidden to step foot on Poveglia since 1968.

How it all began

Tuesday, June 17th, early afternoon

Ignoring the traffic, Lisa ran across Lantern Lane towards a hole in the neighbor's broken-down fence.

A few seconds later, Sophie took off after her. "Lisa, slow down, give it to me! She gave it to us both!"

Lisa had to duck to squeeze through the hole. Following a well-trodden path, she ran through the overgrown yard on the old sawmill property. She came to an abrupt stop, however, when Sophie's best friend Jack suddenly appeared out of nowhere and grabbed her arm. "I heard Sophie screaming inside the house. What's going on?"

Lisa tried to break free but couldn't.

"What's that you're carrying?" he asked. "A painting?"

Jack was almost two years older and more than a head taller. He stretched up to his full height, trying to make himself look taller still.

Sophie came running around the corner and made a beeline for her little sister. Lisa managed to wiggle out of Jack's grasp and gave her sister an indignant look.

"Give it to me." Sophie grabbed hold of the frame.

Lisa tried to resist, her knuckles turning white, but Sophie was too strong. Lisa kept her eyes firmly on the sketch. The frame had become slightly crooked from all their tugging. "Oh, great! You broke it. Now we'll have to glue it back together, otherwise the sketch will fall out and it won't be worth a cent."

"Hey! Would someone like to tell me what's going on here?" Jack asked.

"It's just some painting crusty old Prattle gave us," Sophie said.

"Not true! It's a really old sketch! You didn't even like it. You wanted to throw it in the trash right away, that means it's mine!" Lisa looked like she could spit fire.

"Hmm, are you guys seriously arguing about that thing? What is it? Let me see!"

Sophie took a few steps backwards and held it above her head as if it were a gold medal she had just won at the Olympics.

"Come on, you're making a fuss about nothing. What are you going to do with it? Come on, man." Jack tried to look as disinterested as possible. "Just give that thing back to your sister. Then we can go watch a movie." He gave Sophie a playful nudge.

Sophie reluctantly handed the sketch back to her sister. "Here, I didn't like it anyway."

Lisa grabbed the sketch with both hands and smiled triumphantly. "Thanks sis! Just wait and see. You'll change your tune when this sketch turns out to be really old. One hundred, two hundred..." Lisa pretended to count out a big pile of cash with her fingers.

Feeling very satisfied with herself, Lisa was walking towards the gate when she heard Tom yell. She turned around and saw him running towards her. He was a little bit smaller and more heavy-set than his brother Jack, but he could run just as fast. He wore a frayed pair of jeans and a T-shirt with a skateboard logo. His wispy, light brown hair was plastered against his forehead.

As soon as he reached her, Lisa quickly told him about the sketch. "Sophie and I went to old Mrs. Prattle's this afternoon, you know, the old lady who lives above Sprinkles Bakery. She's always waving to us in that sweet way of hers. Today she waved so enthusiastically when we cycled by that we had no choice but to stop and say hello! We were only in the door when she suddenly produced this sketch and started telling us a long story about how it belonged to our house." Lisa rolled her eyes. "Seriously, she just kept babbling on and on. We've already been living here for a few years, so how come she only produced it now?"

"Maybe she's got dementia? She's really old you know. What did she tell you?" Tom asked, curious.

"Well... do you have a minute?" Lisa joked. "It's a weird story... listen: apparently a professor Kwakkelstein once lived in the farmhouse we now live in. Just before he died he gave this sketch to a neighbor called Mr. Brown, whom he made solemnly swear that when the time came he would give it to the farmhouse's new residents."

"Why?" Tom asked.

"Well, she didn't tell us that, Mr. Nosey... but Mr. Brown passed away before anyone moved into the farmhouse and so, before he died, he gave the sketch to Mrs. Prattle. And then she also had to swear she'd give it to the new residents once they moved in. But at the time, our house was apparently so run-down that Mrs. Prattle had given up all hope of anyone ever moving in, so she hung it on her wall and then completely forgot about it! Until now. Prattle told us that she somehow suddenly remembered this incident today... and so here we are, with a homesick sketch." Lisa grinned at her own joke.

Tom stared into the distance. "Interesting," he murmured.

13

"I always thought she was a bit strange. I mean, she has an ermine as a pet, doesn't she?"

"Yeah, haha, that's true! She even told us that her ermine has been missing since this morning. Well, Mrs. Prattle's getting on in years. She's probably just talking nonsense, I think. I mean, really? It belongs in our home? She must be losing her marbles." Lisa lifted a finger to her temple and made a circling motion. "But anyway... I think it's nice she gave it to us... and hey, if she says it belongs to our house... who am I to disagree?" she winked at her friend.

"Can I see it?" Tom asked, even more curious now.

"Yeah, sure, here it is." She held the sketch up triumphantly in front of his face. "Whatever gibberish Prattle told us, I'm certain it's worth something! My father once showed me a book in his study that had a bunch of drawings that looked just like this one."

Tom studied the artwork carefully. The wooden frame was nothing special and didn't look very old. The clean shiny glass looked normal, too. The sketch was held in place by a cream-colored passe-partout that was slightly larger than the sketch itself. The paper was covered in yellow-brown spots and the edges were torn. The rust-colored ink had faded and was almost invisible in some places. The spidery handwriting with its crazy curly-cues looked like some kind of secret code. There were also little drawings scattered among the text.

"Look Lisa, these figures could be human characters... and the rest, I don't know. Hard to make sense of it. I think Sophie was right, this is just old junk."

Lisa scrutinized the sketch up close. She hadn't noticed the figures before, and she tried hard to identify the other drawings, too.

14

"Maybe it's an old treasure map... or a secret letter. Like in the movies, where it leads us to the gold," Tom suggested enthusiastically.

Lisa laughed at him. "Don't be stupid. This is not going to lead us to a pile of gold. Do you think there were pirates living in Mrs. Prattle's house before her or something? I'm sure it's a genuine piece of art... from a long time ago... you know, really old stuff... it could be worth a lot of money!"

Lisa and Tom were so caught up in their conversation that they hadn't noticed Sophie and Jack walking over to them.

"I heard everything," Sophie said, crossing her arms and standing with her feet spread wide apart.

"You really think that this garbage is worth something?

"Yep, 100%," Lisa answered confidently.

Sophie sighed and changed her tone. "Okay, then I have an idea. We'll stop arguing and sell the sketch... and then split the winnings."

The word 'winnings' instantly attracted Jack's attention. "You could buy me a scooter! Pleeaasse?" He leaned back dramatically, made the sound of an accelerating scooter, and revved an imaginary throttle with his right hand.

"That seems like a fair deal," Tom added eagerly.

Lisa wasn't convinced. "Hmm, dunno... anyway, we need to find out how much it's worth first. I'm not going to sell it to the first person I meet."

"Fine," said Sophie. "Let's find out right now. Where's that book you mentioned?"

"In Dad's study," Lisa replied. She was clearly excited by this sudden distraction from their otherwise fairly normal lives and more than happy to take the lead.

Bursting with renewed energy, they crossed the street and headed up the long gravel driveway.

"After you." Lisa made a deep theatrical bow when she opened the kitchen door.

They threw their jackets and backpacks on the table and followed Lisa into the study.

The room resembled a library. Covering the wall from floor to ceiling was a huge bookcase with thick, dark brown wooden shelves containing thousands of books and a couple of antique knickknacks.

The ceiling was off-white with decorative elements in the corners that had been restored to their former glory during renovation work a few years back. The room was their father's pride and joy.

The walls were nearly twelve feet high. To be able to reach the highest books, each wall was fitted with a narrow mobile ladder that slid along rails attached to the top shelves.

In the back of the room stood a large, ornate, dark brown desk, on top of which sat a gold-colored reading lamp with a green glass shade. A Plexiglas paperweight containing a death's-head moth held a loosely stacked pile of papers in place.

Sophie flipped a switch on the wall, turning on the large and impressive chandelier.

They were almost never allowed into the study unaccompanied. It wasn't exactly forbidden, but it was pretty clear that their father didn't appreciate their nosing around in here. Besides, they didn't like the room anyway. All those old books with their musty smell, the weird stuffed animals, and the strange-looking paraphernalia everywhere didn't exactly make for a festive atmosphere.

This afternoon, however, things were different. They had a mission. Especially Lisa, who, after placing Mrs. Prattle's sketch on the desk, was very serious about searching the room meticulously. She wanted to prove she was right, and she immediately began studying the books carefully. She moved methodically from shelf to shelf, from top to bottom and from left to right. With her hands down by her side and head pointed upwards, she studied the spines on the highest bookshelves, looking for something recognizable. Her dark blond curls fell past her waist and, completely focused and with her lips pouting slightly, she looked even more like a doll than she usually did.

Tom didn't really know what to do or where to begin. He stood by helplessly with a bemused look on his face.

Bored, Jack paced back and forth across the room until he suddenly called out to Sophie.

"Sophie, check this out!" He pointed to the skeleton of a large bird on the second highest shelf in the bookcase behind the desk. The shelf above the bird had been removed to create more space for it. It was roughly 3 feet tall.

Sophie came and stood next to him. "That's a dodo," she said. "A present for my father from his crazy friend Hans."

"Wow, that's totally cool," Jack exclaimed. "Can we take it down?"

"Preferably not. It's really rare. The dodo is extinct now, so if we break it we can't buy a new one."

"Yeah, sure. You always assume the worst," said Jack, brushing aside Sophie's concern.

"Wow, let me see that skeleton!" Tom said. "Get over here Jack and stand next to the desk. If I sit on your shoulders, I might be able to reach it."

Sophie sighed disapprovingly. "Don't break anything okay, my Dad will kill us!"

Tom nodded reassuringly and climbed up on Jack's shoulders. Jack stepped forward and Tom stretched as far out as he could to take the Dodo down from the shelf.

"Ow, my back!" Jack screamed in pain, trying quickly to step back to the desk. Tom teetered dangerously forward and lost his balance. He veered left in an attempt to avoid the dodo, and both he and Jack stumbled towards the far corner of the bookcase.

Lisa looked up, startled. She saw Jack and Tom falling over next to the bookcase. Tom made a last ditch effort to grab hold of one of the ladder rails, but at that very moment the bookcase seemed to slide away from him. A loud creaking noise reverberated around the room and the bookcase shifted about 5 inches to one side.

"The bookcase... oh no, the bookcase is ruined," Sophie said, gasping.

"Ooooww, I think I've broken every bone in my body," wailed Jack, who was sprawled on the wooden floor. From where he was lying, all he could see was Lisa staring wide-eyed at the wall behind him. For a few seconds the room was completely quiet. No one dared say anything, until Tom broke the silence.

"Behind you, drama queen! Look!" he called to Jack, pointing to the bookcase.

Lisa was staring breathlessly in the same direction.

Jack pulled himself up and slowly turned his head.

"Seriously, look!" shouted Tom. "Behind you! The bookcase... there's a hidden room behind the bookcase!"

Tuesday, June 17th, late afternoon

Sophie didn't hear a word Tom was saying. Mesmerized, she used her right hand to trace the edge of the part of the bookshelf that hadn't moved. Her knees were trembling. "Wow," she stammered. Her mouth had gone dry. "The edge..." She slowly ran her hand along the bookcase. "The edge of the bookcase is still intact. Nothing's damaged," she murmured, speaking more to herself than to the others.

Lisa stared at the bookcase as if her feet were nailed to the floor. Her gaze didn't stray, even for a second. Time seemed to stand still.

"There's a room behind the bookcase. A secret room!" Tom repeated loudly, while jumping up and down with excitement.

Hearing Tom's hollering, Sophie finally came to her senses. She could hardly believe her eyes. There was a gap. Part of the bookcase seemed to have shifted a bit to the left and into the wall, creating a narrow opening. The space behind the bookcase was pitch black.

"A secret room in our house?" muttered Sophie.

"That's what I said!" Tom yelled, still jumping up and down. "We just discovered an awesome secret room! Yeehaaw!" Tom threw his hands in the air. He felt like a pioneer, an explorer, an adventurer!

"Look at that," said Sophie, pointing down. There was a dark shiny strip on the floor where the bookcase had just been.

"It looks like some kind of rail," Tom said without waiting for a reaction. "That means there are probably wheels underneath this section of the bookcase." Pointing to the part of the bookcase that had rolled away, he dropped to his knees. Leaning forward and with his cheek pressed against the floor, he tried to look underneath.

"Weird, I don't see anything... maybe the wheels retract into the bookcase so that you can't see them?" When he stood back up a tuft of dust was clinging to his chin. Under normal circumstances Lisa wouldn't have found this very funny, but now she began to giggle uncontrollably. Sophie looked at her sister and started to laugh out loud, too.

"Who would have thought you could have so much fun with Tom the Garden Gnome," Lisa said, tears of laughter welling up in her eyes. That got Tom and Jack laughing, too.

Sophie was the first one to regain her composure. "Guys, this is all very funny but we have to clean up the mess before my dad finds out we damaged his bookcase." She gave her sister a look of urgency and then directed the same gaze at Jack and Tom. "Seriously, if my father sees this he'll be so angry he won't let me go on the school trip to Venice."

"Hang on, I want to know what's back there!" Lisa said firmly. "We have enough time before Mom and Dad get home. If we're quick about it, there'll be nothing to worry about!"

Sophie hesitated for a second, but eventually agreed. "Fine," she said, turning towards the bookcase. "Let's have a quick look and then try to slide it back into place."

"The gap is still too small, we won't fit through," said Tom, who had stuck his arm through the gap to feel around behind. "If we can slide it open just a few more inches, we'll be able to squeeze through." He carefully pushed against the part of the bookcase that had already moved. When that didn't work he leaned against it with all his weight, but still nothing happened.

"Come on Jack, help me out here."

Jack used the bookcase as a crutch and pushed himself up off the ground. He tried to ignore the pain and walked over to where his little brother was standing. Together they pushed as hard as they could.

At first it seemed like nothing was going to happen, but then the bookcase suddenly began to shift. Accompanied by lots of loud cracking and squeaking, it suddenly moved a little bit more. They all leaped back in surprise.

"I think there's something on the rails. The bookcase seems to be resisting our pushing," said Jack.

The gap had widened to about eight inches. Sophie squeezed her head through to see what was hidden behind the bookcase. "I still can't see anything. It's too dark. The opening needs to be bigger."

"Can't you fit through sideways?" Tom asked.

"You want to try?" Sophie answered as if stung by a wasp. She gave Tom a withering look.

Tom shrugged his shoulders and made a face. "Come on Sophie," he said teasing her. "Just turn your body sideways, you'll fit easily."

"Yeah right, you're crazy. If I don't know what's in there, I'm not going in. I know what you guys are like. Once I slip through you'll shut the bookcase and leave me in the dark with all those spiders and God only knows what else. No way, you can do it yourself!"

"Come on Tom, stop pestering Sophie when you don't even dare go in there yourself," said Jack admonishingly.

"Listen," said Lisa, "you two are always acting so tough about everything, but now you want Sophie to go in first? A real pair of superheroes... NOT! So, which one of you is going to volunteer to go in?" She looked both of them straight in the eye, but neither one budged. "Thought so! Well Sophie's right, first we need to make the opening bigger. Come on then, what are you waiting for?"

They all lined up again, ready to push. "Okay, I'll count to three and then give it everything you've got! One, two, THREE!" Lisa shouted.

The four of them pushed as hard as they could. More loud cracking and squeaking filled the room. The bookcase seemed to wobble slightly for a second, and then there was a sharp cracking noise. A long, thin piece of wood shot out from underneath the bookcase and came to rest on the other side of the room.

"What was that?" Jack asked, his voice a little shaky.

"It looks like a paintbrush," Tom said. "Maybe that was what was stuck under the wheels and was jamming the bookcase."

"Whatever!" cried Lisa, "no time to chat. Keep pushing. COME ON!" she urged.

They all pushed as if their lives depended on it and eventually heard a short, dull rolling sound and a soft cracking noise. It felt like the bookcase had rolled over a last piece of wood on the rails, because it suddenly began to slide away into the wall. The gap was now a two-foot-wide opening.

Lisa gave the brothers a steely-eyed look and pointed towards the dark space. "You first."

Tom elbowed his brother. "Go on, you're the oldest."

Jack stepped reluctantly through the opening, with Tom close behind him.

Sophie and Lisa tried to follow the brothers' progress, but it was so dark all they could make out was their shadows.

"Ouch! I bumped into something!"

"What?" they heard Tom ask.

"A wall, I think, or a board. Something hard anyway."

"Hey!" Tom whispered to the sisters from the dark. "We can't see a thing in here. We need a flashlight. Can you get your phone Sophie?"

"It's still in my backpack in the kitchen!" Sophie replied.

"Give me a second," Lisa said. She went to her father's desk and opened one drawer after another, rummaging through a few of them. "Here, this will do!" She grabbed something from the top drawer and showed it triumphantly to her sister. It was a richly decorated, gold-plated lighter imprinted with a catacomb relief and gruesome-looking skulls in the middle of each archway.

"What's that?" Sophie said, appalled.

"Relax, it's only a lighter. Dad bought it in Antwerp last week. He wanted to show it to both of us, but you were too busy studying... as usual." She flipped open the lid of the lighter and gave the wheel a flick with her thumb. A spark shot up from the flint, igniting a flame. It hung in the air for a few seconds before quickly dimming into a small flame. With the lighter in hand, Lisa stepped into the dark room.

Sophie quickly grabbed the sketch from the desk and followed her sister.

"That lighter is like *really* useful," Tom said cynically.

"Yeah, all we can see is you. Your head, I mean," Jack added.

Lisa began goofing around by making funny faces in the flickering light.

Sophie ignored their banter, set the sketch against the wall, and ran to the kitchen to grab her phone.

"I've got it!" she said when she got back to the secret room. With trembling hands she quickly tapped the screen. FLASH! Sophie's telephone instantly shot a bright beam across the room.

"Aah, my eyes," cried Tom, theatrically covering his face with his hands.

"COOL! What's that?" his brother asked excitedly.

"Flashlight Extreme," Sophie said with a smile on her face. "Recently downloaded it. Nice, isn't it?"

"Very cool," Jack said, trying to hide his frustration that he couldn't afford a phone like that.

Sophie put her phone down on the floor so that it lit up the entire space.

"Look at all of this crazy stuff," whispered Lisa as she took in the room. "There!" She pointed to a long wall opposite the opening. "Nearly the whole wall is covered by a gigantic painting, or whatever it is."

"I'm not sure what kind of paintings you've come across in your lifetime, but to me that's just an empty canvas with a frame around it." Jack said.

"Look, there! In the corner on the floor, next to the opening. There's a pile of artist's stuff. That's where the paintbrush on the rails came from!" Tom said.

Everyone stared at the artist's materials on the floor.

"What's that over there on the ground?" Sophie asked.

"A skippy ball!" joked Tom.

Sophie reached down and tilted her phone to illuminate the floor and everything on it.

"Awesome! It's a giant globe," Jack said.

"And next to it? There, back in the corner, what's that?"

Jack looked at the gadget Tom was pointing to. "It's some kind of... actually, I haven't got a clue," Jack said. "That's a pretty odd-looking device. It has all these little spheres attached to it. Shine your light over here Sophie."

"Hey guys!" Lisa walked quickly over to the wall next to the opening. "Voila!" She flicked a switch on the wall, turning on a light hanging from the ceiling.

The others spontaneously began clapping and cheering.

Everyone then suddenly went quiet, as if realizing they were making too much noise. All four looked around in amazement. The burning light bulb lit up the whole room. It was an elongated space, as wide as their father's study and about 6 feet deep, but without any windows. A thick layer of dust covered everything. An enormous canvas with a beautifully ornate wooden frame hung on the back wall. The canvas was about sixteen feet long and almost thirteen feet high. It just barely fit in the room.

"How did they ever get that thing in here? And I mean, seriously, did they run out of paint or something?" asked Tom, staring at the white canvas.

Lisa walked over to him, standing so close to the canvas that her nose nearly touched it. She studied the surface in detail and let her fingers slide slowly over the fabric. "It's a painting alright, but it's been painted over white, the entire canvas."

"Oh," said Tom, sounding uninterested. "Probably not happy with the result."

Lisa looked at her sister, but Sophie and Jack were crouching in front of the strange device with the small spheres. It consisted of a flat, long wooden chest, which looked extremely well preserved. Attached to the top, and sticking out of the middle of the chest, was a metal tube, eight inches long and one inch wide, topped with a sphere. At the bottom of the tube, just above the chest, was a series of metal rods that extended out horizontally on all sides. Each rod was bent ninety degrees vertically, with a sphere sitting on top. The spheres and the rods were all different sizes and lengths.

There were latches on the top right- and left-hand sides of the chest. Jack used his finger to carefully lift up the right latch, but it was empty inside. He closed it and opened the one on the left. "What the heck is that?" he asked Sophie.

They were staring at a glass vial in the chest. It was sealed with a cork and held a clear liquid.

"It looks like water." Jack had already picked up the vial and was shaking it vigorously.

"Are you nuts? Put it down! For all we know it could be poison or hydrochloric acid!"

He reluctantly returned the bottle to the chest, closed the latch and then flicked one of the balls with his fingers, causing it to spin around on its own axis. "They look like planets!"

"Yeah, I think it's some sort of device that shows the earth and all the other planets. Cool."

Lisa was watching her sister and Jack from across the room when Tom suddenly shouted: "Check this out!" He was holding up a dusty old book.

"What's that?" Lisa asked, obviously excited by this new layer of intrigue.

Sophie went over to look, too. "Show it to me." She stuck out her hand and Tom handed over the book. She held it carefully and walked back out to her father's study.

"What are you doing?" Jack asked curiously.

"I want to have a better look in the light," Sophie said, picking up her phone from the floor on her way out.

"I'm coming with you," Jack said quickly.

"Well, actually, we should all get out of here and put the bookcase back before my parents get home." Sophie said. She set the book down on her father's desk, stuck her head through the opening of the secret room and clicked her fingers to make sure Tom and Lisa were following.

Standing side by side, Lisa, Tom and Jack bent over the desk to inspect their find.

"It looks like a really old book," Jack whispered.

"Okay... that's enough," Sophie's hand shot between Tom and Jack and slammed the book shut. "Not now! You seem to have forgotten that we have to get out of here before my dad gets home. We can study the book later. First, let's get that bookcase back where it belongs!"

"Sorry, you're right. Tom, give me a hand," Jack said decisively.

The brothers stood next to each other, each grabbing hold of a shelf in the bookcase.

"One, two, three!" They pulled as hard as they could and the bookcase slid smoothly back into place without any cracking or squeaking. Having expected more resistance, the boys tumbled back into the study, their arms waving wildly in a frantic attempt to keep their balance.

The bookcase looked as if it had never been moved in the first place.

Sophie carefully ran her fingers along the exact spot where the two parts came together. "Wow! That's really weird, you don't see a thing."

Lisa also gave the bookcase a thorough inspection. "Yeah, *really* weird. I don't see anything either." Relieved, she picked up the book and handed it to Sophie. "Let's get out of here now so Dad won't suspect a thing!"

Tom took a quick look around. Apart from the piece of paintbrush he had picked up from the floor, there was no further evidence of their discovery. He used his sleeve to wipe some dust off the desk, turned the lamp off, and followed the others into the kitchen. They looked around nervously, as if they were afraid that someone would catch them red-handed at the very last moment.

"This is all really bizarre. What now?" Tom asked, breaking the silence.

"We'll go back tomorrow!" Lisa said confidently.

"I'm going to hide the book in my room right now so Dad and Mom won't find it... Oh no!" Sophie said suddenly. "We forgot Prattle's sketch."

"So what? Nobody's going to miss that thing, we'll get it tomorrow," Lisa said.

"Well, I'm out of here. See ya!" Tom punched Lisa softly on the shoulder.

"Bye," said Lisa, as she walked out of the kitchen and towards the stairs.

"No one is to breathe a word about this to anyone, okay?!" Sophie warned the others. "This is our secret!"

"I'm not an idiot!" Lisa shouted from the stairs.

"What are you doing this evening?" Jack quietly asked Sophie.

"What do you think? I'm going to dive into that book with Lisa."

"Awesome. I'm very curious too. But I've got to go; my

dad will be home any minute. See you tomorrow. Bye." Jack sprinted out the door after his brother.

A few seconds later, Sophie heard the crunch of gravel as a car pulled into the driveway. She quickly ran up the stairs to her room with the old book under her arm.

"Psst, Sophie... Hey," whispered Lisa, trying to grab her sister's attention in the next room.

Sophie went to her sister's room and pushed open the door. Lisa was sitting comfortably on her bed with her back against the wall balancing her laptop on her knees.

"Show me the book, I'll Google it and see if I can find anything that resembles it. What do you think it is?"

Sophie sat down next to her and put the book on her lap. Then the two of them gave it a thorough inspection. The book was bound in thick, stiff leather. In the middle of the cover hung a piece of leather in the shape of a loop. The book's back flap tapered into a triangle, with a horn button at the tip.

"You can open and close it like this." Sophie demonstrated to her sister how the knot at the back slipped through the loop on the cover. Sophie looked in disgust at the dust on her fingertips. "Did you know that dust consists mostly of dead skin cells? Gross, right?"

Lisa shrugged and carefully inspected the cover. "This is going nowhere," she muttered. "No name, no title, nothing." She pointed to some marks in the bottom left-hand corner of the cover. "What's that? Is there something written there?"

Sophie studied the marks up close and ran her finger over the leather. "L... D... or wait, maybe it's an O? The D or the O is a bit smaller, I'm not sure. Then a V..."

"LDV or LOV?" Lisa asked. "Open the book and see what's inside."

Sophie loosened the knot. The pages were smudged with dark patches and had gone yellow in color. The text was in dark red, almost brown ink. Sophie ran her finger over the pages as she turned them one by one. Everything was handwritten, with drawings scattered here and there. Sometimes the sketches appeared in between the text, and sometimes they covered the entire page.

"The text looks like it's mirrored," Lisa said.

"Yeah, but even when I try to read it in reverse I don't understand a thing," Sophie said.

"Here, this drawing. It looks like your iPhone. Old school style!"

Sophie had to laugh at her sister's joke.

"Wait, go back a bit." Sophie turned back a few pages and pointed. "Then this must be my green backpack!"

They both cracked up.

"Seriously Lisa," Sophie took a deep breath. "This book is probably centuries old, so that's definitely not an iPhone. But what else could it be?"

"A Samsung?" suggested Lisa.

"That's enough." Sophie tried to sound serious.

"But really, I mean it." Lisa tried to keep a straight face, but she couldn't hide a little smile.

"So okay, there's a lot of drawings and a whole lot of text, but if you ask me I think it's written in mirror image and probably in a foreign language as well!"

"Wait a minute!" Sophie let her fingers glide down the middle of the book from the top to the bottom of the page. "There are a couple of pages missing! Here, right smack in the middle!"

Lisa ran her fingers along the torn edges and nodded in agreement.

"If we want to know what's written here, we'll first have to reverse the writing and then figure out which language it is. If we can do that, we can probably translate a few pages word for word," Sophie said.

"It's probably some crazy lady's shopping list." Lisa sat up straight and wrinkled her face. "Ooh, dear diary," she said theatrically in an old lady's voice. "I must not forget to buy milk and eggs tomorrow."

Sophie looked up and tried to keep from laughing as Lisa continued her theatrics.

"And I must not forget to take out my dentures tonight and put the telephone back on the hook."

Sophie burst out laughing. "Lisa, stop it, I'm going to pee my pants."

Lisa jumped up from the bed and put the laptop on her desk. "Let's go downstairs. I smell food. I think Mom's cooking dinner."

At the exact same moment they heard their mother shouting up the stairs, "SOPHIE AND LISA! We're ho-ome, dinner is served!"

"You see. I'm psychic."

Sophie got up and walked back to her own bedroom with the book under her arm. She opened the desk drawer, placed the book inside, and turned around. She looked sternly at her sister, who was standing at the door, and made a zipping motion with her fingers across her lips.

"Duh," responded Lisa. "I won't say a thing."

Downstairs in the kitchen their mother was thumbing through a cookbook. "Hi girls, I heard you giggling upstairs," she said, while running her hands through Lisa's curls.

31

Sophie gave her mother a kiss, saying, "We just found out that long ago people used to keep very interesting diaries."

"Hmm, this feels like one of those 'you had to be there' moments," their mother responded, not understanding.

During dinner, Lisa and Sophie talked about their day and how Mrs. Prattle had given them a sketch, tactically omitting the part about discovering the secret room.

"Wow, what's with the cake?" Lisa asked, a little too enthusiastically, when her mother put an apple pie down on the table.

"Your father and I have a surprise. He will be finished writing an important presentation at the end of the week and has a few days off. We thought we'd go to Paris on Friday for a long weekend!"

Sophie and Lisa leapt up from the table and danced around the kitchen. "Par-is. Par-is. Par-is!"

"That's so cool!" Sophie said.

"Are we going to visit Hans?" Lisa asked her mother hopefully.

"Of course, we'll be staying at his house."

"*Parlez-vous français*," teased Sophie.

"*Un petit peu*," replied Lisa.

"What an awesome day today! First..." Sophie began, before Lisa, who was always there to save her sister from disaster, quickly nudged her to stop her from finishing the sentence.

"Uh, first... uh... the sketch and now a vacation," said Sophie.

"Actually, where's that sketch you were just talking about? Can I have a look at it?" their father suddenly asked them.

Sophie felt the blood rushing to her face.

Her father didn't notice, however, and instead looked at his watch. "On second thoughts, it'll have to wait... I have some work to do on my presentation. I'll have a look at it tomorrow. I'm very curious!" Their father was already walking out of the kitchen towards his study.

Relieved, Lisa and Sophie looked at each other and knew they should leave the kitchen before their mother started asking questions as well. Lisa motioned to Sophie to stand up.

Sophie understood immediately, got up from the table and stretched her arms above her head. "Man, I'm tired!"

Lisa yawned loudly. "Yeah, me too. I'm hitting the sack early. Night Mom," she said, while slipping quickly into the hallway.

"Yeah, night-night Mom," said Sophie, following her sister.

Before their mother could respond, they were already running up the stairs, leaving her standing there in the kitchen with a bemused look on her face.

Wednesday, June 18th, morning

They arrived at school early for a change. Sophie walked into the classroom first. As usual, she took a seat at the back of the class and saved the chair next to her for Jack.

When he came in, Jack waved cheerfully and quickly sat down next to her.

"Were they handing out free gel this morning?" Sophie joked when she saw him.

"Did you two discover anything more last night," he asked, wisely ignoring her remark.

"Well, yes and no," Sophie said, "but I have the book in my bag, we can look at it during break," she whispered.

Jack rocked back and forth on his chair. He looked at Sophie inquiringly. He hadn't stopped thinking about the book and the secret room since he'd left their house yesterday. He had hardly slept, with so many questions running through his head.

"What else did you do yesterday? What did you find out? Do you already know what the text means? Spit it out!"

"Whoa, relax cowboy. I'll tell you everything. Take it easy, you're only drawing attention to us," Sophie said softly.

Jack balanced on the back legs of his chair while, in hushed tones, Sophie told him everything they'd read and discovered. 'We still don't know what language it is. It's not English, otherwise we would have recognized some words."

The front legs of Jack's chair dropped towards the floor and hovered above the ground. His calves tensed as he balanced on the tips of his toes. He was too anxious to sit still, but he listened attentively.

"I already have an idea how we can make the text easier to read, but we still need to find out what language it is."

"Maybe it's the Bible," suggested Jack.

Sophie shot him a skeptical look.

"That's, like, really old, do you think it could be? Jesus! Maybe He wrote the book Himself, or God? Maybe God wrote it?" Jack's eyeballs nearly popped out of their sockets at the thought. "If that's the case, we're billionaires!" He had dollar signs in his eyes already and had to restrain himself from jumping up out of his chair.

Sophie looked at him as if he'd gone crazy. "God didn't write the Bible, nor did Jesus. It's *about* God and Jesus. I'm not exactly sure who did write it, but they certainly didn't."

Jack looked deflated.

"And obviously, it's not the Bible. That doesn't have any drawings in it, does it?" She gave Jack a playful slap on the arm.

"How am I supposed to know?" he said.

"Uhm, maybe by paying more attention in class?"

Jack ignored her and stared sullenly ahead.

"Lisa and I have to go back to the secret room today because we forgot Prattle's sketch and my father wants to see it. You up for another go? You never know what other cool things we might find."

"So we've hit a dead end with the book?"

Sophie looked up and saw that Mr. Hackett was busy with some paperwork.

"Yeah, kind of." She discretely pulled the book out of her bag and slid it onto Jack's lap. "See for yourself, Einstein, but you've got to be super careful. We'll be in serious trouble if Hackett spots it."

Jack took the book in his hands and flipped carefully through it. He looked at the cover first, then at a few pages. "Some of the pages are missing."

"No kidding, Lisa and I noticed that too. Thanks for the tip."

"And look at this!" Sophie pointed to the scratches on the cover.

"L... uh... O... V..." mumbled Jack.

"LOV..."

"Love," he joked. "Maybe someone wrote this book for his girlfriend." Jack stuck up his hand.

"What are you doing?!" asked Sophie, suddenly alarmed.

Ignoring her, Jack quickly slid the book back onto her lap. "Put it back in your bag," he said firmly.

A couple of their classmates turned towards them.

"Ahem," Jack coughed in an attempt to grab Hackett's attention.

Hackett was facing the interactive whiteboard when he heard the noise. He turned around and peered at the class until he saw Jack's raised hand.

"Jack?" Hackett asked. "What is it?"

The tough guy who was facing Sophie a few seconds earlier suddenly turned bright red. Overwhelmed by uncertainty and doubt, he began rocking back and forth again on the back legs of his chair.

"Jack?" repeated Hackett.

"Actually, I have a question about history, is that okay?"

"Well Jack, we're doing math right now. You are aware of that, right?"

Jack looked at the board in surprise. He even felt his ears going red now.

"Sure I did, Mr. Hackett, but I was thinking... oh... never mind, forget it."

Hackett raised his eyebrows. "Go ahead Jack, it's okay. It's always good to ask questions. What did you want to know?"

"It's actually a question about old books," Jack said quietly. Without realizing it, he was now balancing himself perfectly on the chair's back legs.

A buzz went around the class.

"Ssshhh," Hackett commanded the class. "It's okay, what do you want to know exactly?"

"Uhm..." Jack stammered. "Do you know any authors that go by the initials L.O.V.?"

Hackett shrugged his shoulders and sighed deeply. The question seemed to irritate him, but after a long pause he said: "No, Jack, I can't think of anyone right now. Why?"

"I was just wondering," said Jack as nonchalantly as possible.

"Is that all, Jack?"

"Do old books sometimes have leather covers?" Sophie suddenly asked.

The entire class turned around.

"Of course, Sophie. It was quite normal long ago to use leather for book covers. Wait, let me look it up for you."

Hackett opened his laptop and began typing. The whiteboard behind him suddenly came to life, showing a list of Google search results. Hackett clicked on *Images* and several photos of old books appeared on the screen.

The Codex Leicester by Leonardo da Vinci, written between 1506 and 1510, was sold at auction to Bill Gates in 1994 for US $30,802,500.

The class was all eyes and ears now, thankful for the unexpected distraction.

Sophie tried to memorize all the photos. They showed books that looked old, but not as old as the book they had found yesterday.

"Yeah, those kinds of books," Sophie said, "but then older. Are there older ones?"

Hackett looked up at the ceiling, as if he thought he'd find the answer up there. Then he turned back to his laptop and continued his internet search. Various Wikipedia pages flashed by on the large screen behind him.

"This is what I was looking for," Hackett said, making sure the internet page filled the entire screen. The word *Codex* appeared prominently at the top.

"When people first began writing things down, they used scrolls of paper. Later, they wrote on single sheets of paper that were bound together in what we now know as the first books. A book like that is called a codex."

Hackett moved the mouse to *Images*. Most of the photos that appeared on the screen were of pages taken from a codex but then without a cover. The pages had the same yellowish color as the ones in the book they had found.

Hackett scrolled down through the images. "Look, here's one that has a leather cover." He clicked on the photo. "Is that what you mean?"

The image on the screen showed an old book with a leather cover almost identical to their own. Sophie felt a shiver run down her spine. She actually wanted to scream, but then thought about how, in situations like these, her sister would deflect attention from herself by keeping a straight face. She managed to keep that face even when the euphoric sound of drum rolls and trumpets started ringing inside her head. Now that she knew they had found a codex, the answers to their questions were closer than ever.

"Yes, thanks," she mumbled, quickly grabbing her notebook and pretending to focus on her math assignment.

"Why the interest?" Hackett suddenly asked, once again causing the entire class to turn around and look at them.

"Uhm..." They hadn't expected another question and now had to think on their feet. "Nothing special, Jack and I saw it on TV yesterday."

"Okay, now everyone, back to the sums!" Hackett said, already turning to face the board again.

Then Jack raised his hand again. Sophie was mortified. Everything had gone so smoothly; they knew what they needed to know.

"Don't! We'll Google whatever it is you need to know at home!" she hissed.

"What?" Jacked said, shrugging his shoulders. "Relax. Just trust me."

"Mr. Hackett, I have one more question," Jack called across the classroom.

Hackett looked back at Jack. "Let's hear it," Hackett said. He was clearly enjoying the fact that he'd been asked more genuine questions today than he probably had in his entire teaching career up to now.

"Do you know of any books... old books... like, uhm... like the codex books you just showed us, that were written in mirror image?"

Hackett smiled broadly. Looking pleased as punch, he walked out from behind his desk. The classroom went quiet. Everyone waited anxiously for the answer.

"Listen up," he addressed the class, "does anyone know who was famous for writing in mirror image?"

A murmur went around the class. A few names were muttered, but no one gave an answer.

Hackett walked back to his laptop and spoke as he typed. "CODEX." He looked up at the class while he typed. "LE-O-NAR-DO... DA... VIN... CI."

Hackett pushed 'Enter' and the search results appeared on the white screen behind him. He clicked on *Images* again and the screen filled with pictures of various books and writings by Leonardo da Vinci.

"Leonardo da Vinci was one of the greatest artists that ever lived," Hackett said. "He lived in Italy around 1500 and made some of the world's most famous paintings. But he also drew anatomical sketches and came up with all sorts of innovations that were hypermodern for his time. And with regard to your question, Jack, Leonardo also wrote in mirror image. But we're getting very distracted now. Has anyone finished the sum yet?" Hackett gave the class a look that told them to carry on with their calculations.

Jack quickly copied the names from the whiteboard. *Leonardo da Vinci... Codex... old book, paper scrolls*. He then got a shock when he looked at what he had written. He held his breath, focused his eyes, and underlined three of the letters several times. Then he elbowed Sophie.

"Look!" He pointed at the three underlined letters. "L... D... V... " he said softly. "Leonardo da Vinci!" he whispered to Sophie. "L.D.V.!" he said again and pointed to her bag. "Look at the book. It's not LOV but LDV."

Sophie slid the book out of her bag and onto her lap so

she could see the marks. She ran her fingers over the letters.

"You're right! L... D... V..." she said quietly. She felt her sweater beginning to stick to her back.

"Man, I can't stand it any more, there's still half a day of school left," said Jack, suddenly looking completely befuddled.

Sophie raised her hand. "Uhm, Mr. Hackett? Sorry, but may I ask one more question?"

The expression on Mr. Hackett's face went from irritation to surprise to elation and back again. He waved his arm in a gesture that invited her to ask her question.

"Uhm, suppose that a codix..."

"Codex," he corrected her. "With an 'e'."

"A codex, by Leonardo. Would that be worth anything?"

Sophie twisted her hair and tried to look as uninterested as possible. Jack thought it was a great question and leaned back again, balancing on the back legs of his chair. Hackett's laugh resonated throughout the classroom. He took a step forward and addressed Sophie.

"Sophie, Leonardo da Vinci wrote numerous codices during his lifetime. I think more than 10,000 pages in all. But..." To emphasize his words Hackett now gazed intensely at Sophie, "... they are all owned by museums. You can't buy them at a bookstore, and you won't find them on eBay either," he joked.

"How do you know all of them were found," Sophie asked in a serious voice.

"You never know for sure, of course, but after more than 500 years it's safe to assume that there are no more lying around anywhere." He paused for a moment, and then ran his hand over his face and shook his head as if he was trying to remember something. "I just realized that isn't entirely true. Wait a second, I'll look it up."

Everyone watched in nervous anticipation to see what Hackett would do next.

"What I said was that all of Leonardo's codices are owned by museums, but that's not entirely correct. Let me see." Although he had disconnected his laptop from the whiteboard, it was clear to everyone he was busy typing.

"Here it is!" Satisfied that he'd found what he was looking for, Hackett tapped the screen with his finger. "Sophie? You wanted to know if it was worth anything, right?"

Sophie nodded.

Hackett began citing the text aloud. "*The Codex Leicester*, by Leonardo da Vinci, is the only privately owned codex. The codex was sold in 1994," Hackett looked at his class triumphantly. The entire class stared at him, eager for him to go on.

"In other words, *almost* all of the known codices are owned by museums," repeated Hackett, "except one, which has remained in private hands. And in 1994 the owner sold it to none other than Bill Gates! Some of you probably recognize that name, he's the founder of Microsoft."

"One of the richest men on earth!" shouted a boy sitting at the front.

"In 1994 Mr. Gates paid almost thirty-one million dollars for the codex!"

Sophie didn't dare look at Jack, but out of the corner of her eye she could tell from the way he was sitting that he had gone completely stiff. Suddenly realizing that the entire class was looking at them, she slid her bag closer to her under the desk. She grabbed the strap and slowly lifted the bag onto her lap, all the while looking straight at Hackett.

"That's almost 20 years ago, just imagine," said Hackett,

completely oblivious to Sophie's rummaging. "If another codex by Leonardo da Vinci was found, it could fetch several times that amount. Did you happen to find one, Sophie?" He laughed at his own joke.

Sophie held her bag even closer, pulled the drawstring tight, and wrapped her arms protectively around it. She tried to make eye contact with Jack.

He was grinning from cheek to cheek. She'd never seen him look so happy.

"Okay everyone, pay attention. Let's carry on where we left off. If there are no more questions about old books, I'd like to focus on the next sum." Hackett wrote a new assignment on the board.

After school, Sophie was sitting next to Jack at one of the picnic tables in the corner of the schoolyard. Her bag was safe on her lap. Just to be sure, she had transferred her water bottle from her bag to Jack's. The book had to avoid damage at all costs. Jack was sitting unusually close to Sophie. Comrades in arms, like knights charged with defending their castle.

"Hey! Over here!" Jack yelled as loud as he could when he saw Lisa and Tom walking across the schoolyard. He whistled loudly to grab his brother's attention. Tom and Lisa began running quickly towards them.

"Hey, are we going to go back to the secret room this afternoon?" Tom asked. "Lisa said that old Prattle's sketch is still in there."

Jack and Sophie looked at them absentmindedly.

"Hello, earth to..." Lisa waved her hand in front of her sister.

"I heard you." Sophie sounded a little distracted.

"We're definitely going to your house," Jack said. "And after that you and I are going to buy ourselves a smartphone, little bro," he added, grinning from ear to ear.

"Sshh." Sophie looked furiously at Jack. "Shut up, we'll talk about it at home."

"What will we talk about at home?" Lisa asked, looking very serious all of a sudden. "Come on, tell us, what's going on? Did you two discover something?"

Jack nudged Sophie. "What difference does it make if we tell them now or later?"

Sophie looked around nervously to see if anyone could hear them. "Okay," she said softly, leaning in towards her sister and Tom, "but you have to promise – no, *swear on your lives* – that you won't say a thing, okay?"

"I swear," Lisa said quickly.

"Yeah sure, me too." said Tom, nodding his head furiously.

"No, really!" Sophie poked her fingers into Tom's chest.

"Really, really – I swear!" Tom said, somewhat taken aback.

"Stop being such an idiot and tell us. What's going on?" said Lisa, who was never charmed by her sister's bossiness.

"We know who the book belongs to, who wrote it, and what it's worth." Sophie spoke quietly and with an air of mystery.

"Leonardo da Vinci!" Jack interrupted.

Tom didn't immediately grasp the significance of this, but Lisa raised her eyebrows and looked at her sister with a mixture of surprise and expectation.

"It's true, Jack's right! Hackett explained to us that it's a codex by Leonardo da Vinci!"

"You actually showed him the book?" asked Lisa startled.

"Are you kidding? No way, we were totally strategic about it, but... whatever. What matters is that we know what we need to know. It's an extremely old book, written by Leonardo da

Vinci in Italy. It turns out the guy wrote more books like this."

Sophie leaned in even closer to Tom and Lisa. "And apparently, it's really rare. His books are in museums all over the world! He was a mega famous painter, but also a sort of inventor, and almost everything he thought up he wrote down in these books."

Sophie paused for a moment to make sure she had their undivided attention. "I also asked Hackett what something like that was worth. He didn't know exactly, but twenty years ago one of these codices was sold to Bill Gates and that guy is super rich," Sophie exclaimed triumphantly.

Jack jumped up from the table. "It sold for THIRTY-ONE MILLION DOLLARS!" he screamed under his breath.

Lisa grabbed her sister's hand in disbelief. "You mean we could be rich? Richer than rich even?!" she stammered.

"Scooters!" screamed Jack.

"You said that yesterday, too, but what's the use in having a scooter when you can't ride it until you're 16? No matter how rich you are." This brought Jack back down to earth with a bang.

"Stupid rules," Jack muttered angrily.

"You got the book in your bag?" Lisa whispered to her sister, who hadn't moved the entire time and was clinging to her bag.

"Yep, and believe me, I'm so excited I could jump in the air too, but I don't dare to move." Sophie looked nervously around her. "Should we head for home? I want to put the book somewhere safe, and then check out the room again and get the sketch."

When they got home Sophie headed straight for the stairs with her bag. "Go on ahead, you might find some more books lying around. I'm going to put this one away in my desk drawer. And," Sophie shouted from the stairs, "don't forget the sketch!"

"We won't!" Lisa hollered across the room. The brothers followed Lisa into the study and over to the bookcase behind the desk. "Okay guys, help me push."

This time it rolled smoothly into the wall. Lisa stepped into the space first and turned on the light.

Unsure what they were actually looking for, they all began searching around.

Feeling a little on edge, Sophie sat down at her desk and stared at the pages of the codex in front of her. She should have been elated at their discovery and the thirty-million-dollar bonanza, but she wasn't. She wondered if something was wrong. Why wasn't she excited? Why was she so tense? What was this thing lying on her desk? Was it really a codex? How did such an old book end up in their house? Was someone just playing a colossal prank on them? And if it was real, what did Leonardo describe in the book? What had he written?

She pushed the book to one side and snapped open her laptop. With a few clicks she opened Google and quickly typed in the words 'Leonardo da Vinci' in the search engine. She scanned the screen. *Leonardo da Vinci. Codex Leicester. Anatomy. The Last Supper. Flying machines. Musical instruments.* This all sounded pretty real.

Leonardo had been ahead of his time. He discovered and envisioned things long before others did. He had designed things on paper that wouldn't be made until hundreds of years later. He had sketched muscles and organs in meticulous detail long before the technology required to know what they looked like existed. He even designed a bridge that wasn't built until nearly five hundred years after he died.

Sophie opened the book again and felt her heart beating hard in her chest. She flipped through the pages for the umpteenth time. What did it all mean?

Suddenly she knew what to do. She took her phone from her back pocket and swiped her thumb across the screen. When she reached the App Store she searched for 'scanner'. Several scanners appeared in the tiny screen. She scrolled down, dismissing most of them with a frown of frustration.

"QR scanner, no."

"Barcode scanner, no."

"QR scanner, no."

"QR scanner, no-ho!"

"Genius scanner, yes!"

Sophie tapped the screen and read the information accompanying the app. "Turns your telephone into a portable scanner."

"Yes!" she cried. This was exactly what she was looking for!

Okay. Click. A box appeared on the screen asking for her Apple ID. Her parents had always said not to purchase apps without asking first, but fortunately this one was free. She entered her password and the download appeared. After a few seconds the scanner icon popped up on her screen. That was easy!

Now she had to find a translation app. She returned to the App Store and, after finding the app she wanted, repeated the process. Click. Download. Done.

However, when she opened the app she realized she had

chosen the wrong one. This was a special translation app that recognized spoken words and automatically translated them in real time. The app could even read back the translated text aloud. Super cool, but not exactly what she needed. She wanted an app that could translate written text and so she resumed her search. The second download was the right one, she figured. Sophie opened the app and read the description. According to the information, the app was not able to recognize handwritten text.

The frustration caused her to chew off so much of her thumbnail that it started to hurt. But she was determined to translate the book's text and wasn't about to give up now. However, she also knew that typing out the text would take weeks. She had to find an app that could recognize handwritten text and immediately translate it into a form that could be processed by a computer. She had no idea what something like that was called and so she grabbed her laptop.

After several failed search attempts she found the term she was looking for: Optical Character Recognition. "Never heard of that before," she muttered to herself.

She typed the words into the App Store's search box. The screen filled up with app options. She randomly chose a free version. Click. Download. Done.

An entire page of her screen was now filled with her newly downloaded app logos. She was proud of herself for having gotten this far. Nothing could stop her now. She was determined to find out what was written in the book. She took a few deep breaths. She must have been holding her breath unconsciously all the time she had been looking for the right app.

"Okay, stay calm Sophie..." she said quietly to herself. She grabbed the book and began flipping through it. Where to begin? She had to hurry. After turning a few pages her eye was drawn to a sketch on the left-hand page. The blood drained from her face. She felt her stomach turn and had the feeling someone had pressed a freezing cold washcloth against the back of her neck. Why hadn't they seen this before? How could they have missed this yesterday? With a trembling hand she grabbed her phone, opened the scanner app, and scanned the page. She flipped the images using a photo-editing app that was already on her phone. At the same time she opened the app that could translate handwritten text into digital text. Finally, she selected Italian to English in the translation app.

A small hourglass appeared on screen, slowly filling up. The slowest hour glass in the history of humankind, Sophie thought. She felt a surge of aggression towards her sluggish phone.

She examined the page in excited anticipation while waiting for the text to translate. The drawing was of the exact same spherical device that they had found in the secret room.

She jumped at the sound of her telephone's loud ping. The words 'Download complete' appeared on the screen. She tapped to access the long text. Her screen was too small to be able to read it easily, so she emailed the text to herself so that she could read it on her laptop. She set her phone aside, picked up her laptop, and pushed her chair away from the desk and rolled backwards into the room. She read the translated text from the computer on her lap:

The magic of the seven seas.
I went searching.
For something.

The unknown.
The truth.
Time.

This guy was bonkers, Sophie thought as she continued reading. The page was filled with enigmatic theories and calculations. A line written in capital letters above the drawing of the spherical device said: TIME TRAVEL.

Sophie knew that time travel wasn't possible, but she was curious enough to read on. Underneath the drawing of the device were the words:

Dreams are made of this.
History will never be the same.

Sophie felt her shoulders go tense. The writer seemed pretty sure of himself.

She continued reading:

Deus ex machina.
The answer, the orrery.
Use wisely the light.
The seas with their extraordinary powers.
The future is what I see.

"What's an orrery?" Sophie asked herself out loud.

She realized the answer to the question had to be on the next page. But as she was grabbing her phone to scan the right-hand page, she saw a line of tiny slivers of paper protruding from the book's spine. This can't be happening, she thought. The pages missing from the book were the exact same pages she wanted to read. She rolled her chair back to her desk, yanked open the drawer and, feeling extremely irritated, tossed the book inside.

"Stupid fake inventor," she said. She walked to the door but then stopped all of a sudden. Something was wrong. Everything Leonardo had ever imagined had turned out to be true. She couldn't shake the feeling that there was more to all this than met the eye. Her thoughts swung from excitement to doubt and back again. Leonardo had said that time travel was possible using an orrery. But what the hell was an orrery? She had to find out. Sophie walked back to her laptop and typed in the word 'orrery'.

"Enter, stupid!" she said, angry with herself for not having the backbone to accept that this was probably all just pure fantasy.

The results filled her screen. She looked at the images in bewilderment and felt the blood drain from her face again. Her bedroom seemed frozen in time. She looked at the pictures on the screen and thought about the page in the book. The translated text flashed into her head: *Dreams are made of this. History will never be the same.*

She leapt up out of her chair, and it crashed to the ground behind her as she ran as fast as she could through the hallway and down the stairs. She skipped the last few steps. Her shoulder scraped against the wall as she turned the corner and lurched into her father's study, gasping.

"STOP!" Her high-pitched scream was aimed at the secret room. "Stop, stop, stop! Don't touch it! Don't go near the orrery!"

Tom turned around, startled.

"I didn't touch it," he said, holding his hands in the air as if someone was pointing a gun at him. "Seriously, I didn't."

Lisa looked at her sister, wide-eyed with alarm. "What's wrong with you all of a sudden? We didn't do anything."

"You too!" yelled Sophie. "Move! Jack! Move away from that thing!" Jack took a quick step backwards.

Sophie was bent over and out of breath, hands resting on her knees. She'd never run so hard in her life. It took her a few seconds to catch her breath. "That thing..." Still panting, she pointed at the spheres. "That thing... is an orrery. Don't touch it, it's extremely dangerous!"

Wednesday, June 18th, afternoon

"What's the matter with you all of a sudden? The thing's harmless." Jack sounded a little shocked. Everyone stared at Sophie, waiting for her reaction.

Waving her arms wildly, Sophie ushered everyone towards the opening.

"I'll explain in a second. First we've got to get out of the room! Now!"

"But... calm down. First tell us what's going on. Why is that *orry* suddenly so dangerous?" Lisa was trying to make it clear that she didn't like being bossed around.

"Trust me, okay? If you don't listen to me you might never be able to tell anyone what I'm telling you now... and by the way, it's *orrery* not *orry*." Sophie gave her sister a withering look.

"But..." Jack stammered.

"Fine, don't listen to me!" Sophie interrupted angrily. "But don't say I didn't warn you!" And with that she stomped out of the room.

Tom decided to follow Sophie, just to be sure, and Jack did likewise. Lisa crossed her arms and stood her ground. She turned her attention to the device with the spheres. She didn't believe it could be dangerous. Suddenly she heard a noise nearby. The hairs on the back of her neck stood on end. She felt something hairy touch her ankles and she stifled a scream.

"Help! I'm going to die!"

Something white shot along the wall and out into the study towards the hallway. The others ran back into the secret room and stared anxiously at Lisa.

"What's wrong? Well, you're still breathing... you actually look quite good for a dead person," said Tom teasingly.

"There," screeched Lisa, pointing to Mrs. Prattle's pet ermine, which had escaped like lightning out through the study.

"I think she attacked me!"

"Lisa, don't be so dramatic, that creature has sharp claws and teeth. If it had attacked you, you'd know all about it. No blood anywhere, right?" asked Tom.

"What's it doing in here anyway?" Jack asked surprised. "Very weird," he said, trying to figure out where the ermine had come from.

Sophie was lost in her own thoughts. They had to close the bookcase before something bad happened.

"Yeah, really weird. I didn't see her come in when we were here," said Lisa. "But I remember Mrs. Prattle saying something yesterday about it having run away. Let's catch it and bring it back!"

"No way, there's no time! Come on, close the bookcase!" Sophie commanded them.

Together they pulled the bookcase shut until it was back in place.

Now that the danger had passed and they were no longer in the vicinity of the orrery, Sophie was able to calm down a bit. "Let's go upstairs to my room. I'll tell you everything. I'll show you... Lisa, don't forget the sketch!" She looked back at Jack, who was following behind, looking more than a little bewildered. "Sorry I scared you like that. I'll explain upstairs. Can you please make me and Lisa a cup of tea?" Sophie gave Jack a sweet look.

"Please. I'll pay you a quarter of thirty-one million dollars."

Jack straightened up and laughed. "Are you blackmailing me for a cup of tea? Is it okay if we grab a Coke?"

"No problem!"

Sophie walked up the stairs with Lisa, who had the sketch tucked under her arm. "Let's wait for Tom and Jack," she said in her room.

"Oh sure, just because I'm so great at waiting," joked Lisa. "*Patience* is my middle name after all." However, one look at her sister and she knew Sophie was in no mood for her jokes. She changed the subject. "Excited about Venice? Man, I'm so jealous!"

Sophie nodded. "Now that you mention it, I can't wait!"

"Jack likes you," Lisa said abruptly.

Sophie's face turned red. "No way, get out of here. Jack's my best friend. Just like you and Tom. They're the boys next door!"

"Okay, whatever you think yourself," Lisa said.

"Girls!" they heard someone call from the hallway. Jack entered the room triumphantly carrying two large mugs of tea. Tom followed him with two cans of Coke.

Sophie stared at Jack for a second. Nah. She didn't detect anything that indicated he liked her. Jack took a sip of his Coke, sat down in the desk chair, and spun himself around like he always did when he sat there. Just like the others, he was anxious to hear her story.

"Okay, just wait till you see this. The thing is, I discovered something while you were downstairs. I was about to put the book away, but I was so curious..."

"What's new?" Lisa laughed.

"As if I can help it? I was so curious that I started flipping through the book, searching for something that might help us. Hackett said Leonardo was really clever and knew so much... he was right, you know. I looked him up on the internet. The guy did a lot of cool stuff in his lifetime. He designed crazy airplanes and musical instruments, and made really unusual art and stuff. Whatever the reason, he was just a whole lot smarter than everyone else at the time. Strange, right?" Sophie said, looking inquisitively at her friends.

"I was really frustrated that I couldn't read anything in the book, so I downloaded a few apps on my phone. One that scans texts, one that translates handwriting into digital text, and a language translator." She looked at each one of them to make sure they were following her. "I already had a photo-editing app on my phone that could reverse mirror images, turn and crop them, and whatnot."

Lisa, Jack and Tom all looked at each other and then spontaneously burst into applause.

"Wow, I knew you were smart, but this..." Tom said, stunned.

"How do you know all that? How did you know there were apps for that, and how did you know what they were called?" Jack asked, full of admiration.

"I just Googled it on my laptop, quick search, scroll, search again," Sophie said as casually as possible, while secretly enjoying the compliments.

"Anyway, I was hoping everything would work immediately, so I tried to scan a page... the page with the drawing of my phone actually."

Lisa had to laugh, but Jack and Tom didn't get the joke.

Sophie grabbed the book and quickly leafed through the pages. "Here!" She lifted up the book, turned it towards them, and showed them the page she was referring to.

"No way! That really does look like your phone!" Tom said amazed.

"It's just a random tiny sketch, but still." Jack nodded.

Sophie turned the page over. "But then," she took a deep breath, "I saw this page."

Lisa, Jack and Tom's eyes widened when they saw the picture in the book.

"That's the thing downstairs," Jack said.

"An orrery," Sophie said. "It's an old-fashioned name for a planetarium."

"Strange that we didn't notice it yesterday," Lisa said, slightly annoyed.

"That's what I thought. I only just noticed it myself, so I immediately chose this page to translate." Sophie put the book down and grabbed her laptop.

"And this is where it gets really crazy," Sophie whispered. "Look what's written on the page. There's also a bunch of calculations related to time travel. According to Leonardo it should be possible if you reach a certain speed."

"Faster than light," Jack added.

"Exactly. Leonardo wrote that down, too. By traveling faster than light."

"There's just one small problem," Jack said, half jokingly. "No one's ever done it," he said, raising his eyebrows while looking at Sophie. "So, not so smart after all, our Leonardo," Jack said, and nudged Lisa, hoping she would back him up.

Sophie shot Jack a vicious look. "If you don't want to

hear any of this, you can just go home. Go watch a movie or something. In the meantime, we'll be the first people in the world to discover time travel, and we'll make sure to think of you when we're being interviewed by journalists from all around the world, when we're in the newspapers, on TV..."

Jack just stared at his feet. "Alright, alright, I'll keep quiet."

"Good, because I'm not done yet. Anyway, he said that time travel is possible as long as you achieve the right speed. And according to him it's possible using that crazy planetarium downstairs. Now do you understand why I was so freaked out?"

"What do you mean 'with that thing downstairs'? What does it say in the book?" asked Tom, who up to that point had sat listening with his mouth open.

Sophie continued reading. "Underneath the drawing he wrote: 'The answer, the orrery. Use wisely the light. The seas have extraordinary powers. The future is what I see.' I didn't know what an orrery was, so I looked it up on my computer. It translated as planetarium and under 'Images' I saw a picture of the exact same thing downstairs! Get it? Leonardo says that we can use it to travel through time!" By now Sophie was standing and waving her hands in the air in an effort to emphasize her point.

Lisa jumped up from the bed and started playing air guitar in the middle of the room. Jack, Tom and Sophie stared at her in astonishment.

"What? Why are you all just sitting there staring at me? Turn on that *orrilary* and let's go! I want to see a real dinosaur!"

Tom went to join her, but Jack held him back.

"Sounds great, Lisa, but we're not going to experiment with

that thing when we don't know how it works. Your sister's right, the thing could kill us. We could accidentally beam you to another dimension!"

Sophie agreed. "The smart thing to do is first to figure out how it works precisely. That is, unless you want to land in the middle of a battlefield during World War Two."

Lisa stopped playing her air guitar. She slumped her shoulders in theatrical fashion, let out a deep sigh, and sat back down on the bed.

"Can you see if there's any information on the internet about Leonardo and the orrery he invented? To see how the thing works? Lisa asked.

"I already searched, but I couldn't find anything," Sophie said.

"Weird," Lisa raised an eyebrow. "Everything he's ever invented or painted can be found on the internet, but not this?"

"That's what I thought, until I suddenly realized..." Sophie hesitated a second before looking triumphantly at her sister. "It's all very logical actually! Everything about Leonardo and the planetarium is in the codex! In our codex – the codex no one knows about! That's why we can't find out anything about it. We're the only ones who know!"

"Scan the next page, it must say how it works, if it does work, that is," Jack said.

Sophie opened up the book again. "That's going to be a problem, look," she handed the book to Jack and pointed to the frayed edges where the missing pages had been torn out.

"SOPHIE!"

"LISA!" Their mother was standing at the bottom of the stairs.

"Quick, hide the book," Jack said.

"Mom, we'll be down in a minute," Lisa yelled. "Tom, can you beam me downstairs?"

Jack and Tom had a good laugh at this and then headed for the stairs. "We're out of here, see you tomorrow!" They waved as they disappeared around the corner.

Sophie put the book away and turned to Lisa.

"I thought you two would come downstairs, but all I saw were the boys." Sophie's mother was standing in the doorway.

"Your dad called this morning to say that his presentation has been moved forward to today. So he has tomorrow off. And so do I..." She gave her daughters a jubilant look.

"So you'll both be here tomorrow after school?" Sophie asked, realizing this meant they wouldn't be able to explore the secret room.

"It means, Sophie, that we're leaving for Paris tomorrow!"

Lisa began jumping around the room. "Par-is! Par-is! Par-is!"

"We called the school," their mother said. "You can take two days off, on the condition that you learn something there, too. Which is why we're going to visit a few museums."

"That's great, Mom," Sophie groaned. Her mother was already heading back downstairs again.

"Yeah, we thought so too," her mother yelled from the stairs. "Don't forget to pack your suitcases tonight."

Sophie stared at her sister. "What are you so happy about?"

"Look, there's nothing we can do about this little trip. Better to let on we're excited, which is how we normally react when we visit Hans! Otherwise, they might figure out we have a secret. And trust me, we'll have plenty of time to check out the room after the weekend. Every time Dad and Mom take a few days off they end up having to work extra the week after. That means they'll be home late. Which gives us lots of time to explore the room. And enough time to study the *orrery!*"

Sophie should have known that her sister would have already worked out the entire scenario. That would also explain why she reacted so enthusiastically to her mother's announcement that they'd be leaving a day earlier. Lisa had probably been excited *both* about the room and Paris. If she weren't excited about Paris, she would have been fully capable of concocting a story explaining why they couldn't possibly go to Paris at this moment.

"Lisa, you're really something else," said Sophie smiling and shaking her head. She picked up her phone and swiped her thumb across the screen. "Paris is 74 degrees tomorrow. The same on Friday and even warmer at the weekend."

"I'm going to go pack, you too?" Lisa asked. "If we do it now we might have some time tonight to look at the book together."

"Good plan," Sophie said.

They went to the guest room and grabbed their suitcases from one of the closets.

"Well, we won't have to take you out for a walk tonight!" Lisa giggled at her own joke. There on a round glass table in front of them was a stuffed dog sitting on its hind legs. He stared back at them intently. In his front paws was a sign with the words *I'm dead* written on it.

"Ah Lisa, remember!" Sophie tried to suppress an embarrassed smile. "I'm curious as to what Hans will have up his sleeve this time! I'm open to anything, of course, as long as he doesn't give us any more of these dead animals!" she said, nodding towards the dog. "That thing is so freaky. The dodo is the only one I really like. The rest are all a bit weird."

After packing their bags they walked downstairs to the kitchen. Their mother put on the kettle and grabbed her phone.

"Seeing as we're leaving tomorrow, I didn't do any shopping for groceries. I'm going to order pizza. You guys want veggie? She had already begun dialing without waiting for an answer.

Lisa nudged her sister. "Maybe it's a good idea to let Jack and Tom know we're leaving tomorrow. Otherwise they might think we were all beamed off somewhere."

"We'll head over there after dinner," Sophie agreed.

"It'll be here in 25 minutes," their mother said, as she moved towards the living room where she turned on the TV and zapped to the news.

"Come on, we'll go over there now!" said Lisa, throwing Sophie her jacket as she headed for the door. Sophie put it on and followed her out into the garden.

They decided to walk around to the back of Jack and Tom's house. Lisa peered through the kitchen window at the rear of the house. There was a saucepan bubbling away on the stove, but she saw no one in the kitchen.

"Hide! Quick!" Lisa told her sister.

"Why?"

"Come on, just do it, it'll be fun!"

Sophie crawled behind a bush in the garden. Lisa bent forward, messed up her hair with her hands, and knocked on the window a few times with her knuckles. Jack appeared immediately. He opened the door wearing a surprised look on his face. Lisa stared back at him, her face full of fear, her wild curls trembling.

"Jack," she croaked in a low voice. "Jack, get your father. Something's happened. My parents... Sophie..."

Through the branches Sophie could see Jack's face go stiff.

He looked as if he'd seen a ghost. Sophie felt immediately sorry for him. Lisa, however, stuck diligently to her role.

"Jack, quick, I accidentally... beamed them off into space..." Lisa gasped.

Jack put his hands up to his face. He turned around and called his father. "DAD! DAD! You've got to come, quick!" His voice began to break. 'TOM, come help. Lisa's here and... they're gone!"

Sophie heard Tom running towards them, and their father descending the stairs three steps at a time. Jack turned to look at Lisa again. For a second he thought she was crying hysterically, but then he saw that the tears on her cheeks were tears of laughter. It took a few seconds for Jack to realize what was going on. His father and Tom appeared at the door. "What's wrong?" they asked in unison.

"Oh, it's nothing," Lisa said between fits of laughter. "I just stopped by to say that we're off to Paris tomorrow instead of the day after. I said 'We're going away' and Jack suddenly began yelling.

"Jack?" his father said. "Are you pulling our legs?"

"Uh... not really... Lisa..." Jack was speechless.

"Paris, sounds lovely. I hope you have a great time," Jack's father said perplexed and walked back inside.

Sophie had witnessed the entire scene, and out of pure astonishment had remained hiding in the bushes. She had struggled to stifle her laughter, but at the same time she felt very sorry for Jack, who was still dazed and speechless when Sophie re-emerged from behind the bushes.

"Oh, I'm really sorry Jack. I didn't know Lisa was going to..."

Jack stared at the sisters, grimaced, and shook his head.

"Unbelievable, you're a little witch. I really thought you had made everyone disappear with that thing! I thought something terrible had happened. I got the fright of my life... I really believed you!"

Laughing his head off, Tom gave Lisa a big bear hug and said, "Hil-ari-ous! I'm never going to forget this. Jack actually lost for words for once. Brilliant!"

"Lisa, I'm going to get you back for this! Maybe tomorrow, maybe the day after, maybe next month, maybe next year. But trust me, you're going to pay," Jack couldn't suppress a smile, however. "Holy moly, you really had me."

Sophie stepped forward and stood next to Lisa.

"Okay, back to reality. The reason we came is that our plans have changed. We're leaving for Paris early tomorrow morning. That means no secret room for a few days."

"No!" Tom said.

"You can't be serious?" added his brother.

"Sorry, but we can't do anything about it. Fortunately, it's only for a few days. I'll scan a few more pages this evening and send them to you, Jack. Then you guys can see if you can decipher anything else," Sophie said. "And listen, we'll be back on Sunday. If you work quickly and tell us what you discovered on Monday, we might be able to find out on Monday afternoon if that thing actually works."

"I'll email you tonight before nine," Sophie told Jack.

Lisa tugged on Tom's arm. "Come with me," she said, nodding towards the garden.

While Sophie was talking to Jack at the kitchen door, Lisa walked into the garden. Intrigued, Tom followed her. Suddenly Lisa turned around and pushed her hand into the pocket of Tom's jeans. She lifted a finger to her lips before

Tom could react. "Shh! The key to the back door. The alarm code is written on a sticker on the key."

Tom gave her a puzzled look.

"Just in case you guys need to look at the book or go into the room. This way you can get inside when we're gone."

"But... you're crazy, we're not going to break into your house?" stammered Tom.

"It's not really breaking in," Lisa said. "Look. You might not need the key at all. But imagine if you and Jack decide you need more information. This way you can get it, okay?"

She heard a scooter pull into the street. "Oh shoot, we've got to go. That's the pizza guy. The book is in Sophie's desk drawer and... well, you already know how to get into the secret room. Oh, and one more thing, please don't break anything. Seriously Tom. If you break something, then I'm playing dumb!" She looked at him with all the seriousness she could muster.

"Relax, Lisa, we don't even know if we'll need to get into the house. Okay?"

One corner of Lisa's mouth curled into a little smile. Mission accomplished. She knew that in the next day or two Tom wouldn't be able to contain his curiosity. There was no doubt he'd go and investigate.

"Sure, I know. And if you don't need to, no problem, okay?"

"If who doesn't need what?" Sophie had turned around and was walking towards her sister and Tom.

"It's nothing, Tom was just thinking of going to the library tomorrow to check out some books on that Leonardo guy, but I said it might be better to wait until we get back."

To Lisa, this wasn't lying, technically speaking, because her father's study was more or less a library. She couldn't help it if her sister interpreted it differently and was probably thinking that Tom was considering going to the public library.

Sophie gave Tom a slap on the shoulder. "You should go. Take Jack with you to the library and see if you can find out anything about how that thing works."

"Well, if even my sister says you should do it..." Lisa winked at Tom.

He shrugged his shoulders. "We'll see."

They heard the scooter again, the muffled sound of its engine slowly fading into the distance. "Lisa, we've got to go. The pizzas will be gone cold!"

"Good luck in the library," Lisa said, giving Tom an exaggerated slap on the shoulder. Tom walked towards the kitchen door and stood next to Jack.

"Have fun in Paris," they said in unison.

When they walked into the kitchen their mother was slicing the pizza.

Lisa took a deep sniff, taking in the smell of melted cheese and Italian herbs. She tossed her jacket over the back of a chair and grabbed a slice before she had even sat down. She held it above her face and took a bite. A long string of cheese stuck to her chin. Sophie looked at the string of soft cheese that grew longer and longer as gravity did its work, while her sister just carried on eating, oblivious to the mess. She felt a shiver go down her spine. Her sister's eating habits always gave her the heebie-jeebies and she tried not to watch her. Instead she went to the hallway to hang up her coat.

Her father had already devoured half his pizza in a few big bites. His initial hunger satisfied, he turned to the girls. "How did school go this week?

"Wull, wu hadda..." Lisa replied, trying to talk with her mouth full.

"Lisa! Stop, please!" said Sophie, demonstratively sticking her fingers in her ears. "Please finish eating before you start talking. And for God's sake, take the cheese off your chin! Yuck, you're like a big baby."

Lisa shot her sister an irritated look. She swallowed, wiped her chin with her sleeve, and began her story again.

"We had a pretty good week. As good as good can get, in this boring town, I mean," she said, grimacing.

"Whatever," her mother said, who was clearly in no mood for this well-worn topic of discussion. They all went quiet for a few seconds.

"On Monday we spent the whole afternoon outside."

"At the sawmill, you mean?" Her father looked at her questioningly, at the same time shaking his head slightly in disapproval.

Lisa pretended not to notice and continued. "If I remember correctly, Sophie and Jack went skateboarding."

"Yep," said Sophie.

"Yesterday we were late for school. Afterwards we swung by Mrs. Prattle's. And today was boring."

"We were discussing Venice today at school!" Sophie said enthusiastically.

Lisa let out a long, exaggerated sigh.

"Oh Lisa, come on, it'll be your turn next year. And by the way, the school will be celebrating its 100th anniversary next year, so they'll probably organize a special school trip," her mother said.

"I want to go to the sun, to Ca-li-for-ni-yaaaah!"

"Not a chance, you're not going to California. If that's the case, I'll do the year over again," joked Sophie.

"Hey Lisa," her father said, turning to look at her. "About yesterday. I still haven't seen that sketch. Go get it, will you? I'd like to have a look."

"Yeah, cool Dad. I was just thinking... I think I recognize the style, of painting I mean. I think it's a sketch by Leonardo da Vinci."

Sophie swallowed hard and began to cough. She looked for Lisa's leg under the table and gave her a hard kick. But it was too late, her father had heard.

"Leonardo da Vinci?" he asked Lisa. "That would be something else!" he laughed.

"Yeah. Right after we got it I told Sophie that the sketch looked familiar. I saw something like it in one of your books before. Maybe you know which book?"

"If you guys have a genuine da Vinci... Hah! If it's the real thing, then, well... it would be worth millions. But what are the chances of that? As far as I know it's been a long, long time since anyone discovered a Leonardo."

"Dad, if it really is by Leonardo da Vinci, shouldn't we say something to Mrs. Prattle?"

"Of course Lisa, in fact we'll tell the whole world!" Then her father stood up and walked to the door, laughing quietly to himself.

Sophie gave Lisa a worried look. What was her sister up to this time? She felt her cheeks go red and wanted nothing more than to shove Lisa under a cold shower and scream at her.

"I'll be in my study. Will you bring me the sketch later?" their father said.

The nonchalant way in which he referred to the sketch indicated that he didn't think it was worth anything. Their mother cleared the table and turned on the dishwasher.

Lisa stood up feeling excited and seemingly unconcerned that any harm might have been done. "I'm going up to my room."

Sophie ran out of the kitchen and caught up with her sister.

"Before you start," Lisa said, as she walked into her sister's bedroom, "there was no other solution."

"Why did you say that? Why even mention the name Leonardo da Vinci?" Sophie asked, still in shock and not in the least bit convinced.

"I remembered at the dinner table that I'd already said it looked familiar. You were talking about Leonardo da Vinci this afternoon, about the book and all and... while we were eating it suddenly hit me. The sketch looks like one of the pages from that book. That's why I said it."

"But... but..." Sophie said, stunned. "But still, why not discuss it with me first? Why mention the name to Dad?"

"Hello! Dad's an art historian! He advises companies and rich and powerful people about what art to buy. He knows everything about art! He has a library full of books. If it's real, he'll see it immediately. There's no getting around that. That's only if it is a real Leonardo, of course, and we don't know that yet," Lisa said. She widened her stance and put her hands on her hips, attempting to add some weight to her words.

Sophie thought about it. Maybe Lisa was right. There was nothing they could do. If the Leonardo was genuine, their father would recognize it.

"He's been asking to see it since yesterday. I mean, there's no harm telling half the truth, is there?"

"You're right," Sophie said, "but next time discuss your plans with me first, then at least I'll know what's coming. I was so surprised I almost choked. The pizza nearly burned a hole in my throat."

"Don't you think the timing's pretty strange – us getting a sketch from Mrs. Prattle that just happens to look like the stuff in the book?" Sophie was hoping for a reaction from her sister, but all she did was shrug her shoulders.

Lisa picked up the sketch from where it had been leaning against the bed. "The moment of truth."

"If it's real, we're going to have to give it back to Mrs. Prattle. You know that means we'll lose all the money," Sophie said quietly.

"It won't come to that. All Dad said was that we should tell her about it. He said nothing about returning it. And of course it's only fair that Mrs. Prattle gets her share. The sketch belonged to her first. Anyway, what difference does it make? We have the book, and if it's worth more than thirty million dollars, then that's more money than we could ever earn in a lifetime. Even if we split it with Jack and Tom."

Sophie nodded. Thirty million! They'd all be mega rich. It was at the moments like these that she loved her sister the most. Lisa could drive everyone up the wall at times, but there was no one more honest than she was.

"Dad, here it is." Lisa walked into her father's study holding the sketch out in front of her. Sophie came in behind her, unconsciously chewing on a thumbnail. She was almost exploding with curiosity.

Their father stood up, took the sketch in both hands, and set it down carefully on his desk, next to a neatly stacked pile of books about Leonardo da Vinci.

With his left hand he turned up the desk lamp so that it illuminated the sketch brightly. He sat down and tilted the sketch towards him.

"Hmm, I don't know this work. I just had a look through a few books. It's certainly not a sketch I'm familiar with, but I wasn't expecting it to be." He looked up as he spoke.

He bent his head forward again to inspect the drawing closely. It was so quiet in the room that Sophie and Lisa could hear their father breathing.

"I have to admit, it does resemble Leonardo's work. Well spotted, Lisa."

Lisa looked pleased.

"The frame looks newer than the sketch. This side is a bit loose. Maybe because someone tried to remove the sketch from the frame."

"That's our fault, Dad," Lisa said honestly. Sophie and I were both holding it and when we pulled it that piece of the frame suddenly came loose."

Her father looked a bit annoyed. "Imagine if this thing is real..." he said, turning the frame over to see if it could be easily opened at the back. "Sorry girls, this is going to have to wait."

"Oh Dad!" Lisa moaned.

"No Lisa, listen. If – and I emphasize the word IF – if this is a genuine Leonardo, then it's very unique. However, I don't think it is, regardless of how much it resembles his work. I'm more inclined to think it's a very good copy. But if it is the real thing, then it's extremely important that we handle it with care. To safely remove the drawing from the frame I'll need my equipment. If it is real, then we must absolutely avoid damaging it or leaving any fingerprints. It could be phenomenally valuable, including from a historical perspective."

He looked at them and put the sketch down again. "By the way, before you start sharing this with all your friends online – remember, I know you, as the discoverers of the treasure..." their father laughed. Sophie and Lisa started to giggle as if he had somehow caught them red-handed. "I don't want to disappoint you, but the chances that it is authentic... well, the odds are really, really small. I mean it. To be honest, it's pretty inconceivable that a Leonardo has been hanging on Mrs. Prattle's wall for years. And then all of a sudden she gives it to you. You realize that, right? So let's just assume it's a replica."

He took one of the books from the pile. "Look at this..." He flipped through the book until he found what he was looking for.

"Lisa, you remembered it correctly. See? These are texts and drawings in Leonardo's hand. As far as I can judge, given the glass and all, the materials and technique of the sketch look exactly like the images in this book. Even the handwritten scribbles resemble Leonardo's." Their father's finger moved between the sketch and the images in the book.

"As you can see, the texts are written in mirror-image, like they are here, which was typical of Leonardo's work. But, like I said, the chances that this is authentic are extremely small."

Sophie and Lisa looked a little deflated. This wasn't the answer they had been hoping for.

Their father saw their disappointment and said, "When we're back from Paris I'll bring my tools home with me on Monday and we'll have another look. That's a promise!"

Lisa wanted to take the sketch again, but her father stopped her.

"It's best to leave it here. Tonight I'll see if I can find more information about Leonardo's work. We need to handle this carefully."

"But you just said that..." Sophie looked at her father in dismay.

"Girls, let's leave it here. It's sitting safely on my desk. I'll have another look tonight and on Monday I'll remove it carefully from the frame. Okay, off you go. Bedtime in half an hour."

Just then their mother entered the study. "Exactly. Chop-chop," she said.

Sophie and Lisa grumpily made their way up the stairs.

Their mother looked at the ceiling, the girls' footsteps resonating through the floorboards.

"Well, is it anything special?" she asked her husband.

"I don't know. To be honest, I don't think so, I mean, it's inconceivable, a Leonardo and Mrs. Prattle. How could something like that end up there?"

"The girls think it's real," she said.

"Of course they do. If I were their age I'd think the same. It's very exciting. And yes, it could be authentic, but there are countless replicas floating around these days. In any event, I promised them I'd bring home the right tools on Monday and open up the frame. I'm not going to attempt that without the right equipment. If it turns out to be a real Leonardo da Vinci, I don't want to end up being remembered as the art historian who destroyed a priceless old masterpiece." He couldn't help but laugh at his own words.

Upstairs, the girls ran into Sophie's room together. "He doesn't think it's real," said Sophie first.

"I don't think Dad really knows. We'll just have to wait until Monday," replied Lisa. "Let's scan a few pages now and send them to Jack."

"Sure, but what do you think? Is it just a coincidence that we discovered a Leonardo da Vinci book *and* a sketch by him on the same day?" Sophie raised an eyebrow for extra emphasis. "Or..." suddenly feeling inspired, "or... Mrs. Prattle's sketch is the missing page from the book!"

"Yeah, I thought of that, too, but there are several pages missing, not just one, and the sketch is also a lot bigger than one of those pages, so it's still a bit weird. Either way, I just hope it turns out to be real. It looks like the real thing," Lisa said.

Sophie opened her desk drawer and pulled out the book. She turned to the page with the orrery.

"Here! One... two... three... It looks like a new chapter starts three pages before the drawing of the orrery. I think that's where the description of the device starts, the planetarium."

Lisa glanced at the book and nodded.

"I'm going to send Jack the pages from that chapter." Sophie grabbed her telephone and took pictures of all the pages.

"Take a picture of the one on the right as well, it could be part of the same chapter."

Sophie studied the page carefully. The frayed edges were clearly visible between the right-hand page Lisa was pointing at and the left-hand page with the drawing of the orrery. Sophie flipped a few pages ahead to see if there was anything else.

"You might be right about that page on the right. It's probably the last page of the chapter. The next page seems to have a title on it, like it's the beginning of a new chapter."

Pleased with their discovery, Sophie took another photo of the right-hand page and began opening up her apps one by one so that she could transform the pages into something they could actually read. When she was finished translating the last page, she grouped all the images together and sent them to Jack.

Thursday, June 19th, morning

Lisa was sitting in the back seat of the car. The early morning chill didn't bother her. A pair of dark leggings with a striking flame print kept her legs nice and warm. She was listening to music and the motion of the car was making her feel a little bit drowsy. Her thoughts, however, were racing.

Her feet dangled just above the floor in the back of the car and she tapped her heels against the seat to the rhythm of the music. The flame print on her leggings extended from her ankle boots all the way up to her long black shirt.

What did people wear in the old days, she wondered. It was all nonsense, of course, that ridiculous thing in the secret room, but still. Imagine if it were true, that they could travel through time and end up in the Middle Ages next week. What kind of clothes should she wear? She couldn't possibly show up at a castle in her present outfit. When they opened the port to let her in, they'd grab her and throw her in a dungeon, or burn her at the stake. She closed her eyes. What did a castle actually look like in the Middle Ages?

Lisa missed her laptop. She missed having a mobile phone, too. She'd get one after the summer, one like Sophie's. Until then she'd have to sit back and watch how easy it made her sister's life.

Robin Hood, Lord of the Rings – scenes from famous films flashed through her head. There was a good chance the castle's door would be made of solid wood. Dark brown, with big rusty nails and a peephole at eye level. When someone knocked they'd have to look through the slit first to see who was there.

In her mind's eye she sees herself standing there in the dark, in front of an enormous door. She knocks tentatively at first. No answer. Using her fists she then knocks much harder. The castle's residents probably have to walk from the other side of the castle, which explains why it takes them so long to open up. Suddenly a slit opens in the door. An old man with long gray hair stares at her, perplexed. The studs on her boots sparkle in the moonlight. Lisa gives the man a friendly smile, but he slams the slit closed. She then hears him screaming behind the door.

"Get the horses and the swords! A witch, as black as the night, with legs of fire!"

No, Lisa thought, things wouldn't end well if they approached it like this. If they did decide to travel through time, they'd first have to figure out where they were going and what they should wear. Lisa smiled. The drive to Paris had possibly saved her and her friends from being burned at the stake.

She looked out from under her eyelashes. Her father was holding the steering wheel with his left hand while his other hand tapped out a rhythm. An art historian with a passion for electronic dance music. If she had read that somewhere, she wouldn't have believed it.

She felt comfortable. Traveling by car was relaxing, it brought clarity. Everyone in their own space, but all heading in the same direction. She closed her eyes again and lost herself in the music. She thought of all the places they would go if they could travel through time.

Sophie stared at the trees racing by. She twitched her toe for every tree they passed, counting. When she reached one hundred, she started again. This gave her thoughts structure. She thought about the sketch, the room, the book, the planetarium, Mrs. Prattle, and the ermine. What was written on the pages she had sent Jack? She checked her phone. Nine-thirty. No email from Jack. He and Tom were at school, of course. Maybe they had seen the email last night? Maybe they already had more information, had figured something out?

The more she thought about it, the more she was convinced it wasn't likely. Knowing Jack, he had eaten dinner in front of the TV with his brother and father, endlessly surfing channels until they went to bed. They wouldn't see the email until after school.

Suddenly remembering that her father had looked at the sketch again the previous night, she perked up. Why didn't she think of that earlier? Just when she was about to say something, she glanced to the side. Lisa's eyes were closed.

Annoyed, Sophie sank back into her seat. Unbelievable. Wasn't she at all curious? How could she sleep for two hours straight after everything they'd experienced over the past few days?

Imagine if everything in the book was true. Imagine if it was possible to travel to the past, or to the future. The discovery of America, prehistoric times, Indians, the Crusades, flying cars!

Leonardo! If she could, she would visit Leonardo da Vinci. Who was this guy exactly? And how did he know so much? After that, she'd travel to the future, if that was possible. Would there be flying cars and people living on Mars?

She glanced at the dashboard. Ten o'clock. Time was

dragging by very slowly. Then, out of the corner of her eye, she saw something move and she looked over at her sister. Lisa was rubbing her eyes.

"Dad!" Sophie shouted. "Did you take another look at the sketch last night?"

Her father turned down the music so that they could hear him in the back seat.

"I didn't remove the sketch from the frame. I really want to avoid damaging it... I did, however, discover something."

Both Lisa and Sophie immediately leaned forward.

"It's difficult to see through the glass, but I tried to examine it more closely with a magnifying glass. There are irregularities around the edges..." He paused for a moment, "which could indicate that it is not actually a single sketch, but part of a folded sheet."

"Meaning?" Sophie asked.

"I'm not entirely sure, but it could be a larger sketch that has been folded in two, see what I'm getting at? Or a few pages taken from a book. In the early days the pages of a book were actually large sheets of paper all folded up."

Sophie and Lisa exchanged a quick look but said nothing. They didn't need to speak to know what the other was thinking.

"I'll remove it from the frame on Monday and then we'll know for sure."

"Dad, yesterday we were talking about Leonardo da Vinci. Could it be an original?" Lisa asked.

"And how come he was so clever? How did he know all those things? And was everything he wrote actually true?" Sophie asked in quick succession.

Her father lifted a bottle of water to his lips, took a few sips, and switched off the radio. Even from the back seat they could see he lived for moments like these. Nothing gave him a bigger kick than telling stories. Especially to Sophie and Lisa.

"Okay, Leonardo da Vinci." Their father cleared his throat before continuing. "Leonardo lived in Italy more than five hundred years ago. We call that period the Renaissance, which means rebirth. During the Renaissance, interest in art and culture suddenly blossomed, as it was deemed very important.

He was born in 1452 in a small village called Anchiano. He lived there with his mother when he was a child, but at the age of five or so he moved a few kilometers down the road to the Tuscan town of Vinci to be with his father.

His father was a wealthy man who provided Leonardo with a good education from a very young age. Leonardo studied difficult subjects like Latin, geometry and math, for example, and as a result he knew a lot more than other kids his age. However, even though he was extremely intelligent, he never finished school. He loved drawing and painting the most, as well as other subjects that allowed him to draw and sketch, too. Actually, he spent all of his time drawing.

The first artwork he completed on his own was a painting called *The Annunciation*. He painted it somewhere between 1472 and 1475. It took him three years to finish. The painting shows the Angel Gabriel announcing to Mary that she is to give birth to the baby Jesus. In the two years that followed..." Their father paused for the first time. "Actually, no one knows anything about what Leonardo got up to between 1476 and 1478. Like he just disappeared from the face of the earth. Then in 1478..."

"Wait, what do you mean disappeared?" Sophie asked, leaning even further forward.

"Hey, you're still listening!" their father replied, chuffed.

"Sure, Dad. Don't we always?" Lisa laughed.

"It's not that he disappeared as such. It's just that there is no record of him during this period. Then again, that in itself isn't so strange considering it was more than five hundred years ago."

"I think it's strange," Lisa said, indicating to her sister that they should remember this little detail.

"Okay, maybe a bit strange. I looked it up yesterday just to be sure, and it's true. Do you want me to stop or do you want to hear more?"

"More!" they said in unison.

"After that period, Leonardo received increasingly important commissions and lived and work in different places: Florence, Venice, Milan…"

"Dad, I need to pee, can we pull over somewhere?" Sophie interrupted.

"Sure, Sophie. I'll take the next exit. Then I'll tell you about *The Lost Leonardo*, that's a good stepping stone to your sketch," he laughed.

"The Lost Leonardo?" Sophie and Lisa looked at each other with wide-eyed amazement.

Sensing their enthusiasm, their father was now completely in his element. "Okay. So around 1505 Leonardo was working on an important commission in the Hall of the Five Hundred. That's one of the rooms in the Palazzo Vecchio in Florence, named after the five hundred members who governed the city at the time. One of the murals he painted was a large masterpiece called *The Battle of Anghiari*. And – you guys will like this – that too is a mystery. No one knows what he painted exactly. The story goes that during a major renovation a few years later they built a new wall in front of the wall with the Leonardo! On the new wall is an impressive mural by another famous artist, Giorgio Vasari."

"And this is where things get really interesting. Not so long ago, in March 2012, professor Maurizio Seracini and a team of experts drilled a bunch of small holes into the wall and used miniscule cameras to see what was behind it. Their search revealed a black pigment that is identical to the black pigment used on the *Mona Lisa*, which Leonardo painted during the same period in Florence. You know the *Mona Lisa,* right? The *Mona Lisa* is one of the most famous paintings in the world and hangs in the Louvre, the largest museum in the world. We'll definitely go see it this weekend, because the Louvre is in Paris."

The girls sitting in the back seat looked at each other jubilantly. Their weekend in Paris had suddenly became even more interesting than it already was.

"Because of the black pigment, they now assume Leonardo's greatest masterpiece ever is hidden behind that wall. The only problem is that they don't quite know how to get a good look at it without damaging the Vasari, which is also a unique painting. And that's why they don't know what he painted exactly. They believe it depicts four horsemen engaged in battle."

"Why did they build another wall in front of it?" Lisa asked, fascinated.

"From what I understand, no one knows for certain why, but they think Leonardo was experimenting with oil-based paint on stone and that the paint began to run. The story goes that Leonardo hung up fire baskets to help the paint dry faster, but this didn't prevent the colors from running, especially at

This is an image of the mural by Georgio Vasari, behind which professor Maurizio Seracini and a team of experts found traces of The Lost Leonardo in 2012. On this Vasari mural, 40 feet above the ground, a Florentine soldier waves a little green flag with the words 'cerca trova', which mean 'seek and you shall find'. Is this a sign?

the top of the painting. They say the painting remained visible for a few decades, until the Hall of the Five Hundred was renovated somewhere around 1570. There's even a legend that claims that whatever Leonardo painted on the wall should forever remain hidden from human eyes. Who knows?"

Lisa looked at her sister in eager anticipation. A secret room in their house, a book by Leonardo, Prattle's weird sketch, and now they hear that Leonardo went missing for almost two years *and* that there's a lost masterpiece, too! Was Sophie thinking the same thing?

"I really need to pee now," Sophie said. "And I have a mega earache."

Lisa rolled her eyes.

Her father mumbled something in agreement and took the next exit in search of a gas station.

Sophie, Lisa and their parents went and sat together at a picnic table in the sun, where they tucked into some fresh croissants. They were only an hour outside of Paris and expected to arrive at Uncle Hans' place around 12:30.

"Okay, so we're going to the Louvre to check out the *Mona Lisa?*" Lisa suddenly asked.

"Sure, only logical given your sudden interest in Leonardo," their mother laughed.

Back in the car, Sophie immediately returned to her question. "Didn't Leonardo also write a few books about his inventions and stuff? How did he know all those things?"

Her father was delighted to settle into his role again and happily continued his story. "During the Renaissance they had a wonderful name for people like Leonardo: *Homo Universalis*. A 'universal person'. Someone who was good at everything.

He had a well-maintained, athletic frame, was extremely clever, and had many different interests. He wasn't what you would call a scientist, as such, but he did study nature and people very closely.

His observations and beliefs covered a wide range of topics. He didn't eat meat, for example. He thought that people who ate meat made their bodies into tombs for animals. That was a highly unorthodox way of thinking for the time."

"I think I like this Leonardo guy! Eating meat is not good!" Sophie said, a bit too fanatically. No one reacted to her outburst, however. Too often in the past their conversations about meat had turned into endless discussions.

"He tried to understand certain phenomena by making detailed drawings of things and describing situations," their father continued unperturbed. "In order to paint the perfect body, for example, he first had to know how a body was built – what muscles look like underneath the skin, the precise movements of joints. The only way to do that during his time was to dissect corpses."

Sophie and Lisa looked disgusted.

"Leonardo secretly dissected corpses to inspect their insides. He often stole bodies that had recently been buried. He carried them to his atelier where he could study them without being bothered. The smell of decomposing flesh must have been unbearable, but his desire to understand the human anatomy was obviously greater than the repulsive smell. Fortunately, he wrote down many of his observations and thoughts. Today, those manuscripts are priceless. So if Mrs. Prattle's sketch is authentic, then you are both filthy rich!"

Hearing their father's optimistic assessment, Sophie and Lisa gave each other a high five in the back seat.

"So actually... what made him so smart was that he looked carefully at things and thought things through logically," Sophie said.

For a moment everyone was quiet.

"That's right," her father eventually said. "We'll visit the Louvre tomorrow, first thing, then you can see some of his paintings with your own eyes."

"Cool!" Lisa said enthusiastically. For the first time in their lives Sophie and Lisa were looking forward to visiting a museum.

"But first Uncle Hans," their father said.

The car slowed and turned off the freeway. As they approached Paris, Sophie and Lisa stared out the window in awe. They recognized a few buildings from the last time they had visited Hans. The sunlight reflected off the gently rippling waters of the Seine. A few minutes later they saw the top of the Eiffel Tower appear between buildings.

In the distance they saw Hans waiting for them on the side of the street.

Hans and their father had met as art history students. The summer after their first year they borrowed an old car and toured Europe, visiting all the important museums. France beckoned, but it was too far from home. A year later, Hans decided to go anyway. He moved to Paris, the city that stole his heart.

Sophie and Lisa had known him all their lives. Every year, they visited Paris, and every once in a while he made the trip in the opposite direction. The week before Sophie and Lisa had moved into the farmhouse on Lantern Lane, Hans had stayed in the house alone. That way, he had joked, he could break in the guest room and help out with the last remaining odd jobs.

Their father parked the car alongside the curb. Hans motioned to him to drive forward a little further. He pulled a device from his pocket and frantically started pushing the buttons. Eventually they heard a peeping sound and the property's two heavy brown doors began to creak open.

Sophie and Lisa had to laugh at him. He was dressed in dark blue jeans and a light blue short-sleeved shirt, the buttons of which were clearly ready to pop. A pair of blue and white polka dot suspenders ending in brown leather loops were doing their best to hold up his jeans. Hanging from his neck and resting on his bulging midriff was a blue cotton scarf. He looked at them cheerfully through his black horn-rimmed glasses. He had a rapidly receding hairline and the few hairs he still had stood wildly on end, as if he hadn't used a comb in years.

Hans walked alongside the car as they pulled into the garage. After some more frantic button-pushing, he managed to shut the doors again. For a moment it was completely dark in the garage. They had descended a ramp and were now underneath the house with no access to daylight. All of a sudden a bizarre neon installation began flashing in the corner of the garage.

"Isn't that cool?" Hans said to their father. "Hey girls, *très spécial*, right?"

Hans spoke English with a French twist, but they could understand him well enough. He grabbed their father's hand and embraced him, and for a moment didn't look like he was ever going to let go.

"Great to have you here for the weekend!"

Sophie and Lisa continued to stare at the neon contraption on the wall. What was Hans after buying this time? Mounted on the wall were four separate columns, each column comprising twenty-five slogans, all in different neon colors. Weird catchphrases consisting of a single word followed by either *'and die'* or *'and live'* combined to form variations like *'love and die', 'cry and die', 'sick and live', 'kiss and live...'*

"Bruce Nauman," their father said, shaking his head. "Hans, how did you get your hands on this?"

"You really don't wanna know. It's such a *grande* story."

"I could've made that myself," Lisa joked.

"Undoubtedly! That's what makes it so great!" Hans thundered. "Come on upstairs and we'll have a bite to eat. I've prepared my exquisite homemade hotdogs!"

In the meantime, he walked to the car and, without asking, opened the trunk and pulled out the suitcases.

"The stairs is there in the corner, you remember don't you? Oh, and... *attention*! Don't panic when you open the door. It's harmless."

Sophie and Lisa ran ahead up the old stairwell that connected the garage to the floors above. After running up two flights they stopped. This must be the ground floor, but there wasn't a door. They continued on up until they reached the first door. There was a key sticking out of the lock. Sophie hesitated, but Lisa nipped in front of her sister and turned the key.

"Wait! You don't know what's behind the door. Hans said that we should be careful!"

"And also that it was harmless," Lisa replied decisively. "He probably just bought a dog. Hopefully this time it's a live one." Lisa had to laugh at her own joke.

She turned the key and slowly opened the door a crack. She could see into the hallway, but didn't see anything on the marble floor. No puppy waiting, wagging its tail. Lisa was just about to open the door a bit further when something jumped up against it. She caught a glimpse of a small beige claw covered with black spots reaching around the door. Startled, Lisa jumped back. Sophie also retreated in fright down the stairs.

"HELP!" they screamed as they stumbled over each other in an attempt to get away from the door. A loud laugh could be heard from the garage.

"*Ah, bon*, so you've met Rajah?" Hans shouted.

Sophie and Lisa's parents ran up the stairs to see what all the commotion was about. They saw something that looked like a small tiger peering at them from the door opening.

"Shoooo!" Their father shouted and he threw his arms in the air to chase it away. Frightened, the creature ran back inside.

"Hans, have you gone completely mad? A tiger! He could have attacked the kids."

Hans stood on the stairs, still convulsed with laughter. "Relax man, *calme*. Haha, that was hilarious. Come on girls, don't worry, he's completely harmless."

"A tiger? Cute..." Sophie said, more than a little irked.

"Relax everyone. Come on, up you go. Let's go eat some hotdogs. And it isn't a tiger. It's a small Bengal cat. It's fantastic, man! Just *un* normal cat, but it looks like a *petit* tiger.

Hans walked upstairs, still grinning, the others following cautiously behind. Rajah appeared again from the living room. He walked between their legs purring.

Sophie and Lisa then got another fright when they saw

a woman standing next to them, as if she had appeared out of nowhere. They found themselves looking directly into the eyes of a small woman – she was no more than four-and-a-half feet tall – with black hair and even darker eyes.

"This is Wei-Wei, from Vietnam. She speaks French and *un petit peu* English. She'll bring your bags to your room."

The little woman smiled amicably and made a short bow. She grabbed their bags and disappeared again without a sound.

"I met her in the Bibliothèque nationale de France here in Paris. Six months ago, they weren't going to renew her contract. Budget cuts. So I offered her a position at my house. Wei-Wei is a Buddhist, you know… always trying to avoid bad behavior. The perfect foil to my own ways, or so I thought." Hans surveyed the room with a look of satisfaction on his face.

"Doesn't it look a lot tidier and cozier now? And she also knows everything about old Indochina – the habits, the rituals, the art… And she is an a-ma-zing cook!"

"That was never your strong suit," their father said. "By the way, do you have any painkillers? Sophie was complaining about an earache in the car."

"Ah, that's too bad. Of course, I'll go have a look. Make yourselves at home," Hans replied, while placing a bowl of peanuts on the table. "Come on," he said to their parents, "we'll have a *petit vin blanc* to start with." Hans turned around and strode off towards the kitchen.

The living room had been completely transformed since their last visit. The thousands of books that had been piled haphazardly around the room were now neatly stacked in an enormous bookcase that took up an entire wall.

"Wei-Wei sorted them by subject. Super efficient!" hollered Hans, who could see into the living room through a window in the kitchen.

Lisa tapped her sister. "Look behind you," she said, her eyes wide open.

Standing in the corner was a black, plastic, life-sized horse with a black lampshade on its head.

"Cool, isn't it?" Hans was standing in the doorway again. "I also got you two rabbit lamps, in black as well."

Before they could say anything, Hans put his arms around them and led them to the kitchen where their parents were already sitting at the table sipping their wine. They hadn't seen Wei-Wei walk in before them, but when they entered the kitchen the small Vietnamese woman was there, too, and gave them a friendly nod.

They immediately stopped in their tracks, as if they'd slammed into a wall. An overwhelming stench filled their nostrils. Sophie had to gag. Lisa wrinkled her face and tried to locate the source of the atrocious odor. There was a large plate of hotdogs on the table, but that couldn't be it. It smelled like a combination of rotten eggs and moldy cheese.

"Durian," Wei-Wei said softly, her head bowed slightly forward. "You don't like?"

"Sit, sit!" Hans said, gesticulating wildly with his arms. He picked up a large spiky fruit from the table and held it up with both hands.

"You've already had our tasty peaches from the garden, and the apples, pears, and plumbs. So I asked Wei-Wei to find something a bit more unusual. And she came back with this. They import these things from Vietnam. They smell horrendous, but they're really delicious. We'll have some later.

It tastes like a mix of banana, figs, and vanilla."

Hans tapped the side of the fruit with his palm and it made a hollow sound. "Hear that? That's why it stinks so much. It's fully ripe. It's going to be delectable."

"Not for me, the smell makes me want to throw up," Sophie said.

"Oh, stop whining. Actually, Wei-Wei wanted to surprise you with snake wine." Hans giggled like a naughty child. "It really exists, you know? They really drink it in Vietnam! They put a snake in a bottle with wine, and there are even wines with multiple snakes. But I said: 'No, Wei-Wei, we're not going to do that.' I mean, it's *très* cool to have a bottle like that on the table, but then I thought: *Non* Hansy, you can't drink that in front of the children."

Hans grabbed a knife and skillfully sliced the durian open. He then scooped out a big piece with a spoon. Lisa tasted it first and seemed to like it. And when she asked for a second bite, Sophie said she'd try it, too. She took a bite and smiled in surprise.

"No durian, no smell, pitahaya good for you." Wei-Wei said.

Hans picked up the beautiful pink fruit Wei-Wei was pointing at and cut off a slice. "Here, try some of this too, it's dragon fruit."

Sophie felt her phone vibrating. She pulled it out of her pocket and looked at the screen. It was almost four o'clock. A red dot was flashing next to her email icon. They were having so much fun that she had completely forgotten the time. Clearly Tom and Jack weren't in much of a hurry, either. Four o'clock. School finished an hour and a half ago. What had taken them so long to answer?

Hans indicated they could leave the table if they wished.

"Go and check out the rest of the house. It's no fun sitting here with us old folk." He poured some more wine for himself and their parents. Wei-Wei put another board brimming with cheeses on the table. "Your parents and I are just going to sit here and chat for a while and when we're done we can move straight on to dinner without even having to stand up!" He laughed heartily at his own ingenuity.

"Head on downstairs, to the garden. It's nice weather. When you walk to the hallway – the indoor hallway, I mean, not the hallway leading to the garage – you'll see a stairs that takes you downstairs. From that floor you can walk out into the garden. And don't mind the mess. Wei-Wei and I haven't gotten around to that floor yet. Oh... Wait a minute. I just remembered that we have guests downstairs, since yesterday."

"Are you running an Airbnb?" Sophie asked in surprise.

Hans laughed really hard. "You are so funny Sophie!"

Lisa and Sophie exchanged a quizzical look.

Hans said something to Wei-Wei that they didn't understand. "Wei-Wei is going to quickly make our guests something to eat, maybe you could bring it down to them?"

Sophie and Lisa went into the living room and plopped down on the couch. Sophie looked at her phone again. Just as she was about to open Jack's email, Wei-Wei appeared in front of her holding a bowl of porridge and two small spoons.

"Why are you giving us porridge? What kind of guests eat this stuff?"

Wei-Wei didn't understand a word she said. Sophie stood up and walked over to Hans. "Wei-Wei just brought us a bowl of porridge. If that's for the cat, we might as well leave it here."

"Oh, Rajah, completely forgot! Where is that lovely creature anyway? Good you reminded me, Sophie. When you go downstairs make sure to close the door behind you. Rajah is absolutely not allowed to go downstairs, our guests wouldn't like that one bit! As for the porridge, it's fine. We've mixed in some special feed. They're still small and they're really going to need it the next few days. Will you give it to them, together with Lisa?

"I'm sure eet eez fine," Sophie said under her breath, mimicking Hans's accent. She took the bowl of porridge from Wei-Wei and walked downstairs, with Lisa following close behind.

A large cardboard box with two heat lamps burning above it stood in the corner near the door to the garden. A loud quacking instantly filled the room.

"Quick, close the door before that tiger follows us in!" Sophie cried, while peering into the box. Seven fluffy ducklings looked up at her. They stopped their racket for a brief moment, only to start up again twice as loud a few seconds later.

The phone began vibrating again in Sophie's pocket. "Lisa, will you start feeding them so I can take a quick look at Jack's message?"

Lisa nodded.

Sophie opened her mail and read the text aloud. "Yo girls! We completely forgot to check the mail yesterday. This morning was impossible because my father was using the computer. School was boring. One of the twins barfed in class, gross man! Tom got an A for his presentation. We've printed out the pages and are going to look at them in a minute. Having fun in Paris? See you, Tom and Jack."

Sophie replied to Jack's message. "Guys! Congrats to Tom!

Drive down was fun. Dad told us lots of stuff about Leonardo da Vinci. We haven't learned anything more about the sketch. Have to wait till Monday. Very strange: Leonardo disappeared for two years at one point. Maybe he was busy time traveling? We're visiting the Louvre tomorrow, a museum that has some of his work. Hope you guys discover more soon! S&L."

As she typed she thought about how stupid the words 'time traveling' sounded. She considered changing the text, but decided not to. She was curious how Jack would react. Would he think she was being ridiculous or would he also think that it was really weird that no one knows what Leonardo was doing for those two years?

Just as she was about to put her phone away, a new mail arrived from Jack. Sophie quickly opened it. Maybe they'd discovered something!?

"Hey," Jack had titled the email. It contained no more text, just an attachment. It took a while to download it because the network was slow. Sophie was bursting with excitement. What could it be? A cryptic message?

Ping! A short beep indicated the message had downloaded. As she watched the screen, a snapshot appeared of Jack and Tom laughing hysterically and waving. Sophie thought the picture was funny, but she was also disappointed they hadn't discovered anything new. She showed the photo to Lisa, who smiled wanly.

When they were done feeding the ducklings Lisa and Sophie went up to their rooms. Wei-Wei was standing at the foot of Sophie's bed, as if she had been expecting them. She nodded at Sophie and patted the bed urgently with her right hand. Sophie obediently sat down.

Wei-Wei shone a small light in Sophie's left ear so she could examine it. Lisa couldn't recall anyone ever saying that Wei-Wei was a doctor, but as long as she didn't pull out any needles she decided not to complain. Hans appeared in the doorway.

Sophie's face was contorted with pain. Wei-Wei turned to Hans and mumbled something in French. Hans nodded and left the room again. Without asking, Wei-Wei carefully turned Sophie's head to the side to examine the other ear. After putting away her magnifying glass and lamp, she laughed warmly at Sophie and shook her head while pointing to her right ear and walking backwards out of the room.

Hans returned a few minutes later carrying two boxes and a glass of water. "You have an infection in your left ear. It's nothing serious. I have the best stuff for that right here," he grinned. "These pills will help ease the pain. I promise you that in fifteen minutes the pain will be gone. And these are antibiotics, you'll have to take them for three days. Twice a day with a glass of water. And remember... *pas d'alcool!* No alcohol, okay?" Hans laughed.

"Don't you need a prescription for this kind of medicine?" Lisa asked surprised.

Hans casually dismissed her comment. "Not at Uncle Hansy's you don't. I always have antibiotics lying around. Really handy. You're not under twelve, are you?" Hans suddenly seemed a little nervous.

"Come on Hans, that was like a hundred years ago!" Sophie sounded insulted.

Hans quickly read the instructions on the box. Feeling reassured, he held out the pill in his hand again. Sophie took it from him.

"Where did those ducklings come from anyway?" she suddenly asked.

"I was jogging in the Square des Batignolles. That's the big park where I used to go with your father, back when we were students. Before I knew it I was being followed by a string of baby ducks. I was afraid they would die without their mother. So I called Wei-Wei and she showed up carrying a box. The poor things will have to stay here downstairs for a while. I think they need another week or two before they can go back to the pond."

Hans seemed a bit gloomy for a moment, but then he composed himself and put the rest of the medicine and a glass of water on the table next to Sophie's bed, and walked out of the room. "That pill is for the next three days and the other one is for now and tomorrow morning." His head popped around the corner of the door again. "And don't leave them lying around. If that horse in the living room takes one of those pills, it'll knock him out cold." He let out a strange chortle and, as far as Sophie could tell from the rhythm of his fading footsteps, strolled merrily back downstairs.

Sophie opened her fist and looked at the pill. It was a round, light blue tablet with OC written on one side and 5 on the other. She pulled a piece of paper out of the box, assuming it was the instructions, but it was in French.

"Wish me luck," she said to Lisa and then swallowed the pills with water.

Jack and Tom were sitting on top of a pile of tree trunks, from where they could see the entire sawmill. Jack leaned forward holding the prints. He had numbered them in the top corner using the pen he now held between his lips. He mumbled softly as he read the text, which caused the pen to move to the rhythm of the words.

Tom was sitting one trunk lower down so that he could lean his back against the top tree trunk. He gently brushed an ant from his hand with a loose twig. After school they'd gone immediately to the library to borrow a book on Leonardo da Vinci. The book was now lying in Tom's lap. He opened it and randomly flipped through it. The ant was now crawling across the page. Tom sighed loudly and had to force himself not to slam the book shut. He used his hand to swipe the bug off the book. He thumbed through it a little longer, but then quickly closed it and set it down next to him.

"Hand me one of those printouts. Did you find anything yet?" He sounded bored.

Jack motioned for his brother to be quiet. He handed him a couple of printouts without looking up. "Here," he mumbled.

Tom took them and focused on the text. After a few minutes they silently swapped papers. When they were both finished, Tom climbed up to the highest trunk to sit next to Jack. Together they carefully studied all the pages again. One thing was clear: Leonardo was totally convinced that time travel was possible. It had something to do with the planetarium, the device Leonardo called an *orrery*. It was supposed to have several numbered dials on the side that you could turn to set it to a particular year.

"That's weird, I didn't see those dials," Tom said.

"No, me neither. Maybe we just didn't look carefully enough."

The pages they were looking at outlined in meticulous detail how to travel through time, and with which device. But the information on how the planetarium worked was probably on the pages they didn't have.

"Maybe this Leonardo character, maybe he consciously tore

out those pages to keep them a secret?" Tom held up the page. "Look! This is the final page of the chapter that we're reading now, the page in the book that follows the torn-out pages."

Jack nodded in agreement. Tom then read a passage from the last page out loud. "On this page he writes that he succeeded. Listen: *'Those who are crazy enough to think they can change the world usually do.'* I think he meant himself. Does he mean that nobody believed him, but he proved them all wrong in the end, or something like that? At the bottom of the page he goes on about some kind of heavenly connection."

Jack grabbed the page from Tom's hands. He carefully re-read the text:

I must be hallucinating
Watching angels celebrating.
Could this be reactivating
All my senses dislocating?
This must be a strange deception
By celestial intervention.
Leavin' me the recollection
Of your heavenly connection.

Tom began to cheer. "I just know he pulled it off!" He jumped in the air, convinced that Leonardo had succeeded. The answer must be on the missing pages. He felt the adrenaline pumping through his veins. Finally there was something to get excited about again. Tom dangled a key provocatively in front of Jack's face.

"Let's go into the secret room and see if we can find those pages. If we do then we'll know how to work the device."

"Are you kidding me! You have the key to their house?"

Jack bolted upright. "I'M NOT GOING TO BREAK IN!" he yelled angrily, and jumped off the top trunk down onto the ground in one go.

Friday, June 20th, morning

Hans parked his Mini in the underground garage near the museum. Lisa had been hoping they'd take the dark blue Ferrari, but when she'd asked Hans he had simply joked: "Do you have any idea how much gas it guzzles!"

Sophie, Lisa, and their father stepped out of the car and followed Hans.

"Is your ear feeling better now? Those pills are good, are they not?"

Sophie nodded.

"So, Leonardo da Vinci. Your father told me yesterday you want to go to the Louvre to see his work."

Sophie nodded again, a bit lethargically this time.

"Here you are." Hans took a piece of candy from his coat pocket. "A little sugar and you'll be your old self in no time." He looked around. "This way," he shouted to Lisa and her father, who were strolling behind them.

"The great Renaissance master, a genius. You've picked a good artist to like," Hans grinned.

"I'm not sure exactly what dad told you," Sophie said, glancing over her shoulder towards her father who was busy talking with Lisa, "but yes, we found a sketch and think it's one of his."

"Where did you find it?"

"Mrs. Prattle gave it to us."

"Isn't that the old lady down the road from you?" Hans laughed, the sound echoing around the garage off the low ceilings. "No way, that old *dame* couldn't have had a real Leonardo hanging on her wall! I've been in that house before. *Mais non*, I don't believe it."

Sophie looked suspiciously at Hans. She wondered why he had been inside Mrs. Prattle's house, but she wasn't in the mood to ask.

"That's what Dad said, too. He also said it looks very authentic, but he was afraid to open the frame in case he damaged the sketch."

"Why? Your father has the best tools around for inspecting things like that?"

"I know, but he didn't have them with him. He's bringing them home on Monday, then we'll open it up and find out for sure. He thought it might be a folded page, or a few pages from a sketch book."

"Wait a second, this just keeps getting better! You mean from an old Leonardo codex?"

"Yeah, something like that. That's why we thought it would be cool to see his works in the Louvre. Lisa and I have never seen one." When they walked out of the garage Sophie had to squint her eyes against the bright sun.

"Listen," Hans said somewhat conspiratorially. "We're about to enter the Louvre. You naturally have to see Leonardo's works, but that's not going to help you with the sketch. You'd be better off examining another Leonardo manuscript so that... well, you know what I mean..."

Sophie looked at him and wondered what he was getting at.

"Your father is the best in his field, he'll know a real

Leonardo when he sees one. But he's never held an actual codex in his hands..." Hans closed his eyes and seemed to lose himself momentarily in his own thoughts. "A thing like that... you have to have touched it, to feel how heavy it is, how soft that old paper is, and..." He opened his eyes and inhaled deeply, as if it were his last breath. "The scent of a lost era, the rich scent of the paper. Once you've smelled it, you'll remember it forever. When you know what a page like that feels like... the way it brushes against your fingers..." He held his hand in the air and rubbed his thumb and index finger theatrically together. "Oh yes, only then are you able to compare."

"And the value," he continued after a brief pause. "The value of the secrets Leonardo dared to write down, if you only knew..."

"Well, we're out of luck, because there's nowhere we can touch or smell a codex. Or do you happen to be Bill Gates' best friend. If so, we could just swing by?" Sophie said facetiously.

Hans had to laugh at her shrewd remark. "Unfortunately *non*. And the chances of discovering an unknown Leonardo are about as big as the chances of me having *The Concert* hanging on my wall."

"The what?"

"*The Concert*. An extremely beautiful painting by Johannes Vermeer that was stolen from the Isabella Stewart Gardner Museum in Boston in 1990, along with a number of other artworks. It's worth two hundred million and is still missing to this day." He raised an eyebrow and glanced sideways.

"Would be fabulous, *non*? That thing hanging on your wall so you could look at it every day," he chuckled.

"But what I meant to say was that the possibility that there is still another old manuscript or codex by Leonardo out there somewhere is basically zilch. I'm almost certain all of Leonardo's works are known. They're in museums all over the world." Hans paused again for a moment. "There are, however, a few Leonardo da Vinci manuscripts here in Paris."

"Awesome, can we go look at them?"

"Hmm, that's not so easy. Those manuscripts are in the Bibliothèque de l'Institut de France." His eyes darted back and forth as he thought. "We can't just show up and inspect the manuscripts. You can't simply walk into the library. It's only accessible to members of the institute or employees from the institute or one of the five academies. And even then there are strict conditions. At least two members of the institute have to put in a request to the director, Mrs. Arnault, who eventually decides who can go in and who can't."

Frustrated, Sophie stared forlornly into the distance. Hans turned around and saw that Lisa and her father had fallen far behind. He hesitated and then muttered something.

"What?"

"Nothing, just mumbling to myself. Come on, keep walking, we're almost there."

Hans grabbed his phone and made a call. "Françoise?" he said with a French accent.

Sophie tried to follow the conversation, but she couldn't understand a thing. Hans spoke fluent French. He seemed to be trying his best to calm down the person on the other end of the line. He switched rapidly from howls of laughter to wild gesticulations and back again.

"*Merci, au revoir,*" Hans said at the end of the conversation.

"What was that about? I know for sure you said the name of the library where the manuscripts are," Sophie said.

"Little eavesdropper," Hans laughed.

"Can we get in?" Sophie brightened up. "Who is Françoise?"

"Françoise is Mrs. Arnault, the library's director, an old friend of mine. I have a couple of very old books lying around my house that she'd like to have a look at. She's been asking about them for a long time. I just told her she can come by next week. And in return I can visit the library this afternoon to look at a few manuscripts."

"Cool! Then we'll see if they resemble each other!"

"Whoa, steady on, you can't come with me. Sorry. The invitation is for me alone and that's already quite exceptional."

"But what use is that?"

"Hey! I got rid of your earache for you, didn't I?" Hans said suddenly and firmly.

"Uh, yeah," stammered Sophie.

"Well then, just trust me." He winked at her. "And don't tell your father yet, okay? He's got a good job, a family... I have none of that. So just keep it to yourself for now. I'll take care of it. Look, there it is!" He stopped and pointed straight ahead. "Let's wait for your father and sister," he said as he turned around.

Sophie was so caught up in her conversation with Hans that she hadn't paid attention to where she was walking. Before she knew it she was standing in the Place du Carrousel, an enormous square bordering the Tuileries Garden, the public gardens of the former royal palace. From the Place du Carrousel she had a great view of the Musée du Louvre.

Hans noticed her astonishment. "Yep, now *that's* a real museum!" he said proudly, as if he had built it himself.

In the middle of the square, towering above her, was the world-famous glass pyramid. Sophie looked at the thousands of people strolling back and forth across the square. Some were staring at the building while eating sandwiches, and others were taking pictures of each other in front of the glass pyramid. A few street vendors were trying to hawk their wares to the tourists, their cases filled with miniature multicolored Eiffel Towers, gadgets with flashing lights, and candy.

"Wow, awesome!" said Lisa, who was now standing next to her sister. "That pyramid looks really cool in front of such an old building."

"Girls, welcome to the Louvre. The most popular museum in the world," their father said, assuming the role of museum guide. "It houses more than thirty-five thousand works of art."

"We won't be seeing them all today," Hans joked.

"You're probably thinking that's an awful lot of art, but that's only the part of the collection on view to the public. The Louvre owns more than three hundred thousand works of art!" their father said enthusiastically. "Today we'll tour the main attractions, paying special attention to Leonardo da Vinci's work, of course, with the famous *Mona Lisa* as the highlight.

The four of them strolled around the pyramid.

"The pyramid contains almost seven hundred glass panels. If you three go and stand in front of it, I'll take a picture," Hans said. "Just like the good old days!" giving them a cheerful thumbs-up.

After standing in line for half an hour, they finally made it into the museum. The escalator took them deep down into the building. Hans bought a ticket for himself and their father. Like everyone else under eighteen, Sophie and Lisa could enter for free.

"Come on, let's go through the Sully wing up to the ground floor, it's quieter there," Hans said.

Together they headed up the stairs. Sophie and Lisa suddenly felt very small inside the enormous building. Two floors later they turned right and found themselves standing in a room displaying statues from ancient Greece. Compared to the enormous lines outside and at the information booth, it was much quieter here, with only three other people strolling around this particular gallery. It was pleasantly cool inside.

Bent over slightly and with his hands behind his back, their father walked among the statues. He stopped briefly at a few of them to take a closer look.

The next room was busier. A group of people had gathered around a six-foot-tall statue. Their father perked up. "That's the *Venus de Milo*. It's…"

"A hot chick… with no arms," Lisa interrupted her father, a deadpan expression on her face, causing them all to burst out laughing.

Sophie didn't stop there either. "Venus was probably stressed out and started biting her nails…" A group of people looked at them slightly annoyed.

"One must not laugh in the Louvre," Hans said with a wink. "Come on, let's go." He motioned to them to follow him. Hans walked rapidly through a series of rooms towards the Denon wing. Without stopping, they passed through all the galleries until they reached the very last room.

"Michelangelo Buonarroti." Their father pointed to two white marble statutes mounted on large, square, dark gray stone plinths. "Michelangelo was a contemporary of Leonardo. They actually knew each other, but rumor has it they weren't exactly friends."

"Let's head on upstairs to our friend Leonardo's master-pieces. I have another appointment elsewhere this afternoon," Hans said.

After climbing the stairs they turned into the first room, where a series of large 19th century paintings hung ostentatiously on the crimson walls. A girl in her early twenties, wearing a green knitted beret, was copying one of the paintings. Lisa and Sophie looked at each other inquiringly.

"Art academy students are allowed to copy the artworks here as part of their studies. On the condition that their replicas are not the exact same size as the originals and that they clean up after themselves at the end of the day," Hans explained, as the girls did their best to keep up with him.

They walked through another smaller room and then turned right into the next one. Here too the ceiling towered above them. Daylight passed through the square glass panels in the ceiling illuminating the beige walls. A throng of people were admiring and busily photographing something on the wall in the middle of the room. As they moved closer they saw that it was the *Mona Lisa,* which was hanging behind a thick sheet of bulletproof glass.

"*La Joconde*, also known as the *Mona Lisa*," Hans said. "Or a very good replica of it in any event."

"Is it a fake?" Sophie asked astounded.

"Why?" asked Lisa, looking scornful, "All these people didn't pay good money to stand here and stare at a phony, did they? I mean, the whole world comes here to see this painting, right?"

"Opinion is divided on the matter," her father said. "The official version is that this is the one and only *Mona Lisa*."

"You don't really believe that, do you?" Hans said in a

The Mona Lisa (La Joconde) by Leonardo da Vinci, painted between 1513 and 1517, is the most famous work of art in the world.

slightly reproachful tone. "Listen, girls," he said, "this is the most famous painting in the world; it's probably worth a billion dollars, if you can even put a price tag on it. It's so valuable it can't even be insured. So it's all hocus pocus, all that bulletproof glass and stuff. I'm telling you... the real Mona Lisa is sitting safely in a vault somewhere, guarded day and night by two armed men, shielded from daylight and anything else that could damage it. This painting here, which we and ten million other people a year come to look at, is nothing but a copy."

"I don't know, Hans, I'm not entirely convinced, but okay, it's possible," her father responded. "Anyway, try to work your way through the crowd so you can get a better look."

Sophie and Lisa moved slowly forward until they couldn't go any further. Lisa pretended to sneeze really hard a few times without putting her hand before her nose, which made everyone get out of their way for fear of catching something from her. Sophie followed closely behind until they had reached the front and were standing behind a black ribbon. Guards on both sides of the painting monitored every single movement.

"She looks like you," Sophie joked.

"What?"

"Mona Lisa, she looks like you. You have the same smile, especially when you're feeling satisfied with yourself or a situation. You never smile fully either, do you?"

Sophie grabbed her phone. "Move over a bit so I can see you and the painting together, then I'll take a picture."

Lisa looked carefully at the *Mona Lisa* and changed her facial expression a few times until she felt she had mastered the smile.

"That's it! Keep your mouth like that. Don't move."

After taking the picture they wormed their way back towards Hans and their father.

"Well, I'll be… look at that…" Hans stared at the photo in amazement. "You really do look like the Mona Lisa." He winked at Lisa. "However, Hansy now has an errand to run, so let's head to the gallery to see Leonardo's other works before we really have to go."

Sophie and Lisa walked out of the room and into the adjoining gallery.

"To the left, to the Grande Galerie," their father shouted.

Tom ran as fast as he could up the gravel path. Pebbles spat out left and right. He stood with his back against the gate, gazing up the driveway. He wondered if his brother would follow him or not. Yesterday he had taunted him with the key, the same key that he was now clutching tightly in his right hand. Just as Tom was beginning to lose faith, he saw his brother appear on the other side of the street. Jack looked around anxiously as he made his way over to Tom.

"I think we'll have to climb over the fence. Lisa only gave me the key to the house," Tom said, as casually as possible. He didn't want Jack to see he was both surprised and relieved that his brother had shown up.

"What? This is crazy, we shouldn't be doing this. This is breaking in," Jack said, sounding less certain than he wanted to.

Tom looked at his brother. The fact that Jack was standing next to him now gave him reason enough to believe he would follow him. In one go he deftly climbed over the fence and stomped his feet a few times on the ground to make it sound like he was walking away. He heard Jack cursing on the other side, and a few seconds later he saw his brother's head appear over the top. Jack pulled himself over and, still cursing, let himself drop down to the ground. When Tom realized he had actually managed to convince his brother to join him, he began to laugh. Lisa would be proud of him.

"Come on, hurry up," Jack grumbled, "before I change my mind."

Tom turned the key in the front door and walked across the hallway to turn off the alarm.

"Fingers crossed," Jack said. "I really hope Lisa isn't pulling another prank on us. If she's given us the wrong code as a joke, the alarm will go off and we're totally busted."

Tom looked anxiously at his brother. The thought alone of that happening made him instantly break out in a sweat. He imagined Lisa and Sophie doubled over in laughter at the sight of their reaction to the alarm going off.

"I can see you're nervous, too, now you know how I feel. Hurry up! If you don't punch in the code, the alarm's going to go off anyway."

With trembling fingers, Tom typed in the numbers one by one. A short sharp peep sounded, followed by silence.

Jack, who had been holding his breath, let out a deep sigh when he realized they were safe. Tom leaned against the wall and felt his heart beating madly in his chest. He shook his head as he thought about Lisa. His best friend was capable of driving people crazy without even lifting a finger.

Once they'd calmed down they walked to the study. It felt strange, spooky, exciting, criminal and cool, all at the same time, to be secretly creeping through the girls' house.

Mrs. Prattle's sketch was lying on the desk in the study.

Jack picked it up and inspected the strange red cursive letters and drawings.

"Leave it," whispered Tom. "We're here to find the missing pages. That thing can wait till later. Help me push the bookcase back."

Jack put the sketch down on the desk and together they pushed back the bookcase. In the dim light they saw a pair of red eyes staring at them. Jack jumped back in fright. Mrs. Prattle's ermine bolted towards the opening. Acting on impulse, Tom moved his leg to block the creature's path, but the ermine nimbly hurdled it and leaped up onto the desk in one swift movement.

"What the...?" Jack cried out in alarm.

"Come here you stupid creature," Tom lunged towards the ermine, but it jumped aside and avoided his grasp. It landed on the sketch.

"Noooo... stupid beast, get off!" shouted Tom, waving his arms at the animal to chase it off the sketch. With a powerful thrust of its hind legs, the ermine jumped off, sending the sketch flying.

CRASH!

The sketch hit the floor with a bang that instantly broke the silence in the house.

Tom and Jack stood nailed to the floor and stared at the sketch.

"Look, there's something sticking out," Jack whispered.

Tom carefully picked up the sketch and put it back on the desk. "How is it even possible, that's totally bizarre! I swear this place is haunted! That creature gives me the creeps," Tom said in a high-pitched voice as he looked around the room as if expecting to find a ghost.

"Duh, the sketch is sticking out," Jack said. "Let's see if we can push it back in carefully so that no one will notice."

Tom sat down on the chair behind the desk and leaned over the sketch. Remarkably, the glass wasn't broken and the frame was still intact. The only thing they could see was that the gap that had already been in the frame was now a bit wider. The sketch had shifted and was protruding slightly out of the frame. Without saying anything to Jack, Tom tugged on the piece of paper that was sticking out. It dislodged from the frame and fell onto the desk.

"Are you nuts, what have you done!?" Jack looked at his brother, his fists clenched. "We came here to look for the missing pages, that's all. Not to interfere with the sketch. Put it back in the frame. You're making a mess of everything!"

Acting like he hadn't heard him, Tom ran his fingers over the sketch and picked at the edges of the paper. Jack couldn't help but look, too, even though he was still angry.

Tom held up the sketch with both hands and unfolded it.

"Tadaa! Want to bet this is what we were looking for?" He placed it back down on the desk, unfolded it, and then turned it over a few times.

They stared at the discovery in silence for a couple of minutes.

"You're right. These are the missing pages. It's a larger sheet folded double. We have to let Sophie and Lisa know immediately! They'll go crazy when they hear the news!" Jack said.

"Okay, I have a plan. You clean up here and close the bookcase. I'll scan this in Sophie's room and mail it to her. Then we can fold the sheet again and put it back in the frame so that it looks like nothing ever happened."

"And what about the ermine, where did the creature get to?" Jack asked.

"No idea, but it doesn't matter. It must have its own way of getting in and out of the house."

Tom ran upstairs, scanned all the pages, used the email option, and typed in Sophie's email address. It seemed to take forever. When 'Sent' appeared on the screen he quickly pushed the print button. Four copies rolled out of the printer. He removed the sketch from the printer, picked up the copies, and ran back downstairs.

Jack had shut the bookcase and was standing next to the desk waiting for his brother. "Did it work?" he asked anxiously.

"Yep, no problem! The files might be a bit big, though. I accidentally scanned them high-res."

"Doesn't matter, as long as you sent them," Jack said.

Together they pried open the frame and carefully slid the sketch back behind the glass. When they reached the kitchen a feeling of fatigue and emptiness overwhelmed them both. Breaking and entering had taken its toll. Tom reset the alarm and, with the copies in his back pocket, quickly scaled the fence. Jack followed and they walked back home together trying to act as normal as possible.

Hans drove at high speed, but very carefully too, through the narrow streets of Paris.

"Can you please tell me where we're going?" their father asked.

"Oh, nowhere special. I promised to stop by an old friend's, that's all," Hans said.

At the first bridge they turned right. On the other side of the Seine they immediately took another right, so that they were now driving back in the direction of the Louvre but on the opposite side of the river.

As Sophie and Lisa stared at the enormous museum on the other side, Hans made an abrupt turn. They drove down a narrow street to the left of and parallel to the main road. He parked the car halfway up the curb next to an imposing building.

"I'll be right back, five minutes tops!" he said as he slammed the door shut. He retrieved a large brown leather bag from the trunk and ran towards the building in front of them with a funny hop, skip, and jump.

"Where are we?" Sophie asked.

"This is the Institut de France. The entrance is further up around the corner. I have no idea what we're doing here and why Hans is using a side entrance," her father said. He scanned the windows of the building hoping for a glimpse of Hans.

"The what?" Lisa asked, not satisfied with her father's answer.

"It's a scientific institute run by five well-known academies. It's a real honor to be a member of one of these academies and Hans is definitely not a member!" he said with no lack of conviction.

"Institut de France?" Sophie asked surprised. Not waiting for an answer, a smile appeared on her face. She knew why Hans had driven here.

"Dad? Did you know there are Leonardo manuscripts in the institute's library?"

Her father turned around dumbfounded. "That's right, the *Paris Manuscripts*. How did you know that?"

Sophie laughed and shrugged her shoulders.

"I'm sorry Sophie, but we can't get in to see them. Without

117

the right connections it's impossible. As an art historian they might let me in, but only after getting the right introductions. Children though..."

The car door suddenly flew open. Hans jumped in and tossed his bag onto their father's lap.

"This morning I told Sophie you've never held an authentic Leonardo manuscript, right? So there's no way you can say anything meaningful about that sketch you have at home. You first need something to compare it with!"

Sitting behind the wheel again, Hans laughed a very satisfied laugh. They drove away, tires squealing.

The acceleration pushed Sophie and Lisa back into their seats.

"What do you mean?" their father said.

"Dad!" Sophie shouted towards the front. "Have a look in the bag!"

Her father opened the bag and his mouth fell open.

"No, Hans. This can't be real. Hans... Hans! What have you done!?"

"Calm down," reacted Hans, grinning from ear to ear. "I made a deal with the director this morning, she's an old friend of mine. She allowed me to look at some manuscripts... Okay, not Leonardo's, haha. That one just happened to fall into my bag," he said, pointing at the manuscript. They continued to speed along.

Sophie and Lisa remained silent in the back. They couldn't decide if all this was really cool or if things had now gone too far. They could get arrested! Sophie looked through the rear window just to be sure the entire police force of Paris wasn't chasing them.

"No big deal, girls. They'll never know," said Hans,

seemingly able to read their thoughts. "It's almost weekend and I was the last visitor for the day. I'll be a good boy and bring it back on Monday. In the meantime, you can study the manuscript at your leisure. Just don't tear out any pages or draw on it," Hans joked.

"And I'm supposed to be happy that my daughters can stay at your house if they decide to come and study in Paris some day? This could cost me my job, Hans!" their father said angrily.

"Calme! Don't be such a sissy," Hans said suddenly and sharply. "Don't make such a big deal out of it. You're an art historian, one of the best around. Come on, Sophie and Lisa were raised *très* well. So you'll be having a look at the manuscript, *et puis*? It's not like you're going to damage it or anything. And look at the bright side, you get to add to your vast store of knowledge and your two young girls get to develop an interest in *l'art. Merde*, I'm only trying to help." Hans shot an irritated look at their father.

Having got over their initial shock, Sophie and Lisa were now finding it hard to sit still.

"Don't tell your mother, okay? She's capable of turning me in to the police," Hans said.

Their father looked out the window, his fists clenched in his lap. This was way beyond his comfort zone.

After a long silence, during which time they drove through the city and managed to calm down a bit, Hans returned to being his usual happy self again.

"I'm taking your parents out for dinner tonight. Wei-Wei will make something for you to eat. You'll have plenty of time to look through the manuscript. You can have a look too, if you want," he laughed, looking at their father. Hans slapped him on the shoulder with one hand while using the other to park the car on the sidewalk in front of the garage.

Sophie felt her phone vibrating just as her parents were heading down the stairs with Hans. She looked at the screen and gasped when she saw who had sent the message. She gripped the armrest of the couch and blinked her eyes to make sure that what she was seeing was actually real. She stared at the screen. The mail was from her own scanner. A large mail full of attachments had been sent to *her* email address from *her* scanner that was sitting in *her* room in *her* house! She felt her stomach turn. The thought of a stranger in her house – worse still, in her room – at that precise moment made her nauseous. The intruder had accidentally turned on her scanner and given himself away.

Her parents were probably still in the garage. She was just about to run to the stairs and scream down to them to call the police when Lisa suddenly appeared and held her back.

"What's up with you?" Lisa asked, grabbing hold of her sister's arm.

"Let me go. Now. I have to tell Mom and Dad. There's someone in our house!"

"In our house?" Lisa asked, feeling her heart make a little jump for joy in her chest.

"I'm after getting an email from the scanner in my own room. My room! Get out of my way, we have to call the police."

"No!" Lisa said firmly. "Read the mail first, I'm pretty sure it's not a burglar we're dealing with here. I think we just found the missing pages from the codex. And you and I didn't have to lift a finger." Lisa was looking unusually pleased with herself.

Sophie felt her eyeballs burning. "No way! You... what have you done this time?"

"Just check your email. I bet I'm right and that the boys may need some help translating."

Sophie hesitated, but eventually did what Lisa asked. She scrolled down through the menu and opened her email. The high-res files were a nuisance. Downloading them to her phone seemed to take forever.

Lisa stood on the tips of her toes peering intently over her sister's shoulder. The first document opened and Sophie's jaw went tense when she saw the attachment. Lisa read it too and then took a quick step backwards. With her hands on her hips she waited for her sister's reaction.

"How did Tom and Jack get into our house?"

"Are those the missing pages?" laughed Lisa, avoiding the question.

"Lisa! How did they get into OUR house?"

"Don't be such a pain!" Lisa said. "I gave Tom my key and the alarm code. I didn't force them to do it! Actually, the fence was locked so they would have had to climb over that as well. They must have been really keen!"

Sophie briefly covered her face with her hand. She counted to ten and tried to breathe normally again. It's a good thing she hadn't known about this beforehand; she would have convinced Jack not to do it. All this Leonardo da Vinci stuff was going to give her a heart attack.

"Well?" Lisa asked impatiently.

"I think they are..." replied Sophie. She opened all the attachments. "See here. This page looks like Prattle's sketch!"

"Yeah, I think so too! I already suspected the sketch was part of the book, and Dad said it looked like it was a folded sheet. I just hope they didn't damage anything."

Sophie looked up startled. "How are we going to explain that to Dad? He will spot it immediately!"

Lisa shrugged her shoulders. "Just hurry up with the translation! We can't do much from here anyway."

Sophie opened the applications she needed as quickly as she could and then let her iPhone do the rest.

Once the attachments had been translated, they sent the text to Jack. They titled their email: Cops seek teenage burglars.

"One hour, food ready, okay?" said Wei-Wei, suddenly appearing at their side. They were so focused on what they were doing that they both got a terrible fright. Wei-Wei stuck a finger in the air. "One hour, okay?" she repeated.

Lisa looked up, but Wei-Wei was already gone again. With the bag tucked under her arm she walked to the guest room and sat on the bed. She carefully pulled out the manuscript. She still felt a little bit like a criminal, but her conscience quickly lost out to her overwhelming curiosity.

"So this is the real deal," she said in a hushed voice to Sophie, who had followed her into the room and was now pacing back and forth, continuously checking her telephone.

"Our codex and the sketch are the real deal, too. No doubt about it," said Sophie.

She had already forgotten that just a few minutes earlier she had wanted to strangle her sister. But, just like Lisa, she had only become more curious about the manuscript Hans had... well... borrowed. Only for a while, of course, no big deal. He'd return it first thing on Monday. That French institute was a kind of library after all, right? Sophie's internal reasoning helped to calm her down.

Lisa ran her hand lightly over the manuscript on her lap.

"Looking at it, it's exactly the same as the book we found. The same kind of paper, the same drawings, the handwriting in that crazy..."

Sophie looked at her phone again, but she still hadn't received confirmation that her message had been read. She hoped Jack and Tom would check their mailbox again today. Their father gave judo training on Friday nights, which meant they would be free to use the computer tonight. The question was whether they would actually do so. While she considered the situation, Sophie looked at the translated documents on her phone. After a few seconds she became irritated and tossed it onto the bed next to Lisa. "It's driving me up the wall – how can anyone read such a large document on such a small screen?"

Jack and Tom sat at their father's computer, feeling a bit bored. They were home alone for the evening. They loved the freedom this gave them, even when they had nothing to do, like now. And right now they just felt like opening a bag of chips, even though there was enough food in the freezer for a whole week.

"As long as they don't try to send an automatic reply, because that will only send the mail to her own scanner," Tom said.

"Of course she won't do that! Sophie's the smartest girl in her class. She's a super perfectionist, she'll know what to do. She's more likely to lecture us for sending large high-res images when it wasn't necessary," Jack replied.

The boys stared at the screen, waiting for a sign of life from Paris. Jack regretted yet again not having his own phone. This would have been the ideal moment to contact Sophie directly. Instead here he was hanging out at home at his father's desk with his brother, bored silly. They couldn't continue their search without the translation. He shoved a handful of chips into his mouth.

Ping!

"WE GOT MAIL!" Tom cried.

"That thirty million might sound cool, but we'll still have to go to school," said Lisa, reality coming back to bite her.

"The difference being that we'll be going to school every day in a limousine," Sophie laughed.

"Yeah, cool, but if all that stuff in the book turns out to be true..." Lisa hesitated before continuing. "If it's true, man, how awesome would that be? You, me, Jack, and Tom traveling anywhere we like in any year we like! Let's do that first and then we'll sell the book."

Sophie stared off into space. "Lisa, if it's true, we have to visit Leonardo. He wrote all this, we owe that much to him. We have to visit him and tell him he was right. Then we can also tell him that in the future he's world famous and his work is on display in museums all over the world."

"Agreed," Lisa reacted. "If he knows what a museum is. Did they even have museums back then?"

Sophie shrugged her shoulders. "I hope Jack and Tom wait for us. Now that they have all the instructions and maybe even know how everything works," Sophie said, feeling suddenly insecure.

"The good news is that if they try to use the device without us, we'll know straight away whether it's dangerous or not," laughed Lisa.

"Lisa!" Sophie said, appalled by her sister's complete lack of empathy.

Sophie looked at her watch, got up, and stood in the doorway. "Wei-Wei will have dinner ready by now. I'm going to head upstairs. Will you put the manuscript back in the bag? Better still, put it in Hans's study, that way Mom won't see it when they come back tonight."

Lisa stood outside the door to Hans's study. It was the only room in the house with a lock. She hesitated before going in. It didn't feel quite right to enter without permission, but because she didn't know where else to put the bag she decided to go in anyway. The door wasn't locked.

"Why even have a lock then?" she muttered to herself.

She looked around the room, which was minimalist in the extreme. No horses with lampshades on their heads, no stuffed animals, nothing. Just a large, immaculately white desk, a white chest, a burgundy office chair, and a small painting on the wall. Piano music sounded softly from two tiny square speakers hanging from the ceiling. The room smelled of spices. Lisa lost herself in the music and peace and quiet.

She studied the painting closely. It was of a man with long hair sitting next to a harpsichord on a chair with a bright red back. The lid of the harpsichord was open and richly decorated on the inside. Another large musical instrument lay on the black and white checkered floor.

"Lisa!" she suddenly heard someone call from the kitchen. Her sister's sharp voice startled her. She quickly put the bag down on the desk and walked to the door. "I'm coming!"

In the living room, Jack and Tom arranged the four freshly printed pages in front of them on the desk. Tom immediately began studying the text line by line. Jack retrieved the pages they'd already translated and placed those on the desk, too.

Together they carefully inspected all the texts and drawings. For a long time they said nothing, each one busy puzzling, until Jack broke the silence.

"Tom, I've got it! I know how the planetarium works! Look at this." Jack pointed at the page they had decoded earlier. "Look, we already knew this:

> *Dreams are made of this.*
> *History will never be the same.*

That refers to the planetarium. On the bottom it says you need light, remember?

> *Deus ex machina.*
> *The answer: the orrery.*
> *Use wisely the light.*
> *The seas have extraordinary powers.*
> *The future is what I see.*

It's just... we didn't know *how*, until now!"

Tom looked up expectantly at his brother.

"It's the bottle of water and light that make it work. That's why he wrote that you have to use the light wisely. If you do that, you will see the future! It's right here, just look!" Jack said, his voice skipping. He pointed to one of the freshly printed pages.

"He says time travel is easy to explain; to succeed the only thing you need is to move faster than light." Jack looked at his brother, checking whether he was still with him, before continuing. "Now that I think of it, we've talked about this stuff at school, too. Light travels at one hundred and eighty-six thousand miles per second. So if you..."

"What?" Tom yelled. "One hundred and eighty-six thousand miles per second? That's not possible. Some theory that is!" he said, screwing up his face.

"It's totally possible!" Jacked pointed to the text he was referring to. "It says here that the bottle of water doesn't contain normal water. If you shine a light through the sphere from underneath..."

Tom leaned forward. He read the text and inspected the drawing next to it. "If you're right and everything written here is true, then we've got to wait for Sophie. We can't do this without her," Tom said. He tapped his finger on a part of the drawing in front of them. Jack saw exactly what Tom meant and nodded.

"You're right, that's what we need. Sophie has to be here. We can't do it without her," Jack said. "Hide all this stuff so Dad doesn't see it. I'll mail Sophie and Lisa to tell them we've figured it out. When they get back on Sunday we'll explain everything using these pages."

Tom was jumping around the room with excitement.

"If they agree, we can try it out on Sunday," Jack said.

"You think Lisa's going to let an opportunity like this pass? It doesn't matter what Sophie wants, nothing's going to hold Lisa back. And I'm with her!" shouted Tom, who couldn't stop jumping up and down. Unable to restrain himself any longer, Jack stood up and threw his arm around his brother and began jumping around with him, too.

Lisa was sitting up in her bed, feeling quite content. Wei-Wei was inspecting Sophie's ear and nodding her head.

"Better now," she said softly. "Must take pill."

"Okay, I will," said Sophie.

Wei-Wei had already reached the door. She gave them a swift nod and closed the door behind her. Sophie took her pill and then grabbed her phone when it vibrated underneath her pillow.

"Well? Tell me! Is it them?" Lisa asked.

"They know!" Sophie said, staring at her screen in disbelief. "Jack says that they've figured it out. The planetarium is the key, but they can't operate it without us."

Lisa's eyes sparkled. "Can I safely assume now that you're glad I gave them the key?"

Saturday, June 21st, morning

"Wake up sleepyhead." Jack was standing next to his little brother's bed. "We got a message from Paris. I just checked my email. We need to go pick out some clothes today!"

Tom looked inquiringly at his brother. It was the weekend and he still wasn't entirely awake.

"Pick out clothes?" he asked sleepily.

"Yep. Lisa was clever enough to realize we can't visit Leonardo wearing our normal clothes. If we did that, we'd probably be burned at the stake the moment we arrived."

Tom raised his eyebrows. "And what reason would Dad have for suddenly wanting to buy us expensive costumes?" asked Tom.

"Who's saying we have to buy anything?" said Jack. "I just searched the internet and found a place where we can hire costumes for next to nothing!"

"But what are we going to tell Dad? Why do we need those costumes?" Tom asked.

"Ehm... Sophie mailed us a story they made up about the twins in my class having a big fancy dress party next week. Brothers and sisters are invited. They're going to search for their own outfits in Paris today, something that won't look out of place in a castle, or wherever." Jack had to laugh at his own words. "We need something too, so that we fit in."

"Maybe they're right," said Tom, looking his brother up and

down. "I'm pretty sure they didn't have jeans or sneakers back then," he joked. "More likely something cool like what Robin Hood wore. Have you already looked up what they used to wear back then? I mean, we're going to visit Leonardo, right? When was that anyway?"

Jack showed his brother a couple of pictures he had printed out.

"What? Do we have to wear that? That's nothing like Robin Hood!"

"Sorry man," Jack laughed. "I'm afraid this is it. But we won't be alone, look." Jack showed him another picture. "This is what Sophie and Lisa have to wear."

"Whoooaa!!" Tom sputtered when he saw the picture.

"Come on, get dressed," Jack said. "I'm going to go tell Dad about the party, then hopefully we can hire something this afternoon."

Tom nodded, jumped out of bed, and ran to the bathroom. "I can't wait to see you dressed up in that gear," he shouted, before slamming the bathroom door shut.

"Well, make yourselves at home," Hans said to Sophie and Lisa's parents with an extravagant wave of his arm. "If you want to use the Mini, Wei-Wei knows where the keys are."

"What about you?" their father asked, surprised. "How are you and the girls getting into town?" turning his head towards his two daughters, who were eager to go.

"The Ferrari!" Lisa yelled.

Before their parents could say anything they were already running down the stairs towards the garage with Hans. "The Mini had a good kick to it yesterday, didn't it? Well, this car is a little different," Hans beamed.

The rich sound of the engine filled the garage. Hans calmly drove the car out of the garage and drove slowly to the end of the street until he reached the first set of traffic lights. Red. The car stalled. Lisa gave her sister a look of bewilderment. For a moment it seemed as if Hans had lost his nerve. Repaying Lisa's look of bewilderment with one of her own, Sophie then saw the lights turn green out of the corner of her eye.

All of a sudden a wave of gastric acid rose up through her throat. Her stomach convulsed and was pushed back into her spine as Hans floored it. Lisa threw her arms up in the air and screamed, but her voice was completely drowned out by the roar of the engine. They recognized the sound from TV. Formula 1 cars made the same whining noise when they raced by at full throttle. After about thirty seconds Hans braked hard.

"Now *that's* what you call acceleration!" he said, beaming.

Lisa had a blissful grin on her face. Sophie swallowed the bitter taste in her mouth and conjured up a smile as well.

"We need to go slower around here, wouldn't want to have an accident," Hans said. "The streets get narrower here. In a few minutes we'll be at the store I was talking about. That party your friends have got planned seems like a lot of fun. Quite the coincidence..." he winked at them in the rearview mirror, "...isn't it? You having a party that allows you to wear the same clothes as they wore in Leonardo's time?"

Lisa looked at him as if she didn't understand what he was getting at. Sophie deliberately stared out the window.

"Anyway, the store... seriously girls! They've got the most amazing costumes ever. It's going to be one hell of an afternoon!"

131

While Sophie and Lisa were trying on different outfits, Hans went and kitted himself out in Middle Age attire.

"Take a picture of me, just for fun," he chuckled.

Sophie grabbed her telephone. A red light was flickering on the screen.

"Battery empty," she said, deflated.

Hans took the phone from her to see if it was really empty. "You can't print photos with it anyway. Imagine how cool that would be!" he said. "Wait, I have an idea. I'll be right back."

Without waiting for a reaction, Hans ran towards the exit, tossing some money onto the counter as he did so, and shouted something incomprehensible in French at the store employee who looked at him in disbelief as he ran off.

"He's now running through Paris like some kind of harlequin," Sophie said, flummoxed.

"Oh, I really don't think he cares one bit," Lisa said. "But I'd like to know what he's up to."

They changed clothes again, inspected each other's outfits, and then couldn't stop laughing. They looked like ladies-in-waiting in their long ornate dresses.

"Ta-dah!" shouted Hans when he returned a few minutes later. He handed Sophie two small boxes.

"Just down the road is the best electronics store in Paris. What are you waiting for? Open up, pronto! That one is a solar charger so your phone always works. It's already fully charged, so you can plug in your phone right away. The other one is a portable printer that you can use to print out photos instantly.

Sophie stood there perplexed, holding the items.

"Come on! Plug it in and take a picture! Do Uncle Hansy a favor." Hans smiled broadly for the camera. After about a minute, a small photo popped out of the tiny printer.

"Cool! Okay, now let me take yours." Hans grabbed the telephone and took a few pictures of the girls, and the prints popped out of the machine shortly after.

"That's the coolest thing!" Lisa said.

"Here, I've got you something too." Hans handed Lisa a box she instantly recognized.

"Hans! Really? For me?"

"Yeah, otherwise you'll have to wait another year. Now you both have smartphones. Just hide it from your parents for the time being. When you get home, tell them it was a present and all they need to do is get you a subscription. It's the same as Sophie's, and it's already charged, so everything works. You just can't call anyone yet."

Sophie and Lisa threw their arms around Hans' neck and thanked him.

After trying on a few more costumes, they each choose a beautiful dress.

As they were walking to the car, Hans leaned over and whispered into Lisa's ear. "You two are smart girls, and I'm not worried about you at all, but do keep in mind that you're still young. So do me a favor and hold onto this. Just in case you ever need it..." He dropped something into her bag.

Lisa looked at him in surprise and thrust her hand into her bag. At the bottom she felt a long, hard, cold object.

"Promise me you'll always carry it with you when you..." Hans had never sounded so serious before.

"Are we going to rip up the road again?" Sophie asked enthusiastically when they reached the car.

Hans stared at Lisa and didn't move his eyes until she had nodded her head affirmatively.

Monday, June 23rd, afternoon

After what seemed like the longest school day ever, the four of them walked up the gravel path chatting. Tom and Jack were both carrying large bags filled with clothes they had quickly picked up from home.

Lisa couldn't help but make fun of them. "I saw that you both have to wear pantyhose? Maybe you want to use some of our makeup as well?"

"Hmm. Did your father look at the sketch when you got home last night? He shouldn't have noticed anything," Jack said.

"No, luckily he hasn't looked at it yet. He will tonight though, when he gets home from work," Sophie said. "But first you'll have to tell us how that thing works and why you couldn't do it without us."

"Yeah, okay, just hurry up. Go and get your stuff," Jack said.

While the boys walked straight to the study, the girls went upstairs to get their own costumes. When they came back down, packed and dressed, the bookcase had already been moved aside. A light was burning in the secret room and they heard the boys speaking quietly. Lisa walked in and put her bag down on the floor.

Sophie stopped at the desk and studied the sketch. "The gap in the frame is a little bit wider than it was, but you can't really see it. I don't think it's that obvious."

134

"See, I told you," she heard someone say from behind the bookcase.

"Come on, we don't have any time to lose before your parents get home," said Tom. When Sophie walked in he stood up and immediately closed the bookcase behind her. A worried look crossed Sophie's face.

"What if it doesn't open from the inside?"

"Don't worry, Jack and I tested it on Friday. I shut him in just for fun to see if he could get back out on his own."

"And I did," Jack replied venomously.

"Did you bring your phone?" Jack asked.

Sophie turned halfway around and showed him her green backpack as proof.

"We're going to need it, otherwise it won't work."

"So it's not us you need then, just my phone? That's what you were after?"

"Uhm, well... yes. Without your phone we're not going anywhere," Tom said.

Sophie put down her bag of clothes and opened her backpack. She looked inside and realized she hadn't emptied it since Paris. The antibiotics, the painkillers, the solar charger, and the small printer Hans had given her, and even her geography book were still inside. She took her phone from the bag and gave it to Jack. "I want to know what you're going to do with it."

Jack took the phone but said nothing.

"Jack, seriously, whatever you're planning, don't break my phone. If you break it, I'll be in big trouble with my parents."

While Jack studied her smartphone and placed it next to the planetarium, Sophie took out all the loose papers and candy wrappers from her backpack. "Disgusting" she mumbled.

Lost in her own world as she reorganized her bag, she hadn't noticed that the others had already changed clothes. When she looked up she couldn't keep herself from laughing.

"You guys look... fabulous!" Sophie cried.

"And now your turn," Jack laughed, before moving the planetarium to the middle of the room. Tom picked up a few things that were still lying here and there on the floor.

"Look at this," Jack rotated the planetarium so that everyone could see the cogwheels.

"What are those for?" Lisa asked.

"The pages we have say that you can use them to set the year you want to travel to," Tom said.

Lisa couldn't stop laughing. "Guys, seriously, look at us. We're dressed up like monkeys, standing around this crazy thing, and actually thinking we can just beam ourselves off for a quick rendezvous with Leonardo da Vinci?" She stared at her friends waiting for them to react.

"It's going to work," Jack said, deadly serious. "It has to." He indicated to his brother to spread the pages out on the ground. Sophie admired the structured way in which he had numbered everything. At least this way they had a clear idea of what to do. They all leaned over to look.

"Don't get me wrong. It's just that... you guys are suddenly so serious. What do we do if nothing happens?" Lisa said.

"The book is still real and the sketch is too. Okay, together they make up one book, but that alone is worth millions," said Sophie with an enormous grin.

"Yeah, if it doesn't work, then so what. We'll still be richer than rich!" said Tom, equally excited. He threw his arm around Lisa. "But Lisa, believe me, this is going to work. After reading everything, it has to!"

"This bottle here, we thought it contained ordinary water, but it's actually seawater, and not just any old seawater. It's a mixture of the water from the seven seas," Jack said.

"*The magic of the seven seas*," Sophie said quietly to herself. "But wait a minute... the seven seas? That's not really possible, is it? I mean, he didn't have an airplane to fly around the world in. How did he pull that off?"

"Wrong," Jack said. "The seven seas in Leonardo's time weren't the seven seas as we know them today. I looked it up." Jack had anticipated Sophie's comment and proudly pulled a map of the world from his back pocket.

"These were the seven seas in Leonardo's day." As he spoke he pointed to the different seas. "The Mediterranean, the Adriatic Sea, the Black Sea, the Red Sea, the Arabian Sea, The Persian Gulf, and the Caspian Sea. It's still a pretty long drive," he laughed, "but in those days there were enough people who traveled all over the region. And that's probably how he collected the water from all the seas."

Jack knelt down next to the planetarium and viewed the planets from the side. He pushed the metal rods gently with his finger until all the spheres were lined up on the same horizontal.

"If I'm not mistaken..." He maneuvered the last sphere into place.

"Holy Moly!" he exclaimed in surprise. "Check this out! If you look here... try to look through the spheres."

"Through the spheres?" Sophie asked.

Jack stood up to make room for her, but before Sophie could take his place Lisa moved in and squatted on her heels, looking at the first sphere. She moved her head slightly up and down.

"Yeah, I see it too! Huh? All the spheres have tiny holes you can see through." She stood up so that her sister could look as well.

"Jack and I read about that on the missing pages. Each sphere has a tiny little tube going from top to bottom and also one going from one side to the other," Tom said. "That stuff about the cogwheels was on those pages as well."

"Okay, and now what?" asked Lisa.

Jack twisted open the bottle and poured a few drops into each sphere. They all watched breathlessly.

"The water's not running out at the bottom!" Sophie said surprised.

"That's right, too," Tom said pointing to the page he had referred to. "It says here that adhesion keeps the water from running through. That means the water sticks to the inside of the little tunnels, instead of running through."

Everyone looked anxiously at Jack, waiting for whatever came next. "It says on the missing pages that the planets – these spheres – have to be aligned with each other in one straight line and that you then have to pour a few drops of water from the seven seas into each one. Now we need to adjust the cogwheels on the back to the year we want to visit." Jack leaned over the planetarium and started turning the wheels.

"And what year would that be?" Sophie asked.

"1475," said Jack.

"That's when he was working on his first great masterpiece," Lisa said.

Everyone looked at her in surprise.

"What? That's what Dad told us in the car, isn't it? That's when he was painting the annussia... ehm, something like

Announcement, or whatever it's called."

Sophie clapped and bowed theatrically. They all had to laugh because she looked a bit ridiculous in her flamboyant dress.

"So, what now?" asked Lisa, who still wasn't taking it all very seriously.

"I think we're almost there," Tom said. He checked the last missing page together with his brother. "There's a piece of chalk in the side panel, now we just need to write down our destination."

"Where?" Sophie asked.

"There's a small wooden plank made of poplar next to the cogwheels."

"Leonardo painted the *Mona Lisa* on the same type of wood! And before you all get too excited, Dad told us that as well. I do actually listen sometimes," Lisa grinned.

"So we have to write our destination down on that piece of wood," Jack said.

He walked around the planetarium and bent down. "Florence," he said as he wrote.

"What's that?" Sophie cried, jumping back in fright. The ermine had appeared again out of a dark corner.

"Just ignore it," said Tom. "When we came in here on Friday she was here, too. No idea how she keeps getting in, but it's harmless."

Sophie and Lisa watched the creature, which came over and sat next to Jack as if it were the most normal thing in the world.

"Okay, everyone ready?" Jack asked.

"What are you going to do next?" Sophie asked.

"Tom, check the pages to make sure we got everything

right," said Jack, crouching next to the ermine on the other side of the planetarium.

Sophie turned around and quickly grabbed her backpack.

"The painkillers are in my bag! I'll need to bring it just in case I get another earache," she whispered to her sister. Lisa grabbed Sophie's hand and together they leaned slightly forward to read the pages along with Tom.

Tom's fingers ran down through the text. "Planetarium, check. Planets aligned, check. Pour water, check. Date, check. Ehm, Jack, is the date right?"

"Yes, check," he replied.

"Okay, destination... Jack, destination?"

"Yep, also check. Florence 1475, check."

"We're all wearing the right clothes, too. Everything's fine, Jack, up to you now."

Sophie squinted her eyes and tried to focus on Jack's every movement.

"I'm turning on your phone, looking for camera. Wait a second..."

Jack was tinkering with the phone. "Found it! Now the timer, five seconds, check. Okay, I'm going to put your phone in the right-hand panel with the flash pointed upwards. According to the drawings, that's where it's supposed to go. That's why the space underneath the latch on the right was empty.

"Did it work for Leonardo?" Sophie asked.

"Eh, no, not really," Tom said. "He wrote that it didn't work at first because he didn't have anything that produced a strong enough flash. But then... well, then he succeeded. That's what he wrote anyway."

Lisa's eyes shone with excitement. This was the kind of

stuff she lived for. "Come on, what are we waiting for. Turn the thing on!" she cried.

Sophie clutched her backpack and squeezed Lisa's arm with her free hand. Tom was crouched down on the other side and threw his arm over Lisa's shoulder. "Come on Jack!" she cried again.

Jack swallowed and clicked on the timer with trembling fingers.

"The ermine!" yelled Sophie.

"Leave it!" said Lisa. "If we have to, we'll bring her back with us!"

Tom counted down out loud. "Five... four... three... two... one."

Flash! Blinded by the light, everyone squeezed their eyes shut.

"What's happening?" Sophie screamed as hard as she could, but no sound came out of her mouth. The room was completely silent.

The flash had caused the spheres on the planetarium to revolve on their axes. A bright light radiated out of the little tunnels. The spheres themselves appeared to light up as they turned faster and faster.

Sophie's toes were tingling and she had a strange feeling in her stomach. She glanced at her feet to locate the source of the tingling, but when she looked down she saw that her feet were hovering above the ground, she was floating! Terrified, she looked across at Jack. He seemed to be screaming, too, without making any sound. Still crouching and with the ermine next to his feet, he seemed to be rising slowly up into the air. Lisa and Tom were also floating in the air next to her.

Lisa had never looked so happy, this was the first time Sophie had ever seen such delight on her sister's face.

"What's happening?" Sophie yelled, but there was still no sound.

The light radiating from the spheres slowly illuminated the entire room. With a low-pitched buzz, the light seemed to swallow everything within a few feet of the planetarium. She watched in amazement as the ermine vanished into thin air after being touched by the light. She squeezed her eyes shut in fear. When she opened them again Jack was gone as well. Suddenly she felt her hand losing its grip on Lisa's arm, which she had been grasping tightly the entire time. Paralyzed, she looked at her sister. Lisa said something, but all she could hear was the buzzing sound. Sophie looked around her in desperation. Tom had also vanished. The light hadn't reached Lisa yet because she had pulled up her feet. She gave Sophie a thumbs-up and flashed a smile. "See ya," she seemed to say. She stretched her legs. Gone. Lisa disappeared as soon as the light hit her ankles.

Sophie was sitting farthest from the planetarium. She had lifted up her legs so high that her knees were touching her chin. The light rose slowly until it was impossible to avoid it. She closed her eyes and waited for it to engulf her.

Monday, June 23rd, late afternoon

Sophie looked around with a rising sense of alarm. What had gone wrong? The awful smell was overwhelming. When she turned and tried to run, the heel of her shoe got caught in her long dress. She threw her arms back instinctively to cushion the fall, but Jack caught her just in time.

"Sophie! Yo! You okay? We're here! But we should have brought some air freshener..." He laughed sheepishly at his own joke.

"I got here first, then Tom, then your sister. And now you're here, too."

Sophie was still dizzy from hitting the ground. She looked around to try and get her bearings, but she couldn't orientate herself in the dim light. All her feelings seemed to converge in her stomach: pain, dizziness, disgust. The smell of death rushed into her nostrils; the thick, sweet, oily stench of a decomposing corpse overwhelmed her again. She pinched her nostrils and bent over double with revulsion.

Jack did his best to bring her back to her senses. "The planetarium... unbelievable... it actually works! All that light radiating from those little planets. When it touched me everything suddenly went turbo. A second later I was standing here."

"Why am I wearing this?" Sophie stammered. She covered her eyes with her hands, trying to remember why she was dressed this way. She was wearing a long red velvet dress with yellow accents.

"Hello… hello!" Jack waved his arms in front of her face. He tried his best to grab her attention. Sophie tentatively removed one hand from her eyes and gave him a puzzled look. Slowly, things started to come back to her.

"Where is Lisa? Where are Lisa and Tom?" she asked in a trembling voice. "And how…" She forgot to cover her nose as she spoke and was again overwhelmed by the horrible stench. She couldn't even finish her sentence. She gagged and had to bend over. Gastric acid burned her throat.

"Ugh…" she groaned, as saliva dripped from her mouth and stopped her mid sentence. She stood with her hands on her knees, eyes bloodshot. "Jack, where's that stench coming from?" She was almost pleading with him.

"Sophie, relax… breathe! I mean, through your mouth." Jack winked at her as sympathetically as he could.

"Lisa's in the room next to us… with Tom. That's where the smell is coming from. I think you're suffering from some kind of jetlag. It took you ages to get here! We're all fine."

Jack noticed that Sophie still had a dazed look in her eyes. "Sophie, helloooo! We're here! In Florence! In the Renaissance! We did it!" He pointed at the rickety-looking door. "Before the rest of you arrived I took a quick look outside, and we're really here!"

"Huh?" Sophie stammered perplexed. "Did we… Did we really make it?"

"Yes, really! It looks totally different outside, and I saw people walking around wearing the same clothes we're wearing."

Sophie looked him up and down. It was only now that she

noticed that Jack was wearing a strange costume.

"In the next room, where the stench is coming from... he's there! It's really him!"

"What?" she said in amazement. She didn't know if it was real or whether she was just dreaming. Or maybe she was dead? She felt a wave of panic rise inside her. Was she dead and was the stench the smell of her own body decomposing? No, she shook her head, that was impossible.

"Leonardo?" she sputtered incredulously.

Jack nodded and pointed towards the door. "He's in the next room, where the stench is coming from. Tom and Lisa are there as well."

"Really? How do you know it's Leonardo?"

"Well, ehm, I can't understand a thing he's saying, but, you know, he pointed to himself and said 'Leonardo da Vinci'." Then, for some odd reason, Jack flexed his biceps.

"By the way, he's, like, a really young dude, around twenty I think, not nearly as old as in the picture we saw on the computer."

Sophie was slowly regaining her composure. "But, Leonardo... are you sure? I mean, doesn't he think this is kinda weird? Isn't he like completely shocked?"

"Not really. It's almost as if he was expecting us."

"Sophie!" Lisa suddenly yelled from the adjacent room. "What are you doing? Get in here and check this out!"

"Isn't he dangerous?" Sophie stood on her toes so that she could whisper in Jack's ear. "You never know, he might murder us."

Jack couldn't suppress a nervous smile. "Relax." He held out his arms to her and tried to calm her down. "When I fell out of the sky, so to speak, I found myself lying on the ground."

Jack bent down and held his ankle. "I landed awkwardly and my ankle hurt like mad. I was cursing my luck when suddenly he appeared beside me. And it was really strange, I was shocked, but he wasn't at all! He looked me up and down, said something in Italian and then ran off again. I heard him rummaging around in the other room and knocking things over. He was obviously looking for something. Then he came back with a pile of loose sheets of paper and tossed them into my lap. Pages from a book."

"Book?" Sophie mumbled.

"*The* book!" Jack looked at her urgently. "The book we found. The book that's lying in your drawer at home! The pages he tossed to me are from that book."

Sophie looked at him in bewilderment.

"Leonardo crouched down beside me, put a hand on my shoulder, and pointed to the drawing of the planetarium on one of the pages. Then he helped me up and pointed at the planetarium there behind you."

Sophie turned her head and saw the device. A few of the planets were still turning. Her telephone was sitting in the right-hand panel.

"While Leonardo was showing me the planetarium, Tom appeared out of nowhere and slammed into the ground. Leonardo jumped back, startled, but he quickly regained his composure. He pointed to Tom and me, stuck two fingers in the air, and began talking again in Italian. I couldn't understand a word he was saying, but he was calm and composed. He wasn't behaving like a murderer in any case. Lisa appeared soon after that..." Jack shrugged his shoulders. "You know what your sister is like, she saw me and Tom and was instantly at ease, and wanted to look around the house immediately!

Leonardo was quick to spot Lisa's natural curiosity and led her into that room there to show her what he was working on."

"Sophie! Are you coming or not?" Lisa yelled.

"Yeah, hang on!" Sophie yelled back. "I'm putting my trust in you, Jack." She grabbed his hand. "I hope we haven't made a mistake by coming here."

Sophie allowed herself a discrete smile, but it didn't last very long. The smell was so unbearable that she had to focus on her breathing to keep from throwing up.

Together with Jack she entered the room where the stench was coming from. There weren't any doors or windows, and it was even darker than in the room in which they had landed. A single oil lamp cast a slightly eerie light.

Tom and Lisa stood shoulder to shoulder bent over a table, their backs turned to her. In the dim light Sophie couldn't really see what was on the table, behind which stood a man in his early twenties wielding a large, heavy knife. With a macabre, almost demonic smile on his face, he raised the bloody knife with his hand.

"Watch out!" Sophie screamed. The man sliced through the flesh in one fluid motion. Sophie saw blood splatter and heard the sound of bones being crushed.

Lisa turned around and saw the horrified look on her sister's face. "It's okay, Sophie, don't be a wimp. Leonardo's just showing us what he's been doing. Come and have a look," Lisa said casually.

Jack nudged Sophie from behind. She took a few steps forward and was dumbstruck by what she saw.

"A horse," Lisa giggled, "just like the one Hans has in his living room, except that this one used to be alive."

Tom began laughing somewhat nervously. Lying on the table in front of them were the stinking remains of a horse that had been cut up into pieces. Enormous black flies buzzed about above the horse. Leonardo was carefully dissecting the dead animal. Judging by the smell, the carcass was already a few days old. Leonardo made a few more cuts with his knife, producing fleshy, crunching sounds. He needed all his strength to slice through the tendons and bones. Fresh maggots crawled out of the flesh and onto the table. Sophie looked at the wriggling creatures in disgust.

Leonardo used the knife to sweep the maggots onto the floor. He grabbed a rag and wiped the knife clean before setting it back down on the edge of the table. He lifted up a severed shank with two hands, turned it over, and put it back down again. The hair was plastered against the horse's skin. The powerful smell of rotting flesh, clotted blood, and horsehair rose from the table.

Lisa stood on the tips of her toes and leaned in to get a better look. Leonardo walked around the table and stood next to her. He lifted the bloody leg and spoke rapidly while pointing his finger at the tendons, blood vessels, and bones, all of which were clearly visible where the shank had been severed.

Sophie had climbed onto a rickety wooden stool to get a better view of what Leonardo was doing. He didn't look anything like the old man they knew from the internet. She thought of Leonardo's self-portrait, which pictured an old man with a long beard. But standing here in front of her was a fit young man bursting with energy, who had hardly blinked when they suddenly appeared out of nowhere.

Leonardo walked quickly around the table, lifting up a

chunk of flesh every so often to reveal the bones and tendons he had already removed from the rotting flesh. As he explained everything in Italian, he seemed very aware of the fact that they didn't understand him. He tried to clarify his words using gestures, hoping they would understand what he was telling them. Lisa and Tom watched him as if in a trance. His calm, friendly manner helped Sophie to relax, despite the smell.

Then she remembered something and jumped down from the stool. "Wait!" she yelled to the others, and quickly ran to the room they had just come from. Four pairs of eyes stared after her. Even Leonardo stopped in mid-sentence, a long tendon he had just removed from the horse's chest dangling from his right hand.

"I just thought of something," she yelled from the other room.

She came back in carrying her phone. It was a strange scene. On the left a horse in the late stages of decomposition, and on the right Sophie wearing a long velvet dress and holding a shiny telephone.

Jack looked at her quizzically. "What are you going to do?" he asked.

Sophie didn't reply, her fingers moving rapidly across the screen.

"I don't know what you're trying to do, but you do know you can't use the phone, right? There are no wireless networks around here." Jack chuckled at his own joke.

Sophie gave Jack a withering look. "I know that," she said firmly, as she continued typing on her phone.

When she was finished she turned to Leonardo. "Leonardo...?"

Leonardo nodded and waited for her to speak.

She held her phone out in front of him. "My name is Sophie." She quickly gestured for Lisa to keep quiet.

"*Il mio nome é Sophie*," came a voice from the phone.

Leonardo looked at Sophie's smartphone, dumbfounded. "*Cosa c'é di che,*" he said as he stepped towards hers.

"What is that?" said the voice in the telephone.

Sophie smiled broadly and held her telephone up in the air. "We'll explain later," she said, as her telephone automatically translated her sentence into Italian.

"*Va bene!*" said Leonardo, throwing his arms up to heaven in an apparent gesture of gratitude.

"All right!" said the telephone.

Sophie saw that everyone was staring at her in disbelief.

"That's awesome sis!"

"Cool, isn't it? When I was downloading the apps to translate the pages I downloaded this translation app, too."

Sophie was enjoying her friends' obvious elation so much that she forgot to tell them she had downloaded the app by accident.

"But if the battery dies, we're in trouble," said Tom.

Sophie shook her head to dismiss his concern.

"We thought of that as well," Lisa said.

Sophie rummaged quickly through her backpack and pulled out the solar charger.

"How are we going to get back, actually?" Tom asked suddenly.

"Tom! We just got here!" Lisa said sharply.

Listening to their conversation, Leonardo walked towards the planetarium. "You can use this to go back," he said. "It brought you here after all. Don't worry, I wrote everything down. You can return whenever you want. But not just yet.

Let's get to know each other better first. There is... there's so much I'd like to know, so many questions."

"We're not going anywhere," said Jack, clearly relishing his role as the senior member of the group.

"I wouldn't mind getting something to eat, though. Pasta... pizza?" Lisa whispered to Tom.

"Pisa?" Leonardo looked at her in surprise. "You want to go to Pisa? Why?" He didn't understand what they were on about. "We can eat here. Sorry, I'm a terrible host. I completely forgot to offer you something. Sorry, a thousand times sorry."

Leonardo seemed upset by his apparent lack of manners and he looked quickly around the room in search of a solution.

"No big deal," Lisa said, "I didn't mean it that way." She rubbed her stomach. "I'm hungry and just fancy something tasty, like pizza maybe. We're in Italy, right?"

"Pisa?" Leonardo repeated. He shrugged his shoulders. "Why do you want to go to Pisa? Do you have any idea how far that is? It's half a day by horse, and I don't have five horses! You may have time machines in your age, but we can't just head off to Pisa for a bite to eat."

"Pisa!" Sophie said when she understood the confusion. "Pisa! Lisa, he's talking about Pisa, the city, as in the leaning tower of Pisa."

"Well, then it's your phone that's not translating it right. I meant pizza the food." Lisa looked at Leonardo. Holding her hands out in a flat circle, she tried to mimic a pizza. "A pizza, you know, flat bread with cheese, tomatoes, and herbs."

"Ah, bread." Relieved, Leonardo quickly grabbed his coat. "Come, follow me. Let's go get some food, but be careful out there!" He looked them over. "People will want to know who you are. Try to avoid their questions, and under no circumstances let anyone see or hear your talking black box! We'll think of something for that later. And we will have to come up with a really good story about who you are and where you came from." Leonardo quietly sank into thought as he paced the room. "Milan... Pisa... Venice..." Leonardo shook his head. "Rome... all too well known," he mumbled to himself.

"Anghiari!" Leonardo suddenly yelled. "Everybody knows Anghiari, but nobody knows anyone from Anghiari. That's a good start..." Leonardo continued to pace back and forth.

"We'll tell them you're from Anghiari... that you're on your way to Pisa, to your uncle. Yes, that's good. Florence is right in between. You were looking for a place to rest and ran into me."

"Okay," Sophie nodded enthusiastically. "But you ran into us and then? Why are you helping us?"

Leonardo hadn't expected this question, but immediately replied, "I saw you on the outskirts of the city... this morning... when I was walking there... you were on horses... and you were being attacked!" said Leonardo, clearly impressed by his own ingenuity.

"You and a bunch of thieves were fighting, I saw it, and I managed to chase them off. Now you're staying the night here. Tomorrow you'll continue your journey." Leonardo looked expectantly at the four of them.

"Great story," Jack smiled affirmatively, while looking at his friends.

"But the horses," Sophie said, "where are they? What do we say if they ask about those?"

"Ehm..." Leonardo was silent for a moment as he looked at Sophie admiringly. It didn't happen very often that he came across someone who forced him to think on his feet.

"I'll make something up. I'll say that they're at home, at my father's house, that we brought them there.

"Your father's house?" Sophie asked surprised. "So you don't live here?"

Leonardo answered her question: "I'm twenty-three. I live at home with my father and the rest of the family. This studio belongs to Andrea." He spread his arms wide in anticipation of their applause. They would surely know how great an achievement it was for a young man like him to be working as an apprentice at one of the city's most important studios.

Leonardo looked at them with a proud expression, but then quickly realized he hadn't impressed them in the slightest. "Verrocchio?" Leonardo attempted. "You don't know him?" He put his hands on his head in disbelief. "Verrocchio is the best mentor in all of Florence! He teaches me everything – drawing, painting, working with metal and leather, sculpting, etching…"

They all looked sheepishly at Leonardo.

He dismissed their sympathetic gaze, irritated that they didn't know who his mentor was. "This, where we are standing now, is his studio. I work here all day and sometimes all night. Verrochio is away at the moment, so you can sleep here tonight."

"Will he be back soon?" Sophie asked, obviously not prepared to take everything Leonardo said at face value.

"He left yesterday in a furious mood and won't be back for a while, so you don't have to worry about that."

"Furious?" Tom asked.

"Yes, and you know why? Because I helped him!" Leonardo looked livid.

"Why was he angry that you tried to help him?" asked Tom.

"Andrea is working on a commission for the church of San Salvi," Leonardo pointed at one of the pictures hanging on the wall. "He's been working on it for three years already and asked me to help him. I painted the scene on the bottom left."

Tom approached the painting to get a closer look.

"I can see from here that it looks just fine, right?" Lisa shot a quizzical glance at Leonardo.

Leonardo looked crestfallen and bowed his head. "That's precisely the problem. When I finished it yesterday Verrocchio became extremely angry... not at me, but at the situation... at himself. He screamed that I was a better painter than he was. Do you see that paint on the wall in the corner?

They saw the splashes of paint and nodded silently.

"Andrea threw a handful of brushes against the wall and yelled that he would never paint again. Then he ran off and I haven't seen him since. He'll come back, I know he will, but it might not be for a while."

"So," he continued, "you can sleep here tonight. There will be no one dropping by unannounced."

"Okay, so you're a better painter, but can he still teach you things?" Sophie asked, anxious to know more. Before he could answer, however, she fired another question at him, one that she'd been dying to ask for the past hour. "That horse over there, or what's left of it, did Andrea also teach you how to dissect it?" Sophie was clearly struggling with the idea that Leonardo might have killed the horse for nothing.

"Sophie! What are you playing at?" Lisa hissed, poking her in the ribs at the same time.

"No..." Leonardo raised his hands to silence Lisa. He seemed fascinated by Sophie's questions.

154

The Baptism of Christ by Andrea del Verrocchio was completed in 1475 by his pupil Leonardo da Vinci who painted and finished the details of some parts of the painting, particularly the angel on the left.

"It's good that you ask. It shows you use your intelligence wisely. You contemplate things and you display empathy. You could teach my contemporaries a thing or two. The horse was dead when I found it, so it didn't suffer. I'm studying the creature so I can better understand its anatomy. This way its death will also serve a purpose."

Sophie felt ashamed at having doubted him.

"You shouldn't be embarrassed by your questions, making assumptions is usually worse. I like it that you ask so many questions."

Sophie was thankful that Leonardo wanted to make her feel at ease.

"I have great respect for nature," said Leonardo. "To most people, a horse is nothing more than food or an instrument of labor. I believe that we ourselves are part of nature. I don't eat meat or fish. Isn't it absurd to cook a fish in the same water it swam in?" He shuddered visibly and walked to the door.

"But let's get some food first..." he said before turning around again wearing a face full of doubt. "On the other hand, you should stay here. It's too dangerous."

"What!?" Lisa looked like she was ready to explode.

"Look," Leonardo opened the door a few inches. "It'll be dark soon, it's far too dangerous. You don't know your way around, you never know what might happen. I can't risk it. Make yourselves at home, look around, I have nothing to hide from my friends from the future. I'll be back soon."

Before Lisa could react, Leonardo had slammed the door shut behind him. She stood in the middle of the room feeling upset. "Did I really dress up in all this garb for nothing?" Disappointed, Lisa looked around hoping someone would agree. "Look at us," she cried, "just look at what we're wearing!"

Tom and Jack looked at each other. Back home, people would laugh at them for wearing these clothes, but there was nothing wrong with them here. They were both wearing black leggings and knee-high brown leather boots, just like Leonardo. Jack wore a white shirt with puffy sleeves and a sort of dark velvet gown that matched his black and blue hat.

Tom looked like a young prince. He was wearing a dark gray shirt with long sleeves under a tight sleeveless velvet tunic that came down almost to his knees. A wide belt the same color as his boots was wrapped tightly around his waist. When they looked at each other they burst out laughing.

"Okay, okay, maybe it is a little bit weird," said Tom.

"A little bit?!" Lisa cried indignantly. "Look at us! Sophie looks like a bumblebee in that dress and I... I feel like I'm being strangled! And look at this bonnet on my head with these stupid ribbons hanging down the side of my face! They're driving me crazy!" Lisa shouted, glaring at her friends.

When Sophie saw her sister's face she couldn't help but laugh. Lisa wasn't angry very often. The contrast with the ladylike dark green dress she was wearing couldn't have been any greater.

"Tom?" Lisa pleaded, looking for support.

Tom shook his head. "I'd like to go outside, too, and you know I've always got your back, but I believe Leonardo when he says it's too dangerous for us to go out."

Lisa rolled her eyes and looked at him with bitter disappointment.

"I'll go out with you tomorrow," Tom said. "When it's light. We can spend the whole day looking around..."

"We'll go with you too," said Sophie.

Lisa stomped off into the adjacent room to cool down. Tom

wanted to follow his friend, but Sophie held him back.

"Give her five minutes. As soon as she spots something weird there, like a gigantic knife or something, she'll be back here all smiles again. Trust me."

Jack, who had long since accepted the situation, began exploring the studio instead.

Sophie attempted to ease the tension. "That painting they're working on… he and, ehm… Verrocchio? Leonardo really is a gifted painter."

Sophie stood in the middle of the studio, turning slowly around in circles. "I think this is where they always draw and paint." She pointed at things as she spoke. "It's big, has high ceilings, and there's natural light. Look over there, when the shutters are open I bet they have excellent light. A perfect space for painting."

"There are a few pages here that look like the ones in our book," said Tom. "When Leonardo gets back we should ask him what they say."

All of a sudden, a chilling scream was heard coming from the room Lisa was in. The others were instantly rooted to the floor with fear. It was followed by another terrible scream that chilled them to the bone. Then came a rhythmic gasping sound, as if something was being dragged across the floor of the adjacent room. Whatever it was, it was drawing nearer, making a sinister gurgling sound accompanied by heavy thumps.

"DO SOMETHING!" Sophie screamed at the boys.

Jack was the first to swallow his fear. He grabbed the nearest heavy implement he could find. Candlestick in hand, he ran towards the other room.

158

"Lisa!" shouted Tom, who was running behind his brother brandishing a piece of wood he had snatched up from the floor.

Running at full speed, Jack looked into the adjacent room and what he saw took his breath away. "What the... what's..." he stammered, suddenly shaking. Frightened, he took a step back and banged into his brother. They tumbled over each other and fell to the floor. Startled, they crawled backwards until they saw a figure stumbling into the room. It was Lisa.

Lisa shuffled forward... minus her head. Her legs strained to drag her battered body forward. A gurgling noise sounded from under her collar where her head should have been. The body teetered further into the room. Lisa's outstretched arms were shaking. Her severed head lay in her hands. Long strands of wet hair stuck to the skull. Sticky crimson blood dripped onto the floor.

"Noooo!!" Sophie fell to her knees. She thought of her parents and began to shiver uncontrollably.

The boys lay in a heap on the ground. They held on to each other tightly out of sheer terror.

Lisa's mutilated body stopped in the middle of the room and her hands fell lifelessly to her hips, causing the head to drop to the floor in a messy splash. "All I wanted was to go outside... outside..." sounded the gurgle from underneath the top of Lisa's dress.

Tom's face fell. He lifted his leg and purposely slammed it down on the toes of Lisa's foot.

"Ow! My toe... Tom!" Lisa spat out.

"I knew it! You ratbag!" Tom picked himself up and shoved her over.

Lisa quickly poked her head through her collar to catch her

bearings. She stuck out her hand and managed to stay on her feet by leaning against the wall.

Her face turned red with laughter. "You should've seen the look on your faces. Really, I thought I was going to wet myself!"

Laughing too, now, Tom crawled towards Lisa. "When your head fell, all messy and bloody... on the floor, splat!"

Lisa was bent over double. "Ow, my stomach hurts from laughing so much."

Jack went over to Sophie, who was still rattled by what she had seen. "Promise me – no, *swear* that we'll get her back some day," she whispered into his ear.

"Deal!" said Jack. He was sick and tired of Lisa's jokes.

"Come on sis, it was a joke, don't take it so seriously. And it took you guys forever to react to my first scream! You would sooner run away than come to my rescue."

Lisa grabbed her sister's arm and looked at her pleadingly. "It was just a joke..." She hoped that Sophie would forgive her.

Sophie did her best to look angry, but she couldn't hold back her laughter any longer. "Just remember, I'm going to get you back big time for this!"

Lisa sighed in relief. "As long as you can appreciate the humor of it, Sophie dear. I'm really sorry I freaked you out like that."

"Oh, that's nice! So what you mean is that you didn't mean to scare us at all?" Jack said sarcastically.

"Come on, I was just having some fun. What else are we going to do? It's as boring here as it is back home! Can't we go outside, just for a little bit, what could possibly go wrong?" Lisa said softly.

"Boring? A studio with a severed head, a rotting horse, and

an Italian painter who just happens to be world-famous and the subject of every art book worth its salt?" Tom stared at Lisa in disbelief.

"Just a quick peek?" Lisa looked around eagerly. "Aren't you even curious?"

"Five minutes," said Sophie, knowing how impossible Lisa could be if she didn't get her way. "Five minutes, no more. We'll go outside together and stay together. Don't talk to anyone. We'll walk across the street and back again. Okay?" Sophie looked around at everyone.

"I'll lead the way," Jack said, taking charge. He opened the door and carefully peeked through the crack. "It's already dusk, we'll have to be quick if we want to be able to see where we're going." Jack turned around and beckoned to everyone to follow.

"Yuck!" Sophie wrinkled her nose as soon they walked out onto the street. "The smell outside isn't much better than inside. How can they stand it? You could hide a corpse in your house and no one would notice." She shook her head in disgust.

"Watch your step," said Jack, herding everyone over to the right-hand side of the street. "That smell must be poop. I'm pretty sure they just dump it straight out onto the street."

Huddled closely together, the four of them walked about thirty yards down the street and stopped at a T-junction.

Without consulting anyone, Jack turned left into a dodgy-looking alleyway. He looked around to make sure the coast was clear. Catching sight of a raggedy man slowly approaching them, he made himself look bigger by widening his stance. As the person got closer, Jack saw that it was in fact a woman. She was of stocky build with a filthy, moon-shaped face, and her stringy hair was plastered against the sides of her head. Jack attempted to greet her cordially, but the woman looked away and passed them by without the slightest acknowledgement.

Sophie got a fright when the woman brushed past her. She was so focused on avoiding the excrement on the street that she hadn't seen anyone coming. The pungent stench that came trailing in the woman's wake sent shivers down her spine.

"Keep your eyes ahead!" Jack commanded.

"Don't think about the poop… don't think about the poop…" Sophie repeated the words in her head until she was able to focus on what was going on around her instead. "Don't think about…" she said over and over again, "the worst that can happen is that you step on a turd." The thought alone sent another shiver down her spine, but eventually she got over it. She straightened her back and looked ahead so that she could take in everything around her.

It was a narrow, unpaved street littered with the kind of stuff you'd normally find in a sewer. She heard a baby crying and people yelling behind a door, and the clatter of hooves galloping off in the distance. The stench on the street was, of course, atrocious, but compared to the smell of rotting horse flesh it didn't seem too bad.

"Let's turn left here," Jack pointed into a wide street, "then left again followed by another left. That'll take us around the block."

Unlike the cramped, dirty alley they'd just left, this street was paved with rough cobblestones. They were now walking in single file, with Jack up front and Lisa at the rear.

Unusually for Lisa, she hadn't uttered a word since walking out the door. She just looked all around her with a big smile on her face.

The wide street they were walking down eventually brought them onto a square. They stopped and, huddling together, watched the people passing by. The square was extraordinarily busy despite the late evening hour. There was a group of men talking, one of whom quickly looked them over while another began gesticulating furiously and berating the other men loudly for some reason or other. Most of the people were wearing the same clothes as they were, though they did see a man pass by dressed in nothing but dirty gray rags.

Jack scanned the scene quickly and walked over to where the square intersected with a narrow street. "We can see the entire square from here," he said.

With their backs against the wall they gazed out over the square for a while in silence, impressed by the everyday – but for them unusual – comings and goings. Dusk rapidly turned into night. There wasn't a single lamppost or streetlight to shed the slightest bit of light on anything. Two men riding horses came galloping around the corner, their horses' hooves clattering over the stones. Sophie instinctively covered her ears against the noise. When she looked back up again she saw several groups of men gathering here and there and engaging in conversation.

Jack also saw what Sophie had just seen. He urged the others to get a move on. "When we arrived on the square a few minutes ago there were still a few women about, now they've suddenly all disappeared. This doesn't feel right. We should get out of here, and fast." After turning into the dark side street, Jack quickened his pace.

Sophie grew extremely anxious when they found themselves walking in complete darkness.

"I want to go home..." Lisa whispered to her sister.

"There, at the end of the street, if we turn left we'll be back at Leonardo's studio." Jack did his best to sound as self-confident as possible to reassure the others, but he kept looking over his shoulder anyway to make sure everything was okay.

They continued to walk quickly down the side street until they heard a bubbling noise coming out of the wall of one of the houses. They traced the noised to a stone gutter jutting out about three feet above the ground. Curious to know what it was, they had stopped to look when all of a sudden a blob of nasty guck splashed down onto the street next to their feet. The vile muck was followed by a stream of steamy urine.

"Yuuuckkk, someone's on the crapper!" Sophie screamed.

Startled and giggling nervously, they all ran to the end of the street.

"We're almost there!" Jack yelled as he rounded the corner first.

He took a deep breath and tried to remember which of the doors on the street was theirs. Huddled closely together, they slowly walked along looking for the studio.

All of a sudden a door flew open and a dark figure emerged, cursing and raging as he approached them.

Jack's heart was in his mouth, but he did his best to hide it from the others. It was obvious to everyone that the dark figure was heading straight for him. Jack clenched his fists and braced himself.

Tom saw his brother's tensed-up fists in silhouette and quickly planted his feet firmly on the ground.

Lisa heard the approaching footsteps and slowly slipped

her hand into one of her pockets. She had heeded Hans' advice and had secretly brought his ghastly present with her. She grasped the handle and felt the blade's cold edge against her thigh. She'd use it if she had to.

The figure stopped in front of Jack and, gasping, lifted up his hood.

"*Idioti!*" Leonardo glared furiously at Jack and his friends. He shook his head and indicated for them to follow. He slammed the door behind him and began screaming at them. He spoke so quickly that the telephone wasn't able to translate his words into proper sentences. "Stupid.... You think that... evening... arrested... or worse... happens..."

"It's my fault," Lisa said, stepping forward. "I wanted to go outside. I convinced them to come with me. Sorry..." She hoped the sincerity of her apology would alter the mood.

Leonardo grabbed the bloody head that was lying in the corner of the room. "And this?" he roared. "Have you no respect! What's this doing here?"

"I was going to ask you the exact same thing," Sophie said firmly. "Why do you have a severed head in here? Whose head is it anyway?"

"I already told you. Its' the same as with the horse. I want to understand how a body is put together, including the human body. If that means I have to steal a corpse from time to time, then so be it."

"Steal a corpse?" Sophie was genuinely surprised. "How do you steal a dead body?"

"Death. Cemetery. Dig. Drag. Chop." Leonardo saw that the group wasn't entirely convinced by his explanation, but it was also obvious he didn't want to say any more.

"Your turn," he said to Lisa, "that head, what happened..."

"It was a joke," Lisa said. She explained what had happened, re-enacting the performance in which she staggered into the room making gurgling noises.

Still angry at them for having ignored him, Leonardo did his best to keep a straight face. After acting out the final scene in which the head fell dramatically to the ground, Lisa gave him a remorseful smile.

Leonardo appeared to be enchanted by her smile and burst into laughter, causing the others to laugh as well. Confounded, he threw his arms into the air. "I can't stay mad at you, but please don't do that again."

"Even though I think it's gross beyond belief," Sophie said, "would you mind telling us more about the corpses."

"I appreciate your interest, Sophie. More tomorrow, but for now... Come, my friends, it's starting to get cold." Leonardo ushered them towards a table in the corner of the room.

Steam rose from a beautifully decorated bowl filled with tomato soup. Herbs floated on top. Chunks of bread and a plate with a selection of cheeses had been placed on the table next to the soup. Two carafes sat on a smaller table lower down. The large crystal carafe seemed to be filled with milk, but Leonardo couldn't help but notice them staring at the other carafe.

"That's wine, but diluted with water because you are all still young."

"Wine?" Lisa reacted enthusiastically, raising her eyebrows.

"Lisa, we can't be drinking alcohol here," Sophie said. "We don't drink it at home either. Besides, I'm on antibiotics. Remember what Hans said?"

"They've long since worn off, you can drink the wine if

you want. You're just looking for a way out," Lisa said with a twinkle in her eye.

"I've always wondered what it tasted like," said Tom.

"Me too," said Jack.

Leonardo looked at them, waiting to see what they would do.

"We're not allowed to drink alcohol yet, not until we're twenty-one," Sophie said.

Leonardo looked a little dumbstruck. "It's allowed here, every child above the age of five drinks wine, in diluted form of course. What do you usually drink?"

"Water," said Sophie.

"Water? Water is too dangerous to drink, it can make you sick! Only when it comes directly from a spring is it safe." He shook his head. "If you don't want to get sick, you should drink wine, not water."

Lisa took a glass from the table, poured in some wine, and drank it down in one go. "So, that's broken the ice." She looked around the table with an enormous smile on her face.

Tom filled his glass to the brim and quickly followed Lisa's example.

After emptying his glass he put his hands on his head and closed his eyes. "Phew, it's rushing to my head... a kind of... warm feeling... whoa..." he said, giggling.

Leonardo looked on as Jack and Sophie finished their glasses as well. Pleased that his guests had enjoyed the wine, he gave each of them a bowl of soup and a few chunks of bread, and then walked outside. A few minutes later he returned carrying a bale of hay under his arms.

Completely shocked by what he saw when he came back in, he let the hay fall to the floor. Sophie was strolling around the room lighting candles.

She turned around when she noticed her friends had suddenly gone silent. Leonardo was staring at her hands. Sophie didn't understand what was going on and quickly blew out the last candle she had lit. "What?" she said to Leonardo, who looked shell-shocked. "I thought I'd light a few candles, make it a bit cozier in here, that's all. Sorry!"

Struggling to find the right words, Leonardo asked her "What? What is… that?" His eyes were focused on her fist. She followed his gaze and opened her hand. Between her fingers was her father's gold-plated lighter. The catacombs and skulls shone in the dim light.

"*Mama mia*! You have fire in your hands!" Leonardo kissed his clenched fists as if in triumph.

Sophie walked over to him and proudly showed him the lighter. While the others carried on eating the cheese and helped themselves to a second glass of wine, Leonardo and Sophie crouched down in front of the stove. Leonardo tossed the lighter from one hand to the other as if it were a nugget of gold. To his great delight, he then used it to light the stove and started spreading out straw on the floor.

"It could get pretty cold tonight. Summer may have just begun, but the nights are still very cold. Lying on the straw in front of the stove should keep you warm."

When everyone was sitting at the table again, Leonardo took the carafe and topped up their glasses. "This will keep you warm, too," he laughed. "And eat more food."

"My days are mostly spent painting and drawing. Or doing research," Leonardo said.

"Like chopping off a head and drawing it?"

Lisa couldn't keep herself from laughing at her sister's remark, although she didn't really know why she found it funny.

"To make the best painting possible, I first need to know exactly what the horse looks like. And if I am drawing a person, then I have to know exactly what the human body looks like, too, how it's built. I found the horse in a meadow, already dead. The head, well, I dug it up," Leonardo said, somewhat reluctantly revealing his methods.

"Do you actually go digging in graveyards?" asked Sophie.

"At night?" asked Lisa, her face wrinkling in horror. The only thing she was afraid of was the dark.

"Anything that will help me learn," said Leonardo. "Verrocchio has no idea. No one knows. I had to hide that head. Andrea's okay with horses and other creatures, but if he knew I had a skull..."

"Here in the studio I slice away one layer at a time – the skin, the flesh, the fat, the tendons, blood vessels, and the muscles, all the way to the bone. I sketch each layer, that way I can remember everything and understand exactly how the body is built."

"The wine is already working, I see," Leonardo grinned and pointed to Tom who had fallen asleep on his side.

"One last glass and then we'll call it a day."

After draining her third glass, Sophie began to giggle.

"Waddabout all those dwalings and tests," Jack hiccupped.

"You're drunk!" Sophie cried. Lisa leaned against her sister and grinned.

Jack had to laugh, too. He took a deep breath and pulled himself together.

"Your drawings and texts, do you keep them?"

"Yes, I've got hundreds of pages on which I've carefully recorded everything."

"I know," Sophie said hazily. "We found them, that's why we're here."

"I know a good one," said Lisa. "We're here in Florence with a horse that's dead. It reeks of corpse and it's time for bed. Hey, that rhymes!"

They all burst out laughing.

"Oh, I've got one, too." Sophie stuck her finger in the air. "We're here in Florence and it's very smelly... It stinks of bodies, poop and pee."

Leonardo blew out the candles laughing. "We'll talk again tomorrow when you've sobered up."

Tuesday, June 24th, morning

Like a stealthy tiger, Ms. Prattle's ermine snuck its way around the studio unnoticed. With her pricked-up ears and beady eyes, she probed the hay as she honed in on the soft rustling sound being made by her soon-to-be breakfast.

Leonardo deftly opened the shutters without making any noise. He stretched elaborately and took a deep breath, puffing out his chest. The early morning sunshine flooded into the studio.

Sophie was still asleep. She was lying on her stomach, one arm behind her head. Without her noticing, the ermine darted quickly up along her leg and back.

The loud rustling in the hay next to her head soon woke her up. In a split second she saw the ermine leap over her head, its tail brushing softly against her cheek. Unnerved, she looked to see what the creature was up to. The ermine peered at her with a look of sly content on its face. Clasped between her jaws was a bloodied field mouse.

"Shoooo...." Sophie hissed loudly and vigorously waved her hands, forcing the ermine to run off towards the wall. Falling asleep with a dead horse no more than thirty feet away and waking up with a dead mouse next to your head – she wondered what other horrors awaited her today.

In the meantime, all the commotion had woken Lisa, too. She lay on her back with her hands on her stomach, staring silently at the ceiling. It always took her a few minutes in the morning to prepare herself mentally for the day. She had decided long ago that she was a night owl. Later, when she was older and in college, and sharing a place with her sister, she would probably stay up all night hanging out and partying. Her sister, on the other hand, was a morning person. So their paths would probably cross every morning in the kitchen. Lisa heading to bed after partying all night and Sophie up early for a morning run and a healthy start to the day.

More accustomed to the screeching of saws at the mill in the morning, Jack and Tom weren't likely to be woken by the sound of rustling hay. At home their alarm clock went off like a siren on schooldays, but even then their father had to wake them up at least once a week by banging loudly on their door.

Sophie was engaged in animated conversation with Leonardo at the window, the telephone in her hand translating her sentences in rapid succession.

"What's for breakfast?" Lisa asked without receiving a response. "I wouldn't mind a chunk of bread smothered in peanut butter."

Ravenous with hunger, Lisa walked over to inspect the cheese and bread crusts on the table. She stuffed a handful of each into her mouth and started pacing impatiently back and forth. She wanted to go outside, to find some excitement. She stepped over the sleeping boys, purposely kicking Tom's shin with the point of her shoe. Tom sat up grumpily, woken by the pain in his leg.

"Jack! You lazy bum! Time to get up, everyone else is already awake!" Lisa shouted into his ear.

"I picked up some dried fruit and fresh milk this morning,"

said Leonardo. "Over there on the table, help yourselves."

"What are we going to do today?" Lisa asked.

"Dig up a dead body!" Sophie's eyes sparkled at the sound of the words.

"Fine with me, as long as it's not at night." Lisa looked at her sister eagerly.

"Leonardo and I just agreed that we'd go with him to dig up a body this afternoon! He's going to show us how he does it."

"Seriously?" Tom asked. "Can't we just go out for a walk?"

Jack elbowed his brother in the side. "Do you realize how cool this is?" he said excitedly. "If we dig up and dissect a dead body with Leonardo da Vinci, we'll be making history. Even if it gives me nightmares for the rest of my life, it'll be totally worth it!"

"Not just yet, my friends," Leonardo tried to calm everyone down. "Before that I want to show you my studio and my work. Eat something, please. And the orrery, we have to talk about that as well!"

"The toilet is over there!" Leonardo pointed to his 'laboratory' where the dead horse was lying.

Jack and Tom headed in the direction Leonardo had indicated, but not before covering their noses with their hands. "Oh my God!" Tom quickly retreated. "The smell is terrible and there's no door!"

"A door?" Leonardo said, surprised.

Tom nodded. "A door, you know, for the toilet?"

"We don't have doors, why would we? No one has them. The body is a gift from God, you shouldn't be ashamed by it. Not even when you're pooping or peeing."

Jack came back into the room laughing. "Sure, okay," he said. "But I'm only going to go if no one's looking."

Tom ran towards the toilet. "Stay there until I'm done!" he shouted.

"It's different where we come from," Sophie explained. She glanced sideways at her sister and instantly recognized the mischievous grin on her face. "Don't, Lisa!" said Sophie, stepping in front of her sister. "You're going to want to pee in peace later, too, right?"

Lisa realized that she could just as easily become the target of the prank she had in mind. So, for once in her life, she decided to restrain herself.

"What are you rubbing on your hands?" Leonardo spotted the transparent plastic bottle that was being passed around.

"Disinfectant," Sophie said. "It kills the bacteria that can make you sick. Here," she handed the bottle to Leonardo.

He carefully inspected the bottle, pressed down the pump, and rubbed the gel between his hands. "And then?"

"I have some pills in my bag, too. I'll leave them here. One box contains painkillers and the other one antibiotics. They'll come in handy with all these dead animals and poop."

"Antibiotics?" Leonardo leaned in closer. "What is 'antibiotics'?"

Sophie took a moment before answering. "I think they were invented about a hundred years ago. One hundred for us, that is, so around 1900. They contain something that kills bacteria, which helps you recover from diseases. If I'm not mistaken, it's one of humankind's most important discoveries."

Leonardo's eyes glistened. The lighter, the bottle with disinfectant gel, the pills – all these things were now swirling around in his head. He couldn't wait to hear more about the future.

"You said yesterday that the water here could make you sick?"

Leonardo nodded.

"That's because there are bacteria in it. There are bacteria in all the trash lying on the street, and in those decomposing animals, too. When you get really sick, you swallow those pills for a couple of days and they make you better."

Leonardo listened attentively to Sophie's explanation.

Even though the smell in the studio in the morning was still repulsive, it wasn't as awful as the night before. Leonardo had been kind enough to remove the horse's remains when everyone was asleep. Sophie was particularly relieved that the rotting flesh was gone. The studio was warming up in the summer sun, which wouldn't have made the smell any better.

"Are we going to go dig up that corpse soon?" Lisa's voice was a mixture of curiosity and enthusiasm.

"How are we going to get back into the city without anyone asking us what we're carrying?" Sophie sounded concerned. "You said yourself that when people see us they are going to ask questions."

"Yesterday, yes! Today, no!" Leonardo beamed. He strolled happily through the studio. "Do you hear that? Outside?" He cupped a hand to his ear. In the distance they could hear the sound of horns and people shouting. "Yesterday it was better for you to stay inside, but today in the afternoon it will be very busy in the city. No one will take any notice of you!"

"Is it Black Friday?" Tom was trying to be funny, but Leonardo, not understanding, ignored his comment.

"It's the feast day of John the Baptist, the patron saint of Florence. The biggest festival of the year! Everyone in Florence will be out and about, drinking and celebrating. There will be horse races through the center of town, it's going to be crazy. And *Calcio*! It will be a madhouse there! No one will notice us walking around town together."

"Calcio... hmm, no coverage," Sophie muttered as she tried to look up 'Calcio' on her phone. "What's Calcio?"

"You'll see. Leonardo flexed his muscles and showed them an odd karate-like move. "You'll see. We'll go to watch Calcio together. Only the strongest men are allowed to play."

Sophie and Lisa immediately lost interest, but Tom and Jack listened attentively to Leonardo's explanation.

"Awesome!" Tom and Jack began wrestling and tumbling around the studio. Leonardo punched Jack on the shoulder and gave Tom a smack on the back of his head. He grabbed both of them by the neck under his arms and ran through the studio screaming. Tom and Jack broke free and punched him in the side. "Calcio!" the three of them yelled.

"And?" Sophie quietly asked her sister. "Is this what you were hoping for?"

Lisa grinned broadly.

"What are we going to tell Mom and Dad?"

Lisa took a step backwards and gave her sister a serious look.

"Nothing! Really, I mean it! Do you hear me! We're not going to tell them a thing," she said firmly. "They would be livid. We'll think of something, but there's no way we can tell them..."

Sophie nodded, she understood her sister completely. If they told the truth, this would not only be their first experience of time travel but also their last.

"I won't say a thing, but we have to come up with a credible story." Sophie winked at her sister. Lisa nodded and smiled.

"Besides, I have no idea how we'd prove it?" Lisa said to her sister. "How do we know we're not dreaming?"

Sophie shook her head.

"Calcio!" Jack and Tom gave Leonardo a high five. The three of them stood gasping in the middle of the studio, exhausted from their wrestling match.

Leonardo threw his arms around the boys' shoulders and winked at the girls. "We'll go into town in a couple of hours, my friends from the future, but first take a look at this. What do you think of this painting? I've been asked to work on it."

Hanging on the wall was a painting about three feet high and six feet wide. A pale woman in a beautiful red and blue dress was seated on the right. Next to her was a low, ornately decorated marble table. On the left-hand side of the painting was a terrace.

"An angel needs to be painted here in the foreground, on the grass. In the backdrop I'm going to paint trees and a mountain, then it will be done." Leonardo pointed proudly to the area he was referring to.

"This is Andrea's initial design, now it's up to me to finish the painting!"

"Cool! Do you already have a name for it?" Sophie asked curiously.

"*L'Annunciazione*," said Leonardo. "The Annunciation," sounded from her telephone.

"Wait a second," she said. "Say that again."

Lisa's mouth fell open. Sophie covered her mouth with her hand.

"What?" Jack asked. "What's wrong?"

This is The Annunciation, painted by Leonardo da Vinci and his teacher Andrea del Verrocchio between 1472 and 1475. Leonardo painted the angel in this masterpiece using lead-free paint. When this work was x-rayed (researchers use x-rays to look for old coats of paint hidden underneath the top layers) the angel, unlike everything else in the painting, did not show up on the x-rays. It was completely invisible.

"Did you say 'The Annunciation'?" Sophie had never sounded so serious.

Leonardo nodded his head almost imperceptibly.

"What are you getting at?" asked Jack.

"The Annunciation is world-famous," Lisa said. "Dad told us that in the car on the way to Paris."

Sophie immediately added, "Leonardo, this painting... this painting is still known five hundred years from now, books have been written about it... internet, lectures, exhibitions! It will go down in history as your first real work of art!"

Lisa stared at the painting, her mouth still open. Sophie had a glint in her eyes. They were suddenly very aware of the fact that history was being written before their very eyes.

"Really?" Leonardo looked proudly at Sophie. "I haven't even really started yet."

"Maybe it's time you did," laughed Lisa.

Leonardo turned around and ran his hand over the canvas. World-famous, he could live with that. When he turned back around, Leonardo had a resolute look on his face. He bent down and picked up a few paintbrushes from the floor. "Would you like to witness my first strokes of paint on the canvas?"

Four pairs of eyes glistened in the sunlight as they watched him. Feeling revitalized, Leonardo started to mix different colors of paint.

"What are you going to do with that?" asked Sophie while leaning forward to look at the piece of metal that Leonardo had in his hand.

"This is lead, and this is vinegar," he said, showing them a transparent bottle. "The lead reacts to the vinegar and then I mix it with the paint."

"Lead? Are you crazy! Why would you mix lead with paint?"

Leonardo was surprised by the intensity of her reaction. He struggled to find the right words. "Everyone uses lead in their paint, it helps it to dry quicker. And it's better for the paint, it preserves it longer! If you say that this painting will still be around five hundred years from now, then that seems pretty essential to me.

"Don't you know that lead is poisonous? If you were to ingest it..." Sophie looked at him crossly. Leonardo brushed off her concern.

"People don't lick paintings," said Leonardo, continuing to drop vinegar onto the metal.

"Is it possible to paint without mixing in lead?"

Leonardo looked up and nodded. "In theory, I suppose..."

Everyone looked at Sophie. At times, her intelligence made her very hard to follow.

"Lisa, you wanted proof to show that we have actually been here, right? What if Leonardo paints the angel using paint that doesn't contain lead? That'll be our evidence when we get back. X-rays can't pass through lead. Jack, remember?" Both Jack and Tom nodded.

"When Tom fell and sprained his wrist at the sawmill they had to take x-rays. Jack was only allowed to stay in the room with Tom if he wore a lead apron to protect him from the radiation." Tom instinctively grabbed his wrist and nodded again.

"What?" Leonardo didn't understand any of this. "What are you talking about?" Leonardo asked again. "What is an 'x-ray' and what does it have to do with lead? And what kind of proof are you talking about anyway?"

"Wait, I'll show you," said Sophie. "Lisa, go stand over there." Lisa went and stood in front of a bare wall and waited for more instructions from her sister. "Good, now mimic that woman in the picture hanging in the Louvre, Mona."

Lisa was always game for a bit of fun. She turned slightly to the side, laid her right hand on her left wrist, and looked into the camera as seriously as she could.

"You're actually a bit too young and too skinny," Sophie joked. Shaking her head, she looked at her sister while she figured out what to do. "Wait." She draped some cloth over Lisa's shoulder. "Take a deep breath, chest forward, try to make yourself a bit bigger." Lisa breathed in deeply, puffing up her cheeks in the process.

"Yes, perfect!" Sophie cried. "Don't move!" Sophie grabbed her telephone, took a picture, and showed it to Leonardo.

He looked at the picture flabbergasted. He grabbed her phone and continued to stare at the screen. He'd never seen anything like it. "But..." he stammered. "That, what you just did... it's perfect... I'll never be able to come even close... it's so good, so... real."

Afraid that Leonardo might panic or lose confidence, Sophie quickly explained that photography was a completely different medium than painting.

After reassuring him, Sophie explained how x-rays worked. "Doctors use them to take pictures right through your body, which allows them to see the stuff inside you, like your bones, for example."

Leonardo slapped himself on the forehead. He couldn't believe his ears. "They can see through your body?" Feeling a little overwhelmed, he sat down on a stool. "But what does lead have to do with it? With my paint? What proof are you talking about?" Everyone was waiting to hear Sophie's explanation.

"X-rays pass through everything, except lead. If you

promise to paint the angel with lead-free paint..." Sophie smiled, pleased with her own ingenuity, "then everyone in our time will be astonished!" Sophie saw that her sister finally understood where she was going with this.

Lisa added to her sister's explanation. "Five hundred years from now, all important artworks are meticulously examined over and over again. Paintings are even carefully restored to their original colors in museums. Sometimes they discover a different background hidden underneath all the grime. And with the real masterpieces, it's not uncommon to x-ray the paintings. My father explained all of this to us once. They do it to see if older drawings were painted over."

"So what you're saying is that if I paint my angel with lead-free paint, everything in the painting will be visible on a special x-ray, except the angel?" Leonardo smiled at the thought that he was now an accomplice in the cunning plan Sophie had just thought up.

"Exactly! If you do that..." Sophie looked proudly at her sister.

Lisa nodded in agreement. "Sophie's right. If you paint the angel with lead-free paint, we'll look it up when we get back home. If the angel isn't visible on an x-ray, then we'll know that all of this really happened... that it wasn't a dream."

Leonardo stood up and shook Sophie's hand. "Perfect! I will paint the angel with lead-free paint!"

Jack patted Sophie on the back. "When we're home I'll check online to see if we can find anything about that painting. If you're right..."

Smiling broadly, Lisa looked at her sister. "Well, there you go. Super stuff, sis!"

Leonardo was sitting at the table writing furiously on a grimy sheet of paper. "That phone of yours, it really is something else! When you made that tiny painting…"

"You mean photo?" said Sophie, correcting him.

"Ehm, yes," Leonardo replied. "When you took that photo – the thing that looks like a tiny painting, taken with what you call a phone – there was a flash of light! That flash is precisely what's been missing in my attempts to travel through time with the orrery. Here, look! I've been writing down instructions for how to use the orrery. I was convinced my theories and calculations were correct. Everything was spot on – the planets, the water – but success has eluded me because I lacked the right source of light. But now, with your phone… with that flash!"

Leonardo returned to his furious scribbling, all the while explaining to Sophie what he was writing down. She looked over his shoulder and saw him make a very precise sketch of her telephone. "When you travel back to your own time, it will be the first time I get to see it actually work. I mean, I built the time machine and everything, but without that light I could never get it to work. Today I'm going to witness exactly that!" said Leonardo a little nervously.

"Everything will turn out all right," Jack tried his best to act cool. "Don't worry, everything you wrote down is correct. It'll work just fine…"

When he was finished drawing Sophie's phone, Leonardo put down his pen. "And then what? When you're gone…" he shook his head sadly. Leonardo was worried and wondered whether he would ever be able to travel through time himself without Sophie's telephone. He had built the machine primarily for his own use, so that he could learn more about the future.

Lisa glanced at Leonardo and felt a wave of compassion rise up within her. More than anyone else, she could relate to his desire to discover new worlds. She hoped he would be able to do it without Sophie's telephone, because her sister was definitely going to take it back with her.

Lisa felt around in one of her pockets. "Jack's right, it'll all work out," she said. "I know for sure you'll find a solution. Why don't we go outside for a while? Didn't someone say something about digging up a corpse?" She already had her eyes on the door.

Leonardo regained his composure, pointed outside, and gave them all a very serious look.

"Listen to me. This is not a joke. We have to stay together no matter what. Don't lose sight of me whatever you do. And no messing around either, the consequences could be catastrophic!"

The sun was at its highest when they walked outside and the heat enveloped them like a warm blanket. In one fluid motion they all tossed their hoods and hats back inside before Leonardo shut the door. Sophie and Lisa watched in amusement as Tom and Jack leaned down and picked at their leggings, irritated by the feel of the fabric on their legs. Back home they'd be sporting cool shorts and a pair of sneakers. They certainly wouldn't be wearing dark leggings and high boots.

The boys walked awkwardly down the dusty street in their suffocating costumes. Together with Leonardo they moved through the bustling narrow streets in a sort of shuffle. The air was warm and had a musty smell to it. Sophie and Lisa followed the boys closely to avoid being shoved aside.

Leonardo suddenly raised his hand and everyone froze. They could hear shouting coming from further down the street.

"Quick! Move aside!" He pushed Sophie, Lisa, and Tom against the wall. "Here!" he yelled, pulling Jack towards him. The two of them stood with their backs pressed flat against their friends. Up the street people scattered in every direction, many pressing themselves flat against a wall, some seeking safety by leaping through an open widow.

In the distance a group of men on horseback thundered towards them. The sound seemed to pour into the streets. The horses' hooves pounded the ground in unison. Clouds of fine sand and gravel shot up into the air. Sophie felt like all her senses were on fire as the horses passed by. A deafening noise penetrated her ears. She smelled the horse's sweat and felt their warmth. Once the riders had passed, everyone stepped back onto the street cheering and laughing.

"It's the horse race!" Leonardo bellowed. "Did you see that? We're in the lead!"

When he saw the blank look on Sophie's face, Leonardo began to explain. "Florence is a big city, one of the biggest in the world! The city is divided into four districts. Today those four districts are battling each other in horseracing and Calcio. And our district is winning the horse race!" he rejoiced.

The noise grew louder and the people rowdier as the group neared the public square. Leonardo forged a path through the crowd, continually looking back to make sure everyone was following. This definitely wasn't a good place to lose sight of each other. Once on the square, the group was nearly trampled by the masses. Thousands of people were crammed together, sweating and carousing.

Before Leonardo could react, a drunken man stuck out his hand and Lisa, who was walking at the rear, got cut off from the rest of the group. She smelled the putrid stench of alcohol on his breath when he began speaking to her in Italian. Lisa caught a glimpse of Sophie, who was walking a few feet ahead and had turned around to see where she was. Lisa tried to slip past, but the man grabbed her arm forcefully and didn't seem to want to let it go any time soon. Lisa shook her head frantically and did her best to make it clear that she didn't appreciate his behavior. She tried as hard as she could to break loose from his grip, but without success. The situation didn't get any better when the man's pudgy friend decided to join them.

She recalled the advice Hans had given her, slid her free hand into her pocket, and grabbed the knife. She was holding it so tightly that her knuckles hurt. The men were busy talking to each other, every now and then glancing in her direction. Lisa was conscious of the fact that she was the main topic of their discussion. When the other man wrapped his arm around her waist she realized she had to do something. She immediately began screaming and pointed at something behind them. While they were momentarily distracted she hit back with all her strength. The point of her shoe landed full force between the man's legs, forcing him to double over in pain and let go of her arm.

The drunken man looked up, his face contorted with pain, and turned on his companion. Convinced that he had just kicked him, he knocked him to the ground with a single punch. Lisa dropped to the ground and crawled quickly through their legs, rapidly making her way through the crowd until she caught up to her sister. A huge brawl was now breaking out only a few yards behind her.

"What's going on back there?" Sophie asked her sister.

"1-0 to me," Lisa said gasping. She nudged her sister. "Come on, keep walking, or before you know it we'll be in trouble."

Halfway across the square, Leonardo came to a halt. "Calcio!" he cried. He picked a spot next to a wooden barrier that surrounded a sand-covered field. Jack and Tom threw their arms over each other's shoulders in brotherly fashion and watched the men on the field with mounting excitement.

"Calcio is played between two teams, each with twenty-seven players. You have to throw that leather ball over there, the red and white one, over the barrier behind your opponent," Leonardo quickly explained.

"Like football on sand?" Sophie asked.

Leonardo nodded. "Football... yes, you can use your feet. In fact you can use everything: your feet, your hands, whatever, but you're not allowed to kick your opponent in the face. After that anything goes. Slapping, kicking, choking, as long as you get the ball over the barrier. That's how you score a point, a *cacce*!"

Sophie and her sister looked at each other uncertainly. "Choking?"

"Yeah!!!!" Jack and Tom were hopping and cheering.

Right in front of them, a player managed to steal the ball by stomping hard on his opponent's face. With the ball under his arm he took off straight across the field, managing to avoid several opponents until he was brutally tackled to the ground. Several extremely muscular men pounced on him and began roughing each other up as they tried to gain possession of the ball.

"They're nothing but barbarians!" the sisters said simultaneously, both horrified.

Jack and Tom whooped as they watched the spectacle. They imagined themselves running across the field, the strongest and fastest of them all, and everyone cheering them on.

Suddenly a loud horn sounded signaling the end of the match.

"Our turn now," said Leonardo, his chest swelling with pride. "See the men walking onto the field wearing black leggings, that's our district!"

"Why aren't they wearing shirts?"

"Weren't you just watching? Shirts would be torn to shreds in an instant. And they'd be able to catch you from behind and tackle you more easily, too."

Not much later, the man with the ball was buried under a mountain of players right in front of them. After much pushing and pulling, one of them managed to escape with the ball under his arm. The others pulled themselves to their feet and gave chase. One player, however, remained motionless on the ground, blood pouring from his mouth and out of one ear. After a quick inspection by a few of his teammates he was carried off the pitch.

"Ouch," said Leonardo, almost apologetically, "I think he's just had all of his teeth knocked out. I hope he recovers quickly, he's on our team after all."

A loud voice amplified by a horn blared out something in Italian across the field. Jack and Tom could hardly stand the excitement.

"We've got to win, Leonardo," shouted Jack, jumping up and down behind the barrier. "Woohoo!!!" He raised his arm into the air to point at something when all of a sudden the players on the pitch began to cheer. The man with the horn made another announcement and everyone looked in Jack's direction.

Leonardo's face went white.

"What?" Jack suddenly saw that everyone was staring at him. Perplexed, he looked at Leonardo. "What's up?"

"Stay calm," said Leonardo, putting both his hands on Jack's shoulders.

"What? What do you mean stay calm? What's going on? Tell me!"

Lisa glanced at the pitch and saw that the players were still staring at Jack. She couldn't stop herself from smiling when she realized what was about to happen.

"What? Why is everyone looking at me?" Jack said, before it dawned on him what was going on and he went pale.

"Okay, you have to hurry, otherwise they'll come and get you themselves."

Jack looked helplessly at Leonardo.

"A moment ago, the man with the horn asked who wanted to replace the man who was carried off and you put up your hand..."

Jack began to shake his head furiously. "No! I was pointing at someone on the field, I didn't raise my hand!"

"You want to try telling them that?" Leonardo said quietly. "Sorry Jack, you'll have to do it. If you don't they'll come and get you. I can't protect you from all those men."

"No, no, no!" Jack stood in front of Leonardo shaking his head.

Tom threw an arm around his brother's shoulder and slapped him on the back reassuringly. "You've got this man!"

For the past thirty minutes Sophie had been carefully analyzing the game. She pulled Jack close and whispered in

his ear. "If you stay on the right... those two guys there..."
She kept pointing until she was sure Jack was looking at the
right men. "That dude with the bald head and the one next
to him with the greasy black ponytail..." Jack nodded, "those
two are a lot slower than the rest. You're faster than they are.
And the fat one in defense... he's constantly covering the left
side. So your best option is to run down the right. That way
you'll only have to steer clear of the big guy with the blond
hair. He'll probably try to tackle you by your ankles. If you
jump in the air the moment he starts to dive, hopefully you'll
be able to avoid him."

The crowd began cheering again.

"Come on, hurry," Leonardo said firmly. "The crowd is
getting restless, you have to go, and fast. Take off your shirt."

Jack pulled off his tunic and removed his shirt. He slowly
and reluctantly climbed over the barrier.

Lisa jumped onto the fence, grabbed Jack, and whispered
something in his ear. Without anyone noticing, she pressed
the knife into his hands. Momentarily stunned, Jack nimbly
slipped it into his leggings.

Jack looked out over the field, turned around, and stared at
Lisa. "Thanks," he said as he walked onto the pitch.

A deafening applause erupted as Jack, bare-chested, stepped
onto the pitch. Each and every man here was a hero. The
crowd was going mad. Nobody had been brave enough to
volunteer as a substitute. Except for Jack, even if it was by
accident.

The largest man on Jack's team walked up to him and
clapped him reassuringly on the shoulder. The difference
between them only became really apparent when the man was

standing next to him. His muscular arms were thicker than Jack's thighs. The only advantage Jack had was his height. Despite the difference in age between them, Jack was just as tall as the other men.

When the man slapped him amicably on the back, Jack's eyes nearly popped out of his head. He shuddered at the thought that the gesture was meant to be reassuring.

The horn sounded again and the ball was tossed back onto the pitch. Jack kept to one side in the hope that he could stay out of harm's way. The scuffles took place mostly in the middle of the field where the teams fought each other fiercely for possession of the ball.

Jack shot across the field like a rabbit attempting to avoid the worst of the violence. He wasn't even looking at the ball. He only had eyes for the opponents who occasionally tried to grab him. His speed came in handy. With their large, bulky bodies, the men couldn't keep up with him.

After what seemed like an eternity, a whistle suddenly blew.

"The last three minutes," Leonardo cheered. "Your friend's going to make it."

Tom stood behind the barrier with clenched fists. He watched his brother's every movement.

"Jack, watch out!" Sophie screamed as hard as she could.

Jack saw the ball being thrown in his direction. Up until that point he had managed to keep himself out of the game, but now came the moment of truth. Catch the ball or run away? Jack quickly realized he didn't have a choice. His teammates would pummel him to pieces if he missed the ball on purpose.

As the ball flew through the air he adjusted his body and with outstretched arms jumped up and caught it. Gotcha!

A man with a square jaw charged towards him with his fists clenched. Out of nowhere, one of Jack's teammates jumped on the man's back and tackled him to the ground. Jack looked around frantically. No other teammates were nearby. He was completely on his own.

He ran down along the right-hand side of the field. The two slowcoach opponents Sophie had pointed out tried to stop him. He accelerated and slithered around them like a snake. The bald man's hand grazed his calf, which immediately began to burn.

With just ten yards to go his confidence began to grow. Then, from the left, the man with the blond hair suddenly started closing in. The enormous man was charging right at him with outstretched arms. Jack tucked the ball firmly under his arm. The man bent forward as he made a dive for Jack's ankles. Jack jumped and his foot scraped along the man's left ear. The man fell to the ground, groaning in pain.

Jack just managed to keep his balance and carried on stumbling forward. He threw the ball over the barrier just as the horn sounded.

Euphoric, Leonardo climbed the fence screaming wildly. The crowd was in hysterics. Jack crumbled to the ground when he saw his teammates rushing towards him. Twenty-six enormous men piled on top of him. The cloud of sand they kicked up obscured the view of the field. A few seconds later, Jack was sitting on the shoulders of a huge man and being paraded like a hero in front of the crowd.

"We won!" Leonardo screamed. "And Jack scored the winning point!"

Tom and the sisters stood proudly along the side of the pitch as the players carried Jack across the field like a trophy.

Leonardo ran over to him the moment they set him back down on the ground.

"Did you see that?" Jack triumphantly flexed his muscles.

"Unbelievable!" Leonardo reached out and pulled him over the railing. "Unbelievable!" he repeated. "You're the hero of the day!" cried Leonardo, tossing Jack his clothes. "But now we have to get out of here. You're the reason we won, and now the other team can't wait to get their hands on you. Let's leave before there's trouble."

Waving his arms wildly, Leonardo showed them the way. "Come on, we're almost there."

Jack followed close behind Leonardo, walking tall and bursting with pride. No longer afraid of anything or anyone, he wormed his way through the crowd. The others could barely keep up. The crowds thinned out the farther they got from the pitch. When they reached the city outskirts the streets were almost deserted.

Sweating and still reeling from the experience, they walked through the empty streets towards the cemetery. On a public holiday like today, the cemetery was probably the last place anyone would want to be. So for Leonardo it was the ideal opportunity to dig up a body without being seen.

Leonardo pulled a heavy shovel from the bushes running along the cemetery's periphery. "I hide it here so I don't have to carry it through the city every time." He crisscrossed the cemetery with the shovel in his hands before finally crouching over a grave that looked like it had just been filled in. He ran his hand through the dark soil.

"This is what we're after. The earth is still moist, so the grave must be a fresh one!"

Leonardo pushed his shovel into the dirt and began digging furiously. The others gathered eagerly around the grave, curious as to what he might find.

Jack went and stood next to Lisa, discretely pulling the knife from his leggings. He handed it back to Lisa. "Thanks, but where did you get it?" he whispered.

Lisa quickly slid the knife into her pocket and shrugged her shoulders.

Jack looked at her inquiringly, but Lisa took a quick step forward. As Leonardo continued to dig, sweat began to appear on his forehead.

"Need any help?" Lisa asked, not sure what to do.

"Yes, Jack, help me out here."

Lisa looked surprised, but Jack quickly grabbed the shovel and immediately began digging. He fell into a rhythm as he dug deeper into the soil. Leonardo monitored his progress closely until Jack suddenly hit something.

"Stop!" Leonardo snatched the shovel out of Jack's hands and threw it on the ground behind him. He dropped to his knees inside the grave and continued digging with his hands.

"We have to be really carefully now, we don't want to damage the body. Do you really want to see this?"

Tom looked horrified when he saw a piece of cloth sticking out of the ground, but he didn't protest. The others mumbled their consent. Leonardo used his hands to carefully brush away the remaining dirt around the lower body. As he repositioned himself in the grave to free the upper part of the body, Sophie leaned forward to help.

"Remove the dirt from there." She swallowed when she saw a bloody mouth appear. "I think I know who this is." She looked at Jack.

"One man's trash is another man's treasure," said Lisa, thumping Jack on the shoulder.

"Lisa!" Sophie looked angrily at her sister.

"Cry baby! There's no harm in trying to lighten things up with a little humor!"

When Leonardo had freed the head they knew for sure. Lying in the grave was the lifeless body of the man who had been carted off the field seriously injured during the calcio match.

"He didn't make it after all." Leonardo made the sign of the cross and quickly inspected the body. A few of his teeth were broken, but the rest of his body was completely intact. "Probably a broken neck, but an otherwise sound body. Perfect for my research."

He beckoned to Jack and Tom and the three of them lifted the corpse out of the grave and lay it on the ground. Leonardo pulled a rag out of his pocket and brushed away all the dirt from the body. When he was done he went and got a long purple coat from a bag he had hidden in the bushes. He quickly dressed the corpse in it.

"Now he looks lively enough to come for a stroll with us." He winked at the others, picked up the body, and in one fluid motion threw it over his shoulder. "Can you clean up my stuff… there, in the bushes? I know a few backstreets that will take us to my studio without being seen. If we bump into anyone, I'll think up something. People are getting hurt all the time, and you can't really see that he's dead. If someone asks, I'll say he's drunk."

Leonardo walked across the cemetery with the lifeless body hanging over his shoulder. When he saw a rough-looking group of men approaching along the street they had just walked into, he slowed his pace. He tried to walk in front of Jack so as to hide him, but he could tell by the look on the men's faces that they had already spotted him. They stared at Jack and started calling him names. When one of them threw something at him, Jack had just enough time to duck. He slipped behind Leonardo and ran to the end of the street.

"Who were those men?" Jack asked Leonardo after they had caught up to him.

"Fans of the other team. They're angry at you, obviously. By now everyone will be drunk and the atmosphere will be getting grimmer." Leonardo shook his head. "We should get a move on, there are a lot of people in the city who will have a bone to pick with you. It's important we get back to the studio as quickly as possible. Come on, this way!" Leonardo turned left into a quiet alley that led to the street where his studio was located.

The body landed with a thud on the examination table.

"It's boiling outside, there's no time to lose. I need to work fast before the smell becomes unbearable."

Aware of what was about to happen, everyone stared in horror at the body on the table.

"I think you should go, this isn't something kids should see. I'm going to sever his head and his legs. Then I have to slice him open."

No one protested. Even Lisa realized this was a bridge too far for them.

"Actually, I just want to go home before they discover we're gone!" said Sophie, who hardly dared think about the consequences on the home front.

Tom nodded vigorously in agreement.

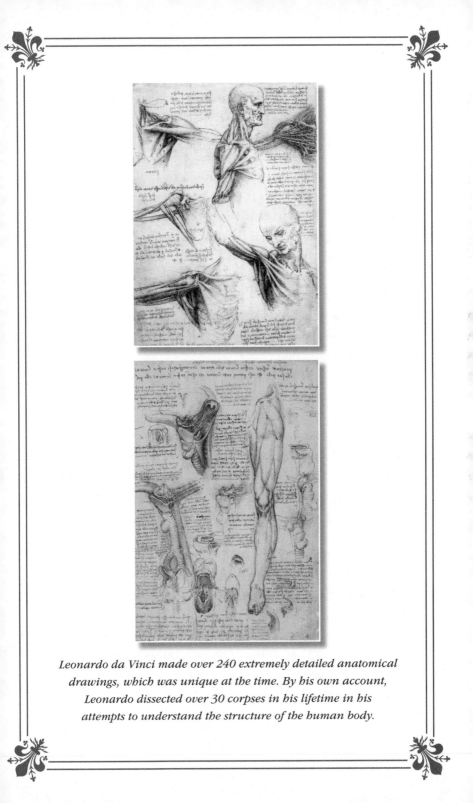

Leonardo da Vinci made over 240 extremely detailed anatomical drawings, which was unique at the time. By his own account, Leonardo dissected over 30 corpses in his lifetime in his attempts to understand the structure of the human body.

"Besides," Leonardo continued, "it's no longer safe, now that half the city is out to get Jack."

Jack laughed sheepishly and rubbed his calf. He could already feel the pain in his muscles.

"Friends," Leonardo said, sounding a little sad. "I'd like nothing more than to spend the next few days and weeks, years even, with you, but that's not possible. It's too dangerous for you here, you have to leave as soon as possible. Come, let's go over to the orrery so you can prepare yourselves."

Everyone was quiet for a few minutes, until Leonardo broke the silence. "Come on, hurry up. I'm really, really anxious to see how this thing works!" Leonardo tried to sound upbeat, but it was obvious he was putting on an act.

"It's your invention!" Sophie looked at Leonardo surprised.

"Yeah, I know that, but I've never succeeded in using it. This is the first time I get to see the orrery in action."

As they crossed the studio, Lisa picked something up off the floor and walked back to Leonardo's 'laboratory'. Without anyone noticing, she set the object down on the shelf next to the knives Leonardo would soon be using.

Ms. Prattle's ermine crawled out of the darkness and sat on the same shelf next to the knives. "Wait here, I'll come back for you in a minute." Lisa gently petted the creature, hoping she would stay there and felt around in her pocket.

She discreetly pulled out her own telephone. If she didn't know better, she would have thought the phone was her sister's. She turned it on, opened the photo app, and set the timer to five seconds. It would start counting down when she pushed the button. She walked back to the studio with the telephone concealed in her hand.

"Everything's in place," Jack said to Leonardo. He moved the planetarium to the middle of the studio and adjusted the rods to align all the planets. He then carefully opened the bottle and poured in the water before adjusting the date and writing down the destination. "Now all we need is to place the telephone in here. The flash will set everything in motion and then we'll be on our way home."

Leonardo was paying close attention. He was euphoric. This was exactly how he had envisioned it. "Angels," he said. "You are all angels." He bowed his head and thanked the four of them for coming to visit him.

After they had all hugged, Sophie turned off the translation app so she could activate the flash. Leonardo waved one last time and walked to the laboratory so the light wouldn't hit him. The others gathered around the planetarium as Leonardo hid behind the table.

"I'll do it," Lisa said abruptly. Sophie shrugged her shoulders.

Lisa took the phone from her sister and, without the others noticing, swapped it for her own phone. She placed her phone in the panel of the planetarium and pushed the button to set the timer in motion.

"Byyeeee!" they yelled in unison.

"The ermine!" Lisa cried suddenly, running back to the laboratory.

"Lisa!!!" Sophie cried in panic. "Quickly!"

Lisa saw the surprised look on Leonardo's face as he crouched behind the examination table. She pulled out Sophie's telephone from her pocket and tossed it into the open backpack she'd left next to the knives.

She gave Leonardo a big wink and pointed to the backpack

as she picked up the ermine. Carrying the animal, she ran quickly back to the planetarium. She took her place next to her sister just in time.

FLASH!

While the studio lit up, a deep buzzing sound forced Leonardo to cover his ears. After a few minutes, the light returned to normal and he stood up. His friends from the future were gone.

He picked up the backpack from the shelf. Sophie's telephone was lying on top. Everything was still there: her geography book, the pills, the printer, the solar charger. He walked back into the studio with the backpack thrown over his shoulder, shaking his head in disbelief.

He knew what he was going to write next, the words were already in his head.

Was it just a hallucination.
They came as four together.
Will they come again?
It is too much, it is too good.
Too good to be true.
Heaven, earth and time.
And I am left behind.
Searching for the divine connection.

Monday, June 23rd, late afternoon

Both Sophie and Tom were lying on the floor in a daze. Lisa sat with her back against the wall with the ermine on her lap. Feeling quite content, she absentmindedly stroked the creature's stomach. Jack stood in the middle of the secret room dusting his clothes off.

"Everyone okay?" Jack asked, breaking the silence. "Tom?"

Tom pulled himself to his feet and smiled at his brother.

Sophie stood up as well and then sat down against the wall next to Lisa. "What time is it? Do you think they missed us?" she whispered hoarsely.

Tom silently picked up his regular clothes from the ground. He took off the costume and put on his jeans and t-shirt.

"Much better!" he said, relieved, running his hands through his hair. "Come on, you guys need to change back into your normal clothes quickly, too. Before you know it the police will be at the door. Then what would we say? That we were having a fancy dress party and got lost?"

Tom carefully pushed open the bookcase and peeked around the corner. "I don't see or hear anyone. I'm going to have a look." He slipped out of the secret room and into the house.

"No, don't go, we first have to agree on our story," Lisa called after him in panic.

All three of them held their breaths as they tried to follow the sound of Tom's footsteps.

Tom returned, panting. "You're not going to believe this! Time has stood still! The newspaper in the kitchen is from today. I mean, yesterday... yesterday for us, which means today. And the sketch is still lying there..." he said, tripping over his words.

Sophie perked up. "You mean it's still Monday?"

"Yes!" Tom cried. "Yes! Time just stood still here! We went and visited the past, but no one noticed we were gone, get it?"

Sophie poked her head through the opening and saw the sketch lying on her father's desk, just as they had left it.

Lisa smiled. "Just like what we wrote down on the planetarium, right? Good to know it actually works, this way we won't need to make up any excuses. Cool!" Feeling very satisfied, she stood up and carefully put the ermine down, giving it one last friendly pat on the head. "Hurry up, that means Mom and Dad could be home any minute."

They changed their clothes as quickly as possible.

"Ugh, I think I can still smell dead horse on my clothes and in my hair!" Sophie said disgusted.

"Don't be such a drama queen, hurry up!" Lisa pushed her sister towards the exit and swept all the clothes into a pile in the corner.

"Wait, my phone!" Sophie shouted.

Lisa bent down, removed the device from the planetarium, and put it in her pocket.

"I'll give it to you in a second," she mumbled, ushering everyone out of the secret room. In the hallway they hastily said goodbye to the boys.

"Not a word! We'll see you tomorrow!"

They hugged each other a little awkwardly and then the boys scurried off home.

Sophie and Lisa sprinted up the stairs. Sophie reached the bathroom first, turning on the shower and greedily drinking from the faucet while waiting for the water to warm up. She spoke with her sister in between gulps.

"The first thing I'm going to do is scrub away the smell… and wash it out of my hair!"

"Me too!" Lisa said, inspecting a long curl of her own hair in disgust.

After showering and drinking loads of water, they both felt a lot better. Refreshed, they went to Sophie's room.

"Sure we weren't just dreaming?" asked Lisa, who then sat down on the bed and looked at the clock as if it were lying about the time.

Sophie shrugged her shoulders, twisted her wet hair into a knot, grabbed her laptop, and flopped down next to her sister on the bed.

"What are you doing?" Lisa asked.

"Looking for proof! You wanted to know whether or not we imagined everything, right?" Sophie typed hurriedly, and quickly scrolled down through the various websites until she stopped at Leonardo da Vinci's Wikipedia page. She placed her hand in front of her mouth in disbelief at what she read.

"Lisa?!" She removed her hand and stared at the screen with her mouth open. "It says it right here!" She pointed to a few paragraphs and read them out loud. "When *The Annunciation* was x-rayed, Verrocchio's work was still visible but Leonardo's angel was not."

Lisa's cheeks began to turn hot. Her sister's ploy had worked. Leonardo, the painting, everything was real. Art historians had discovered the trick a long time ago!"

Sophie was completely in her element now and continued to

search enthusiastically for more information about Leonardo. "Here! Here's some information about *The Lost Leonardo*, what Dad was talking about." She carefully read the text. "Leonardo was working on it in Florence in 1505. Dad was right."

When she heard her mother calling she immediately shut her laptop.

"Okay Lisa, remember, this was just another boring day at school." Sophie winked at her sister and they both ran downstairs. Their parents might not have missed the girls, but for Sophie and her sister it had been two days since they had last seen them. When they got to the kitchen they hugged their mother warmly.

"Whoa... What's going on with you two?" she said, pleasantly surprised.

Sophie and Lisa realized their behavior was odd and did their best to quickly regain their composure.

"Nothing Mom, we just thought you deserved an extra hug every once in a while," said Lisa with a broad smile, before greedily shoving a handful of cashew nuts into her mouth.

After dinner they followed their father to his study. He sat down at his desk and carefully laid out his shiny tools, one by one. His systematic approach had a soothing effect on Sophie. She had adopted his approach to work, too, and made it her own.

He pulled on a pair of thin white gloves and turned up the lamp on his desk. Without saying a word, he carefully lifted the sketch and thoroughly inspected the front and back.

He peered over his glasses and quickly glanced at Sophie and Lisa's tense faces before continuing. He began loosening the back of the frame using an object that was a cross between an ice pick and a screwdriver. He removed the sketch from the frame with the utmost care.

He then picked up a magnifying glass from his desk and, breathing deeply, meticulously inspected the sketch. To examine the material even more closely, he occasionally brought the magnifying glass right up to the paper.

He ran his fingers along the edge and unfolded the sketch. Sophie and Lisa anxiously followed their father's every move. He turned the sheet over, carefully examined the paper again with the magnifying glass, and then removed his glasses.

"Sorry girls," he shook his head. "It might look very authentic, but it's only a copy."

For a few seconds time seemed to stand still. Sophie and Lisa looked quickly at each other. "That can't be," Sophie said. She was shaking her head emphatically. "No, it can't be. Everything written down there is true. I know for certain, otherwise we couldn't have done it!"

Lisa pinched her sister on the arm without her father noticing.

"What do you mean?" he asked. Sophie quickly composed herself. This wasn't the moment to give the game away.

"I mean... I mean, how is that possible, it looks so real?"

Her father nodded. He removed his gloves and picked up the sketch again. He ran his hand slowly over the paper. "I understand, Sophie. I admit, it is a very, *very* meticulous forgery. It had to be made by someone with a thorough understanding of art, of antiquity, but this..." He shook his head again. "Here." He handed the sketch to Lisa. "Again, I'm sorry girls, it would have been so much fun."

Disappointed, Sophie ran upstairs to her room without saying a word and angrily slammed her door. Lisa, who was less intense by nature, thanked her father and walked to her own room, deep in thought. She lay on her bed and stared at the ceiling for a few minutes without moving a muscle. The sketch being a fake didn't make any sense. Something about this just isn't right, she said to herself.

The sketch had frayed edges, just like the pages torn out of the codex. The texts and drawings accurately matched the other pages in the chapter.

Someone had to have seen the real codex pages, otherwise Prattle's sketch couldn't be such a good imitation. Someone well versed in art. Someone who didn't want Prattle's sketch ever to be identified as an authentic Leonardo. Someone who knew what was written on those pages. Someone who knew about the secret room just like they did. Someone who had had access to the sketch before they did...

As she lay there thinking about it, all the pieces fell into place. How had she not thought of this earlier? She knew who the culprit was. She jumped up from the bed with a smile on her face. She knew who had discovered the secret room before they had, but she decided to keep the discovery to herself for now. Her friends didn't need to know. She would tell them when the time was right, but not just yet.

Tuesday, June 24th, morning

"And? What did your father say about the sketch?" whispered Jack. Hackett hadn't arrived yet, but Jack didn't want anyone in the class overhearing them.

"It's nothing," hissed Sophie.

"What's nothing? What do you mean?"

"He said the sketch is a fake!" Jack looked at her dumbstruck.

"I know, it's crazy, right? Lisa and I can't get our heads around it. Everything written on those pages is true... and yet it's a fake?" Sophie couldn't accept the fact that she didn't get it and stared angrily straight ahead.

Jack shrugged his shoulders exaggeratedly. "Bummer!" he said categorically after a few seconds. "I mean, bummer that we don't know how the sketch could be a fake, but the most important thing is that it works!" He looked at her triumphantly. "And in a few days from now we're also going to Venice!" His eyes sparkled as he took out his notebook and put it on the desk.

"I had expected you to react differently..." Sophie looked at Jack inquiringly.

"Well, okay, I don't get it, but I don't want it to spoil anything right now. It's actually a good thing, because now your father will no longer be interested in the sketch!" Satisfied with his own explanation, he began drawing an ermine in his notebook.

"Give me a sheet of paper. I couldn't find my backpack this morning. Lisa had it last. She still has my phone, too!"

Jack passed her a page from his notebook.

"Lisa!" Sophie shouted as loud as she could when she saw her sister running with Tom towards their bikes after school. "Lisa, have you got my phone?"

Lisa felt around in her jacket pocket and pulled out her own telephone. "No, sorry, don't have it," she said with a goading smile as she put the telephone back into her pocket.

Sophie looked furious. "Give me back my phone! You have your own, don't be so annoying."

Lisa raised her eyebrows. "This isn't your phone, it's mine."

Sophie gave her an irritated look. "You took my phone out of the planetarium yesterday, right? That means it's my phone!"

"Um, yes and no," Lisa chuckled.

"Lisa, cut it out! Give me my phone, now." Sophie took a step forward, thrust her hand into Lisa's jacket pocket, and in one swift movement removed the phone.

"Will you please give me back my phone?" Lisa stood in front of her sister defiantly.

"Maybe you didn't hear me very well, but like I said... yes and no. Yes, I took it from the planetarium, but no that's not your phone."

Sophie now smelled a rat and decided to inspect the phone. She turned it on and immediately saw it was Lisa's. "But... if this is the phone you took out of the planetarium yesterday... then where's mine? Lisa!"

Lisa didn't say anything.

"Lisa!" Sophie looked angrily at her sister. "If it was your phone that you took out of the planetarium yesterday, then that means that was the one you used to transport us back from Florence."

"Bingo! You're on your way to winning a washing machine," Lisa said teasingly.

"That's why you were suddenly so eager in Florence to put the phone in the planetarium. You switched the phones, but why? Where's mine?"

"You have only one help line remaining," Lisa said. "Do you want to use it or do you want to continue playing?"

"Lisa," Sophie nearly roared, "where... is... my... phone?"

"In your backpack," Lisa taunted her sister.

"Okay then, *where* is my backpack?"

"Uh, let me think. Oh yeah, at Leonardo's place," said Lisa, taking two quick steps backwards just in case.

"What?"

Jack grabbed Sophie tightly before she could jump on her sister.

"Lisa! What have you done? If my phone's lost, Mom and Dad will be really mad at me. And I need it for Venice, and it's really expensive, and, well, I just need it! How could you do this to me?"

"Didn't you hear Leonardo? He sounded so disappointed when he said he had never managed to use the planetarium successfully. That's so unfair. He's the inventor of a machine he can't even use himself, even though that's the one thing he wants more than anything in the world. Your phone gives him that opportunity; don't you think that's only fair?"

"Okay, totally sad for Leonardo. But if you feel so sorry for 'Mr. Inventor' why didn't you just give him your phone?" Sophie said furiously.

"Mine doesn't have any apps. It's completely blank, Leonardo wouldn't be able to do anything with it. He's smart enough to figure out how to use the apps, and with the translation app – which is on your phone and not on mine – he'll be able to go anywhere in the world."

Even though Sophie was astounded by her sister's revelation, she felt her anger ebbing away. Jack and Tom, who had been watching the exchange breathlessly, stood by, slightly stunned.

"Fine, that was very kind of you. But I want my phone back before we go on our school trip. I really need it."

"Oh, really? Then we'll have to go back to Florence again," Lisa said, her eyes sparkling.

"Leonardo here we come." Tom took a step forward trying to reproduce the sound of a flash.

Sophie looked irritated. "Lisa, something tells me that was part of your plan all along." She rolled her eyes. "And it's only because you were doing something nice for Leonardo, otherwise…" She clenched her fists menacingly. Sophie gave Jack a steely gaze. "We have no time to lose, we have to go immediately. Tomorrow's the last day before we go to Venice, and Mom was planning to be home in the afternoon."

The four of them hesitated for a moment until Tom and Lisa high-fived each other and, feeling very sure of themselves, hopped on their bikes.

"See you later," Lisa yelled. "We'll get changed into our costumes." The two of them set off towards home whooping with excitement. Sophie and Jack got onto their bikes, too, and followed.

Jack moved the bookcase aside with a loud crack.

"Where are we going?" Lisa asked excitedly. "The Jurassic?"

Jack acted as if he didn't hear her. He waited to see what Sophie would say.

"No, just Florence, I need to get my phone back. That's the whole point, isn't it?"

Jack bent over and began writing.

"Wait," Sophie said. "What year are you writing down?"

"1475," Jack answered. "The same as last time."

"No, wait... give me a second to think." Sophie closed her eyes and tried to remember what she had read about Leonardo last night in bed.

"Write down 1505! The planetarium is his invention, he should get the opportunity to use it. Lisa's right about that. If we return the same day we left, he'll never have that chance and that wouldn't be fair. We need to go back a few years later. And, before you ask, I don't know exactly where he was in the years after we left – Florence, Rome, Milan, wherever – but what I do know is that we have to find him. There's no room for error!" She looked sternly at Jack.

"And in 1505?" Jack and Tom asked in unison.

"I know for sure that Leonardo was in Florence in 1505. And I know where." Sophie saw that her sister grasped what she was getting at because she had been there last night when Sophie had read it out loud to her.

"The Hall of the Five Hundred," Lisa quietly concurred.

Jack trusted Sophie blindly and did what he was asked. "I didn't expect to be using this thing again so quickly," he said gleefully.

"I did," Lisa laughed.

"Lisa, promise me one thing. We just go back and get the

phone, nothing crazy, okay?" Sophie looked almost pleadingly at her sister.

"I'll try my best," Lisa said with a wink.

Jack did a few push-ups. "You never know, if they see me again they could come after me."

"Jack, it's been thirty years!" laughed Sophie. "They definitely won't recognize you anymore. Come on, change quickly so we can go."

Dressed again in their costumes, they took up position around the planetarium. Jack went through his set-up routine. They spoke nervously amongst themselves while Jack carefully poured the liquid into the planets.

"Do we have everything?" Tom asked.

"Stop!" Sophie suddenly yelled. "We can't go yet!"

"Why not?" Tom sounded surprised.

"That's Lisa's phone, there are no apps on it, nothing. Without a translation app we won't be able to understand a thing!" she said, throwing her arms in the air for extra emphasis.

"But he still has your phone," Jack said, "so we can still talk to him." Jack took a step forward to accept their applause, which was not forthcoming.

"No," Lisa's fingers picked at a loose thread on her dress. "Sophie is right, we can't risk it."

Sophie was genuinely pleased with her sister's unexpected support. "We're taking a huge risk already in assuming that Leonardo is actually there. I know he's there, but then again you can never be certain."

Sophie shook her head. "Maybe we'll need to ask someone directions or something. We have to download the translation app onto the phone," she looked desperately at her sister. "But we can't ask Mom and Dad to pay for a subscription. How do we get your phone working within a day so we can download the apps?"

"I know how!" Lisa pulled something small out of the pocket of her dress and handed it to Sophie. "Here, it's your SIM card," she looked at her sister with a wry smile.

Sophie stared back at her sister, her mouth wide open. "Why do I get the feeling you already had everything figured out before you even swapped phones?"

Lisa nodded silently and pointed to the phone and SIM card in Sophie's hands.

After inserting her own SIM card into her sister's phone, Sophie rapidly ran though the entire program. She registered the phone to the provider and downloaded a bunch of apps. She handed it to Jack when she was done.

"What do you think Leonardo looks like now?" she asked her sister.

"And old man with long gray hair, just like on the internet."

"I think so, too," Sophie said. "Do you think he'll remember us?"

"Of course he will!" Lisa said confidently. "He couldn't forget us if he tried!"

Jack began counting down. "Three... two... one...!"

FLASH!

Tuesday, June 24th, afternoon

Lisa jumped up and brushed the powdery sand off her dress. She quickly ran to the end of the street. The day was extremely hot and dry. A cloud of pale dust rose up every time her foot hit the ground. At the junction she stopped abruptly, gazing down one street and then the other. She savored every little detail: the smell, the trash on the street, the noise from inside the homes, and the people in the distance.

Keeping a close eye on her sister, Sophie pinched her nose theatrically. "Oh my god, the smell hasn't changed!"

Tom, still a bit dazed, nodded in agreement. The streets were still covered with discarded food and waste. The smell lingering in the air was a pungent mix of rotting fruit and stale urine.

Jack tried to ignore it. He walked to the studio and stared through the windows. "No Leonardo," he mumbled, just loud enough for the others to hear.

Tom took a quick look inside as well. "Nope, I don't see anyone." He caught up to Lisa and jumped deftly over a small rock on the side of the street, reacting as if he'd just pulled off a skateboarding stunt.

"Let me look." Sophie stood next to Jack and stared inside. "This is not a studio anymore. Look, everything is different. That's probably why we landed on the street."

Jack took another quick look and had to admit Sophie was

right. There was a dining table in the corner of the room surrounded by several three-legged wooden stools. The house in front of them was definitely not being used as a studio now. There were no paintings hanging on the walls and no art materials lying around.

"Maybe we should ask one of the neighbors if they know where Leonardo is? What do you think? One thing's for sure, he's not here." Jack shrugged his shoulders. He seemed a bit baffled.

Sophie shook her head. Her hands rummaged through her dress pockets until she found the phone and then looked around warily to make sure no one was looking. She pulled it out, ran through the menu, and looked closely at one of the images. She zoomed in while simultaneously trying to orientate herself.

"We can't just go knocking on someone's door. What would we say?" Sophie's voice was trembling slightly. She switched off the telephone and put it back into her pocket. "Wait! I think I know where Leonardo is. All we have to do is figure out how to get there."

Jack sighed deeply, clearly indicating that he wanted a better explanation.

"Leonardo is working on an enormous artwork in the Palazzo Vecchio, Florence's city hall. In fact, it's supposed to be his greatest work of all! I'm sure we'll be able to find him there." Sophie tried to sound as upbeat as possible. Finding the city hall couldn't be too difficult, she thought.

"Let's go left here," Sophie said. "We first need to find the big square where we were the last time." She pointed towards the narrow street that led to the square.

"I wouldn't do that," Lisa said. "Tom and I have been standing here for a while watching and it's crazy busy over there. I don't think it would be very clever to walk through the square. If something happens, or if someone asks us something, we're toast."

Sophie shook her head. "Trust me, I'm certain we should go that way." Feeling sure of herself, she started walking down the street. "If we go to the right, we'll have to walk all the way around, and I really want to find Leonardo before it gets dark!" Sophie stopped, folded her arms, and waited, hoping that Lisa would follow her.

"Okay," Lisa said, "so the choice is between walking around or getting killed? Fine, we'll do it your way so!" She cocked an eyebrow and looked first at her sister and then at the boys.

"Aaaggh! You always have to get your own way, don't you?! I hope you're right, Lisa! We'll take your route," said Sophie, and they all followed her. Jack continued to look around furtively with his fists clenched, just in case someone recognized him.

They stopped briefly at the first junction.

Lisa was half humming a tune while Jack and Tom just stood around waiting, and Sophie was doing her best to find her bearings in the hot city.

"I know where we are," Sophie said. "This is the same route as last time, but in the opposite direction. If we turn here, we'll eventually end up at the cemetery."

"Because you want to dig up another body?" Tom said.

Lisa laughed at the joke, but Jack and Sophie, being older, were less easily amused.

"No laughing allowed," Lisa said with a French accent.

"Pfff," Lisa rolled her eyes when Sophie and Jack didn't appreciate her joke either.

Sophie and Jack walked on as Tom and Lisa playfully made their way down the street. To avoid any trouble, every time they passed someone they pretended to be engaged in conversation with each other.

"Look, there's the cemetery!" Jack pointed to the end of the street.

Lisa and Tom ran past him and quickly rummaged through the hedges and bushes surrounding the graves. They walked back after checking the last bush. "No shovel, nothing."

"It's been thirty years," Sophie said. "Maybe he's learned enough and doesn't need to dig up bodies anymore?"

"Why are we here anyway? Where to next?" Tom asked impatiently.

From the cemetery, which was situated on a hill, they could see the entire city.

"We have to reach the other side of the square and I think I remember how to get there from here," Sophie said. She closed her eyes and tried to recall how they had walked with Leonardo. "This way!"

They walked down a series of quiet streets quickly and without incident. Sophie knew exactly where she was going. The few people they encountered along the way didn't pay them much attention. After a while they looked at each other, tired and dehydrated from the oppressing heat.

"We should have brought some water and something to eat. I'm hungry," Lisa said. "And thirsty."

"Me too," Tom grumbled.

Jack panted as he walked ahead. "How much farther?" he asked in a whiny voice.

Sophie took out her phone and stared at the screen for a

bit. "Walk to the end of this street. We're halfway there," she finally said. "It's taking a lot longer because we're walking all the way around."

"How do you even know that?" Jack asked. "I thought the phone didn't work here. You can't just look up the route, can you?"

"If only it were so easy. Before we left home I quickly downloaded a map of Florence. Because the screen is small and I can't type in the location, it's not working as well as I had hoped. To make matters worse there are no street signs and the city isn't the same as in our time, but I'm doing my best."

Lisa stomped on the ground. "Fair enough, but I really need to eat and drink something or I'm going to get really grumpy."

Tom laughed and threw his arm over her shoulder. "Correction!" he said. "We want to eat and drink something because we are already grumpy."

Jack and Sophie exchanged a look of dismay. "Let's just keep walking," said Jack. "The sooner we find Leonardo, the sooner we can get something to drink. He'll sort us out."

The group stopped at the end of the street.

"A market!" Lisa's eyes glistened in the sunlight. She looked left and right. Eyeing all the food, her mouth began to water.

"Lisa!" her sister whispered. "Lisa, forget it! You said yourself we shouldn't cross that other square because there were too many people..."

"Sophie's right, we can't risk it. That market on the left of the square is even busier than it was on the other square. I think we should keep to the right and cross it as quickly as possible." Jack motioned for them to leave, but Lisa and Tom clearly had their doubts. With their stomachs rumbling, they stared at the food as if it were calling out to them.

"Lisa, seriously." Sophie tried her best to convince her sister.

"We don't even have any money, so we can't buy anything anyway." She turned around and without hesitation quickly walked across the square with Jack, certain her sister would follow.

Lisa inspected her pockets and figured they were big enough. She pulled Tom closer before he could follow his brother.

Tom giggled as she ran her hands over his costume. "Are you trying to tickle me?"

"How many pockets do you have?" Lisa asked without the slightest hint of emotion as she carefully inspected the people at the market.

"Ehm…" Tom checked his clothes. "Four!"

"Okay." Lisa took a deep breath and nodded her head a few times before whispering in Tom's ear. "Listen, this is totally against my principles and I've never done anything like this in my life…" She glanced one last time over the square and calculated their odds, "but I'm so hungry, really! Chances are we'll be spending the next few hours looking for Leonardo, and what happens if we can't find him? We have to eat before we die of starvation!"

Tom nodded, he agreed with her on that. Not entirely understanding what she was getting at, however, he shrugged his shoulders.

"Follow me and stay *very* close!" Lisa walked along the left-hand side of the square and pushed her way quickly through the crowd. Tom ran after her, dodging people and never letting the distance between them become more than a few feet. They bumped into each other a few times when she briefly stopped and looked around. Like a sly fox, she maneuvered her way around the rows of baskets. After a few minutes they were standing on the edge of the market again.

Tom didn't understand a thing, but suddenly he noticed that his tight blue velvet uniform was heavier than it had been a few minutes before. He looked down surprised. His pockets were bulging with tomatoes.

He glanced quickly at Lisa. She looked like a deformed zucchini with lumps in her dark green dress. All the pockets were filled with food. He couldn't believe his eyes when he realized what had happened. "What? How?" he stuttered before being interrupted by a loud roar.

Lisa looked back over her shoulder and saw an enormous man charging through the crowd in their direction.

"Run!" she screamed. "Run for your life."

Tom didn't hesitate for even a second and ran like crazy towards the street corner where a surprised-looking Jack and Sophie were waiting for them.

"Where were you guys?" Sophie asked angrily.

"Run!" screamed Lisa, as she dove into the street with Tom to escape the angry market trader.

Frightened by the sight of the vengeful man running in their direction, Sophie immediately turned and followed them.

Jack saw the man, closed his eyes, and briefly thought of the victorious match. "Calcio!" he said quietly to himself. He took a deep breath and stepped deftly aside to let the angry man pass. As he bulldozed by, Jack stuck out his leg and the man tumbled forward and slammed onto the ground.

As the man lay moaning on the street, Jack quickly retreated. After a few hundred feet he heard Sophie call to him from a side street.

"This way!"

The four of them continued running, crisscrossing a number of streets, until they were sure they were no longer being followed.

Sophie leaned against the wall shaking her head. "I don't know what to say, you only ever do what you want anyway."

Lisa retrieved four apples from her pocket and threw one to each of them. "Bon appétit, and you're welcome."

Jack and Sophie were livid, but at the same time so hungry that they quickly sank their teeth into their apples. They ate the juicy fruit in silence. Lisa looked at her sister and friends and was glad to see that the fruit had the desired effect; everyone looked a lot happier.

Sophie reluctantly admitted that it was a delicious apple. "What else did you nab, you little thief?"

One by one Lisa pulled the fruit and vegetables from her pockets.

"No way!" Sophie burst out laughing. "I bet you even had a recipe in mind!"

Lisa hadn't grabbed things randomly. In her pockets she had the exact ingredients needed for a well-known dish. They all started laughing uncontrollably. Jack contributed to the hilarity by theatrically mimicking the angry market trader smacking against the ground after he had tripped him.

"Okay, very funny, but there's no time to lose. We've got a mob of angry barbarians on our tail again, though this time they've got a good reason, I have to say. And we really need to find Leonardo before it gets dark, otherwise it'll be too dangerous," said Sophie, suddenly dead serious.

Everyone seemed to agree and so they set off again, Sophie walking in front with her phone in hand. They came to a stop in front of a colossal building. She studied the building from top to bottom.

"I think…" she looked at her phone, zoomed in, and did a little jump for joy. "Do you see that enormous dome on the roof? Up there? This the Florence Cathedral, this is the Duomo! That means we're almost there. It's just a few minutes away."

They carried on walking, feeling both excited and determined. Side by side they scampered onto the enormous square. Buildings towered high above them on all sides. Impressed by their surroundings, they looked around in amazement.

"Which one is the Palazzo we're looking for?" asked Tom suddenly.

"That square one," said Sophie and Lisa in unison.

"The Hall of the Five Hundred," Lisa said. "Dad told us about it. I recognize the building from the internet."

The Palazzo Vecchio was Florence's city hall, but it looked more like a Roman fort. The cubical building had a fortified look to it, with solid masonry interspersed with marble arches and battlements. The defense systems on the roof facilitated the pouring of burning fluid, the shooting of arrows, and the throwing of rocks from behind protective barriers.

Sophie studied the entire building and spotted a grotesque marble statue near the entrance. "They have absolutely no shame here, do they?" she said. "I hope we haven't seen more of Leonardo than we had bargained for…"

"Why are the statues always naked? Can you imagine it? A statue of our own mayor on the square not wearing any clothes! Gruesome!" Jack joked.

"I have the feeling I've seen that statue before," said Lisa.

Sophie walked around the sculpture, nodding her head.

"We'll ask Leonardo when we find him, maybe this really is one of his works."

They continued to inspect the statue, letting out the occasional embarrassed chuckle, until they were sure they could sneak into the building without being noticed.

Sophie stopped in the middle of the beautiful interior courtyard.

"I don't know the way from here. I only downloaded a map of Florence. I didn't think the building would actually be this big."

"Doesn't matter," Jack sounded sincere. "You already got us safely through the city, we should be able to figure out this last bit, too."

A young man standing at the top of the stairs attracted their attention.

"Leonardo!" Tom's voice ricocheted across the courtyard. The man froze. He looked at Tom suspiciously.

"No, birdbrain!" hissed Sophie.

Tom ignored her and walked enthusiastically towards the staircase.

"That's not Leonardo," said Sophie in a soft voice, hoping Tom would hear her this time. She exchanged tense looks with Jack and Lisa. "That man is, like, thirty years old. That can't be him! Leonardo must be at least fifty now, which means that's definitely not him!"

The man waited expectantly at the top of the stairs as Tom started to ascend the staircase.

This isn't going to end well, Sophie thought. She racked her brains trying to find a quick solution to the situation. Suddenly, a figure with a long beard appeared from behind the younger man and pushed him aside.

Tom was startled by the figure with the beard at the top of the stairs. He realized he had made a mistake and quickly stepped back.

After the two men exchanged a few angry words, the bearded figure slowly descended the stairs.

"Leonardo?" Lisa looked up at him, her eyes glistening.

Leonardo spread his arms. *"Amici!"*

"Friends!" said Sophie, "I don't need any help with that one."

She grabbed her telephone and turned on the translation app.

"For thirty years I've been waiting for you. That you arrive at this precise moment, here at the Palazzo, now that it's ready, that can't be a coincidence." He wrapped his arms around his friends.

"How are you? What have you been doing all these years?" Jack asked curiously.

Leonardo didn't respond, but instead looked at them full of emotion. "I'm so happy to see you again, especially now... my friends from the future."

"Why is it so special that we're here right now?" Sophie could no longer suppress her curiosity.

Leonardo laughed heartily. "You'll see for yourselves tonight!"

"What's happening tonight?"

"Patience!" He laughed and patted Sophie lightly on the shoulder. "I assume you can stay one night?"

"But you no longer have the studio?" Jack said, confused.

"No, I don't work there anymore. So you already know that? I'm busy working on something very big, my most

*This is how Leonardo da Vinci must have looked in his late fifties,
as this is a self-portrait painted by the famous artist around 1510.*

important piece yet." Leonardo winked at them and pointed up to a room on the first floor.

"Oh, wait here for a moment, I'll be back in a second." Despite his age, Leonardo took the steps two at the time.

"Do any of you know what's up there?" Sophie asked.

Lisa nodded. "The Hall of the Five Hundred and... *The Lost Leonardo!*"

"What's the Hall of the Five Hundred?" asked Tom.

"Dad told us that in 1505 – which is now – Leonardo was working on his greatest artwork yet, here in the Palazzo Vecchio," Lisa said. "That's how Sophie knew we'd find him here."

"And what's *The Lost Leonardo?*" Tom asked.

"That..." said Lisa, "that is a work of art that can no longer be seen in our own time. There are a lot of books written about it, though. They say a wall was built in front of it, meaning there's no actual evidence that it even exists. Just a bunch of texts and sketches that show what it would have looked like."

"Whoa! There *is* evidence!" Sophie joined the discussion. "Not so very long ago, in March 2012 – I mean, in our time – researchers drilled tiny holes into the front wall so that they could insert mini cameras or whatever to look behind it. They discovered the same pigments that Leonardo used for his other known artworks."

Lisa continued the story. "That's right. That's why they call that work of art *The Lost Leonardo*, because everyone in our time thinks it's behind the front wall but nobody knows for sure."

"*The Lost Leonardo?*" What are you talking about?" said Leonardo as he came back down the stairs again looking very cheerful.

Lisa cleverly changed the subject. "What were you doing up there?"

"I was just asking my assistant to hang up a few fire baskets." He gave them a mysterious look. "Now that my old studio no longer exists, we're going to sleep here tonight, upstairs in the Palazzo. In the room where I am currently working, to be precise."

"Fire baskets?" Sophie's mouth fell open. "Does the paint still need to dry?" She asked the question even though she already knew the answer.

"The paint still need to dry?" Leonardo looked at her with a frown. "No, the paint is dry. The entire work is finished actually, except for a few minor details. It is amazing, even if I say so myself!"

"But..." Sophie didn't get it. She was sure her father had told them the paint had started to drip, which is why Leonardo had hung up the fire baskets. That's what was written in the history books.

"No, I'm having my assistant hang up some fire baskets so that the room is well lit when we return later on this evening. Otherwise it will be too dark to see the work properly."

Lisa looked at her sister and shook her head furiously. "Let it go Sophie, let it go," she whispered.

Sophie reluctantly kept quiet. She had already been anxious to know more about *The Lost Leonardo*, but now she was absolutely bursting with curiosity. "Where are we going now?" she asked. "Can't we just have a quick look first?"

"Patience, Sophie, the work isn't going to walk away on us. Besides, I'm in a hurry – I mean, *we're* in a hurry."

They all looked at him inquisitively.

"I've been invited to dine with Giovan Francesco Rustici

this evening." He adopted an aristocratic air. "And you are going with me, as my guests! I'll tell them you're the children of a foreign friend. That will explain your strange tongue. But one important thing: that device you call a 'phone', you have to turn it off, okay? We can't be seen with that!"

"Disgusting!" Leonardo spat, as they passed by the marble statue of the naked man outside.

"Isn't that statue yo..." Sophie caught herself just in time. "Who made that statue?"

"That brat you saw standing on the stairs," Leonardo growled. "I should have shoved him harder..."

"What's his name?"

"Oh, Michelangelo, an insufferable show-off. He has also been commissioned to paint something in the Hall of the Five Hundred, but so far he hasn't done anything but draw a few sketches, pfff..." Leonardo didn't even try to hide his irritation. "By the way, I still have to think of something to eat for tonight. Do you have any suggestions?"

"I thought you had been invited?" said Jack.

"Yes, but this is different. Tonight is a small gathering of prominent men. Artistic talent and scientists from Florence. I'm not actually a member of the group, but Giovan asked me to come along."

"That's not really an answer to Jack's question," Sophie said.

Leonardo bowed his head and smiled. "You're right. For this gathering every guest is required to bring along something to eat. I really have to think of something. Oh, and it has to be something out of the ordinary!"

"Can you get your hands on some beef?" asked Lisa, and,

just as it had thirty years previously, her smile again enchanted Leonardo.

He nodded. "I can, but I don't eat meat, you know that!"

Sophie gave her sister a goofy smile. "No way Lisa, this is just too much!" She knew immediately what her sister was up to.

"Have you ever heard of Spaghetti Bolognese?" Lisa had to laugh when she asked the question.

Leonardo pursed his lips and shook his head.

"No way, you've got to be kidding me!" Sophie burst out laughing.

"What?" Lisa said, shrugging her shoulders innocently. "Someone had to invent the recipe at some point or other, didn't they?"

"Okay, but let's make it without meat. Leonardo can tell the other guests that it can also be made with ground beef."

Sophie looked at her sister, hoping that she would agree. The mere idea of eating meat was enough to horrify her, and she knew that Leonardo felt the same way.

"Okay, we should also let the Italians discover a few things for themselves, I suppose," giggled Lisa. She rummaged through her pockets: flour, basil, onions, celery, garlic, and carrots. "Tom, you still have the tomatoes?"

Tom removed the tomatoes from his pockets and held them up triumphantly.

"If this Giovan guy has oil, stock, and wine, then we'll be able to cook the meal tonight."

"You mean we don't have to pick up anything else?" asked Leonardo. He was delighted that everything was going so smoothly. As they walked through the streets of Florence, he continued his story.

Most of the homes in Florence stood on narrow, unpaved streets and alleyways littered with filth, but the street they were now walking down was breathtaking. It was paved with beautiful stones and free of trash. The homes on the street were large and well maintained. Leonardo saw the astonishment on their faces.

"Giovan is a noble. This neighborhood here is the most well-to-do in all of Florence."

They stopped in front of an impressive building and Leonardo knocked on the beautifully crafted door a few times. A few seconds later the two wooden panels opened elegantly inwards. Two immaculately dressed servants held the doors open as Leonardo and his guests walked through.

The hallway, the stairwell, the paneling – everything appeared to be made of marble. Gold leaf mirrors hung on the wall, and candles flickered everywhere.

Jack threw his arm over his brother's shoulder. *Look at us now*, he thought. They'd never been in a house like this in their entire lives.

As Sophie walked down the hallway with Leonardo, Lisa made funny faces in every single mirror she passed. Sophie turned down the volume of her phone to make sure no one could hear it. Leonardo saw her slip the phone into her pocket and pointed to the stairs.

"Follow the wizard with the long gray beard!" Lisa joked, causing Tom to burst out laughing.

"Shh," Jack tried to shut him up before he got them thrown out.

Another well-dressed butler-type held the door open for them on the first floor. Leonardo paused in the doorway to allow them to enter before him. Before they had a chance to look around, several middle-aged and elderly men stood up and introduced themselves, first to Sophie and Lisa.

"Italians certainly have good manners," Lisa immediately joked, "but I don't understand a thing they're saying."

Leonardo walked into the room and spoke in a voice loud enough to make everyone stop talking. Sophie hid behind Jack and crouched down on her knees. She brought her ear close to the pocket in which the telephone was hidden so she could understand what Leonardo was saying. When he finished she stood back up and shuffled forward again. All the men applauded and bowed to the friends, before returning to their seats at the table. Leonardo went over to them, pointed to an adjacent room, and then took his place at the table along with the other men.

"Does anyone know what that was all about?" asked Jack.

"That area over there with the table is the dining room and we're standing in the entrance to the kitchen," said Lisa. "I think we're supposed to start cooking."

Sophie nodded. "I heard everything."

"You've got the phone in your pocket? That's what you were doing, wasn't it?" Tom asked her.

"Yep, I have the volume turned down so that you can only hear it when you press your ear right up to it."

"What did Leonardo say?" asked Tom.

"He said he was grateful for the invitation, blah-blah-blah, that we were the children of a friend from a foreign country, and that we don't speak any Italian, but that we are fabulous cooks! That's when they all began applauding."

Lisa laid out all the ingredients from her pockets on a long table and motioned to Tom to do the same.

231

Communicating with her hands, she made it clear to the kitchen servants that she wouldn't be needing their help. She picked up a large knife and prepared to chop the vegetables. It might not be as challenging as a rotting horse, but she was still eager to get started.

Tom stood in silence next to her and helped where he could.

From the kitchen, Jack and Sophie watched the wonderful scene in the dining room. Judging by their raised voices and animated gestures, the men sitting around the table were exchanging incredible stories. Some of them stood up every now and then to add emphasis to their tales.

"Do you think we can join them later?" Jack asked softly.

Sophie nodded. "Why not? And we'll be able to chat with each other as well. No one will give it a second thought!"

Jack gave her a satisfied grin. "Cool, eh?"

Occasionally, Leonardo looked over at them from the table to see if everything was going okay. Sophie gave him a nod of her head each time he looked, just to reassure him.

"Out of the way, it's hot!" Lisa and Tom walked into the dining room carrying hot plates of pasta. Leonardo jumped up and took two plates from Lisa. When he felt how scorching hot the plates were, he glanced at their hands. Tom had wrapped his hand in a towel, but Lisa was stoically holding the plates with her bare hands. Leonardo set the plates down on the table as fast as he could to keep from burning his fingers.

Lisa bowed and, together with Tom, accepted the applause. One of the men stood up, waved to the servants, and shouted something in Italian. Soon afterwards the servants returned carrying a couple of extra chairs.

"Pasta Bolognese!" shouted Lisa, pointing at the plates.

"Pasta Bolognese?" she heard the men say, some of whom were already nodding their heads in approval after tasting her dish.

The man who had just summoned the servants stood up again and began speaking expansively. At that same moment Sophie felt something prickly rub against her ankles. She glanced underneath the table and found herself staring straight into the eyes of a porcupine sitting next to her feet. With her mouth wide open and eyes fixed on the porcupine, she elbowed Leonardo.

Sophie tapped her pocket to make clear they should both bend down so that they could talk using her phone.

"A porcupine?" she said softly, her head almost touching her knees.

Leonardo laughed. "Yes, Giovan is a special man. A friend of animals, too. The porcupine is tame, that's why he's cuddling up to your leg!"

Fascinated, Sophie stared at the creature. She'd never seen a tame porcupine before. When she went to sit up straight again Leonardo grabbed her arm.

"It's fate," he said. "Fate has brought the porcupine to you tonight, and now you have an excuse to keep crouching down so that you can listen to the translations on your telephone!"

Sophie's squeezed her eyes shut. *Leonardo's right about that,* she thought.

He sat up again and rejoined the conversation.

"Giovan, she has discovered your porcupine!" Leonardo shouted.

Giovan laughed. "That means she's a good person," he said. "The porcupine will only sit next to people it trusts."

The table fell silent momentarily. "Leonardo, I want to thank you for introducing us to your special friends. We may not understand them, but my gut instinct tells me that they're good people!"

"And they can cook, too!" someone shouted.

Sophie sat back up grinning and glanced at her sister. "There's a porcupine underneath the table!"

Lisa looked at her in surprise, grabbed her glass, and emptied it in one go.

"Lisa, that's wine!" Sophie's attempts to keep her sister from drinking alcohol were doomed to failure it seemed.

"Yeah, yeah," Lisa said. "If you saw a porcupine underneath the table, you're the one who's drunk!"

Sophie continued to stare intently at her sister, until Lisa looked under the table. She sat back up, flabbergasted. "There really is a porcupine underneath the table," Lisa said giggling.

All of a sudden there was a commotion on the other side of the table. A couple of small sculptures were being passed from hand to hand.

Jack marveled at a small clay horse when he got it in his hands.

Leonardo bent down and Sophie followed her. "Those are Giovan's sculptures. I taught him how to make those beautiful horses."

Leonardo was keen to exhibit the extent of his influence, but he was immediately embarrassed, too, by his behavior. He tossed a couple of breadcrumbs to the porcupine and added, "Giovan is a fascinating gentleman, a very kind man who treats the poor and his servants well." He laughed, hoping Sophie would quickly forget his boastful remarks.

Sophie sat upright again, but about ten seconds later a large brown bird appeared out of nowhere and flew past her face. All the men laughed and clapped.

The bird landed in the middle of the table with a heavy thud. It was an enormous eagle that moved its head quickly as it looked around the table. Its claws made a loud scratching noise as it rocked from one leg to the other. One of the men provoked the bird by tossing it a piece of bread. The bird instinctively leapt up and nabbed it out of the air with its beak.

"Giovan," Leonardo said softly, making sure everyone acknowledged the man who stood up as their host.

They all went quiet when Giovan began speaking to the bird in a friendly voice. A few men clapped their hands softly until the bird opened its beak and flawlessly spoke a few words in Italian. The men applauded in amazement. The eagle flapped its wings and flew back to the corner of the room.

Sophie looked at Leonardo, her eyes bulging. He grabbed a few more pieces of bread for the porcupine and together they bent down again.

"I told you he had a special relationship with animals. That bird you just saw, the eagle, it required enormous patience on Giovan's part to teach it just a few words!"

Sophie looked at him with her mouth agape.

"Somewhere in the house he also has a room full of snakes."

Shivers ran up and down her spine. "Please don't tell Lisa that."

"A bit chilly!" said Sophie, as she wrapped her arms around herself. She had had a wonderful evening, but still she didn't appreciate the cold outside on the street. It was already late and she was missing her usual mug of hot tea and her soft bed.

"Did you enjoy it? Your pasta was a huge success!"

Leonardo kept a steady pace as they walked through the narrow streets, which were growing darker by the minute. "It's good that we left when we did, it's almost midnight, and that's not the best time to be out on the streets."

"That was so awesome!" said Lisa. "When I went to the bathroom I even found a room full of snakes!"

Sophie froze at the idea that her sister had discovered the snakes. Lisa saw the astonished look on her sister's face and quickly calmed her down. "No, I didn't do anything to them, and no I didn't steal one... I just thought I'd mention it."

When they reached the deserted Palazzo Vecchio they followed Leonardo up the stairs to the Hall of the Five Hundred. He turned around and looked seriously at his young friends.

"We met each other for the first time thirty years ago. For me..." he paused briefly and then took a few deep breaths. "For me, our meeting has been the most important event in my life." He thought deeply and nodded a few times. "I am so very grateful for having met you. Because of you... everything changed. I've learned so much, I've experienced so many things, all because of you. And I'm very grateful for that!" He stretched out his arm and pointed up to the hall. "This artwork is an homage to our friendship. An homage to you!"

Not knowing what to make of Leonardo's words or what to expect, they entered the hall full of curiosity. The Hall of the Five Hundred was an enormous room approximately one hundred and fifty feet long and sixty feet wide. The fire baskets the assistants had hung up provided just enough light to be able to see everything. The ceiling was covered in huge paintings framed by beautifully decorated wood engravings. They could see that there were windows on the shorter side of the hall, but no light shone inside because it was dark outside.

One of the long walls was completely bare. Leonardo was right when he said Michelangelo hadn't progressed much beyond doing a few sketches.

What they saw on the other wall, however, stopped them in their tracks. The painting covered a large section of the wall and extended up way above their heads. Their gaze moved slowly from left to right and from top to bottom. Jack and Tom took a step back, stopping only when they bumped into the wall on the opposite side of the room. They stared silently at the imposing image on the wall with wide eyes and open mouths.

Sophie and Lisa stood next to Leonardo in the middle of the hall. What they saw took their breath away. Sophie tried to take it all in. Lisa bit her bottom lip as she scrutinized the figures on the wall. The longer she looked the more excited she became.

"Oh my God, this is soooooooo cool!" she shouted. Never before in her life had Lisa had been so unguarded in showing her emotions. "Wow, unbelievable!" She covered her mouth with her hand as she continued to stare at the painting. She ran across the hall, threw her arms in the air, and jumped up onto Tom's back.

Lisa's enthusiasm infected the boys as well. They both joined her in jumping jubilantly around the hall.

Sophie remained standing next to Leonardo, her fists clenched. What she was looking at couldn't be real. *The Lost Leonardo*. Who would ever have imagined that this was what was really hidden behind the double wall?

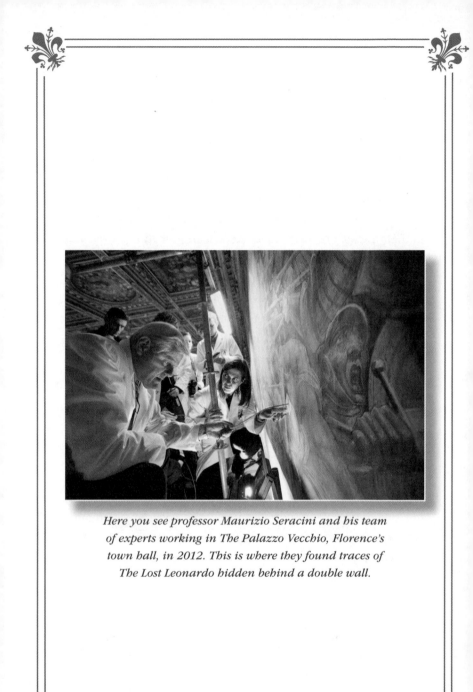

Here you see professor Maurizio Seracini and his team of experts working in The Palazzo Vecchio, Florence's town hall, in 2012. This is where they found traces of The Lost Leonardo hidden behind a double wall.

A million thoughts ran through her head. What were the implications? What would her father think? What would the world think once the truth came to light? What would the consequences be if everyone knew *The Lost Leonardo* actually existed? What would happen to them if the whole world learned what had been painted on the wall? *Who* had been painted on the wall?

Leonardo looked at her in tense anticipation. "And?"

Sophie's mouth fell open. "And?" she reacted. "And? Leonardo! Leonardo, have you any idea what...?" She shook her head.

"This... this..." she couldn't finish her sentence because Lisa had jumped onto her back.

"Do you know who that is?" Lisa shouted as if Sophie hadn't quite figured out who was in the painting.

"Anghiari!" Leonardo beamed. "You remember, right?"

Tuesday, June 24th, evening

"Anghiari?" Tom yelled. "That's us!" He jumped into the air with delight and gave Lisa an enthusiastic high five. The sharp slap resonated throughout the room. "Look! Look at that!" He couldn't stop bouncing around, saying the same thing over and over again: "That's us! That's us!"

Jack had stopped jumping around and was now standing dumbstruck next to Sophie. They could hear Tom and Lisa still screaming behind them. The painting was of them, the four of them, there was no doubt about it.

"Do you still remember? Thirty years ago?" Leonardo asked. "When you wanted to go outside I needed to come up with an excuse, just in case someone asked you where you were from? Do you still remember that?"

Jack and Sophie nodded affirmatively. For them it had literally happened yesterday. "Anghiari," Sophie said, louder and louder, with Jack repeating it in the same rhythm.

"*The Battle of Anghiari*! People have written about that, too." She looked excitedly at Leonardo. "That's what the history books call it! They claim that there's a painting of the battle of Anghiari on this wall and that you painted it!"

Leonardo corrected her story. "Then they almost got it right. It's not the battle *of* Anghiari, but the battle with the people *from* Anghiari!"

"That's right," Sophie said. "You were going to say that

you came across us just outside the city. That we were riding horses and were attacked by thieves. You had come to our rescue. The story was that we were from Anghiari and just passing through."

"That's exactly it, Sophie!" Leonardo clapped his hands enthusiastically. "Look!"

On the wall above them were four people riding horseback and fighting with a band of thieves. Exactly the story Leonardo had come up with at the time.

"After you left, a lot of people came by asking questions, people who had seen you. People who had seen *you*, Jack!"

Jack puffed out his chest with pride and thought again about scoring the winning point.

"I ended up telling them that story. I said I met you outside the city just as you were being attacked. I told them you were fearless and that the thieves ran off with their tails between their legs. They believed the story, it matched perfectly with the expectations they had of the unknown calcio hero who scored the winning point." Leonardo had to laugh when he said this. "Lots of people thought it was a great story." He pointed to the painting on the wall. "It's all there on the wall. You are all sitting on horses and fighting the thieves, who are being trampled by the horses, too."

"It looks so real!" said Sophie. "We look so real!"

"I can paint a little bit," Leonardo said with a smile.

Jack and Tom were painted at the top, sitting on horses and wielding long knives in their hands. Sophie was painted in the middle. She was expertly riding what looked like a wild horse. On the left side of the painting Lisa sat almost backwards on one of the horses. A thief lay on the ground under the horse's hooves. Another thief was crouched down and shielding

241

himself from being trampled. Leonardo had captured the horses' physiology in perfect detail, as well as their passionate spirit. Tom, Jack, Sophie, and Lisa were painted so well that it was like they were looking at a photograph. The painting was an unprecedented masterpiece.

"So, how do you like it?" asked Leonardo.

"It's awesome, just... wow," said Sophie.

Jack nodded in agreement.

Sophie wondered whether she should tell Leonardo what would eventually happen to the painting. During rebuilding work fifty years from now they would erect a second wall that would hide the painting forever. This painting would be remembered as *The Lost Leonardo*. If she told Leonardo this now, he might be able to prevent it from happening.

She looked around in desperation until she locked eyes with her sister. Lisa was shaking her head – No.

"Come here," Lisa whispered to her sister, pulling her closer. "Sophie, you can't say anything..."

Sophie frowned and looked at her sister.

"I know you, you're all about the facts, the truth, but trust me, just let it go," Lisa said, trying to convince her sister. "If we tell him everything, we don't know what will happen, how that will affect the future? So don't, okay?"

Sophie nodded. "You're probably right."

Lisa laughed. "Always!" she said, emphasizing her point with an exaggerated wink. "And remember, they eventually end up finding traces of it behind the wall. I promise you that in a few years the truth will be revealed. The world will discover, all on its own, exactly what's painted there."

"And then what?" Sophie sounded shocked.

"Uhm, then we'll be world famous," said Lisa, "but that also means we can forget about traveling through time ever again. And that's why we should make good use of it while we can. It's our secret, ours and Jack's and Tom's, how cool is that?"

Sophie could find no reason to disagree. It was indeed very cool.

"But Sophie, don't you remember the real reason we came here?" Lisa said, suddenly giving their conversation a lighter twist.

"My phone!" Sophie immediately shouted.

"Uhm, yes..." Leonardo mumbled, "that's a long story."

He looked around as if hoping a simple explanation would magically appear on one of the walls. "So the thing is... I no longer have it."

"What do you mean you no longer have it?" Sophie stuttered. "Seriously?"

"She always says that," Lisa said.

Sophie gave her sister an irritated look. "Seriously, my bag should be lying around here somewhere, with my pills, my book, the charger, the printer and, most importantly, my phone. How could you lose it? You're supposed to be the clever one, right?" said Sophie with a mix of sarcasm and annoyance.

Leonardo paced back and forth across the hall as he talked, looking around for something soft to sit on. "Let me start by giving you something." He took a large, shiny, round tin out of his pocket. "Here."

Sophie took the tin and immediately removed the lid. She looked at Leonardo, dumbstruck by what she saw inside.

"A portable orrery," he said. "Much more practical."

Tom reached over and grabbed the tin from her hands.

Together with his brother he carefully removed the planetarium and set it down on the ground. Jack carefully unfolded all the rods, turning the instrument into something that looked like a real planetarium, but smaller.

"Because it no longer sits in a wooden chest, you have to write the destination and year on the bottom. This here is where you place the bottled water from the Seven Seas and that's where you put the phone. It's important that you hold these metal wires. That way you remain connected to the portable planetarium and it can travel with you through time. I've tested the wire and it's strong enough. Everything else works the same."

Leonardo proudly examined his own design. "The other one was too big. You can take this one with you everywhere you go." He winked at Lisa. "My guess is you're not done traveling through time just yet! By the way, the other one, the big one…" He looked a little embarrassed. "It's gone, someone took it, so I actually had to make a new one."

"Took it?" Lisa was the only one to react to his comment. She stared at Leonardo and wondered if her intuition was right. Had someone beaten them to the punch? Had someone else found about time travel, too? Leonardo seemed to be able to read her mind and nodded, holding a finger to his lips.

"About ten years after you all showed up," Leonardo whispered, looking around to make sure only Lisa could hear him, "I was working on a painting of a young woman with an ermine. It made me think of you. I was focused on my work when suddenly I realized there was someone watching me. I had no idea how long he had been standing there, but before I could say anything he had vanished.

This paining by Leonardo da Vinci is called Lady with an Ermine and was painted around 1489.

"An ermine?" Lisa said.

"Yes," Leonardo nodded. "The stranger took the orrery, and the ermine disappeared as well. I have thought about it for years, but the reason for the visit still baffles me."

"An ermine?" Lisa repeated softly. Now she was certain. Someone had indeed beaten them to it and she had a strong suspicion who.

"The little orrery is just awesome," said Sophie, who had nearly forgotten that both her backpack and phone were gone.

Leonardo's surprise gift had lifted the mood. He sat down on a pile of clothes he had gathered together and told them what had happened to Sophie's telephone and backpack.

"Thirty years ago, in the studio. You were already gone. Suddenly I found your backpack and all the stuff inside."

"Suddenly?" Sophie glanced at her sister but Lisa ignored her remark and indicated to Leonardo that he should continue his story.

"I found the backpack and was burning with curiosity. I wanted to know everything, but initially I... initially I didn't dare touch anything. I was afraid someone would find out and I didn't know what the consequences might be." To emphasize his anguish Leonardo gestured to the heavens in desperation.

"I hid the backpack in a really safe place in the studio, but I never found the time to carefully examine everything. There was a constant stream of visitors stopping by with commissions and requests for paintings. Every time someone knocked on the door I had to frantically hide everything. It made me nervous. One day they even put me in jail..."

Sophie looked at him horrified. "Seriously?"

Leonardo nodded his head somberly. "Maybe I was acting a bit strange at the time. I was losing my mind. I had a lot of secret activities going on – digging up bodies, examining your things – I think they locked me up because I was acting so odd." He laughed quietly to himself. "I came really close to losing it. When they finally let me out of jail a few months later I packed up all my stuff up and left Florence. I went looking for a place where I could examine your things in peace."

"Did you take the planetarium with you?" Sophie felt her entire body go tense as she waited for his answer.

Leonardo grinned from ear to ear. "Of course I did, Sophie! And to answer your next question, I succeeded in using it. I traveled with the orrery myself. I met a man, a genius, and he… he was so happy to see me. And Sophie, your telephone!" Leonardo shook his head in disbelief. "He was so excited about it, that thing is miraculous!"

"What do you mean!" Sophie asked surprised.

"Where did you go? What did you do?" asked Lisa, every bit as curious as Sophie.

"Okay, as I was saying," Leonardo continued, "I left Florence to go east, towards the coast. I had heard stories about an island that no one ever visited anymore." Leonardo breathed in deeply through his nose and let the air escape slowly through his mouth. "Poveglia. That's the name of the island: Poveglia."

They all stared at him, breathless. Sophie shook her head. "I've never heard of it," she said. "Did you find it? Did you go there? What's it like?"

Leonardo raised his arms in the air to calm Sophie down. "Whoa! Please, one question at a time. It definitely wasn't easy traveling to Poveglia because no boats went there. In the end I had to build my own boat and sail there myself."

"Why didn't any boats go there? An island off the coast is

always worth visiting, isn't it?" Sophie shot him a questioning look.

"Well, Sophie," said Leonardo, while shaking his head, "it's not a very inviting island. Which is why it was the perfect location for me to go about my business without interruption."

Jack and Tom sensed the tension in Leonardo's voice.

"Why doesn't anyone want to go to that island?" Tom asked intrigued.

"Because it's haunted!" said Leonardo in a deliberately deep voice to make sure he had their full attention.

"Haunted?" Lisa immediately sat up.

"I had heard about Poveglia before," Leonardo said. "The story goes that a long time ago thousands, if not tens of thousands of people were brought there..." He paused for a moment. You could feel the tension in the air.

"People suffering from the plague, people on their deathbeds. The entire island is one big mass grave for plague victims."

"What?" Sophie sounded like she'd been stung by a wasp. "What kind of horrible island is that? And what were you doing there?"

"Legend has it that the island was used as a sort of dumping ground for people suffering from the plague, to keep them from contaminating others. That's one way to stop the plague from spreading, I suppose. In those days if you got sick they simply dumped you on Poveglia... to die."

Sophie felt the hairs rise on the back of her neck. "Oh, what a terrible place. I would never, ever go there!"

"I'd go," Jack said undaunted.

"How do you know all this is true?" Sophie asked Leonardo. "You said it was just a legend and that it happened a long time ago. Maybe somebody just made the story up."

"Unfortunately, I know for certain that it's true," said Leonardo in a sad voice. "I lived on the island for almost two years, completely alone. I examined all your things – the book, the telephone, everything – and I... I found the bodies – men, women, children..."

Sophie gulped at the thought of Leonardo on the island all by himself, surrounded by mass graves.

"For almost two whole years I closely examined and sketched the bodies – or what remained of them after so many years, which was mainly bones. I learned an awful lot about anatomy during that period."

"Enough," Sophie said, unable to take any more. "I get it, and I also understand why you did it, but can we stop talking about it! Ugh, the thought alone, that island..."

Everyone had gone quiet. They were all thinking of the gruesome image of thousands of bones and skulls buried on some haunted island.

"And the backpack... you examined everything, but where is the backpack? Sophie needs to get her phone back before she goes to Venice," Lisa suddenly said.

"It's buried on the island." Leonardo said it as quickly as he could in the hope that it wouldn't come across as bad as it sounded.

"Buried?" the sisters said simultaneously in a high-pitched voice.

Sophie's eyes nearly popped out of their sockets. "My backpack? Buried? On that island? Why? How?"

"Sorry, I'm so sorry. Before going back to Florence two years later, I buried your backpack and everything in it so that no one would ever find it. That was the reason, remember? That was the reason I left Florence in the first place. I had no choice but to leave your stuff behind on the island."

Sophie reacted by clenching her jaws and saying, "I'm leaving for Venice in two days, I need to have my telephone before then!"

Distressed, she wondered how she would tell her parents that she'd lost her phone.

Lisa gave her sister an encouraging pat on the back. "We'll think of something. Really. Trust me!"

"But Leonardo, what else did you do on that island during those two years?" Lisa continued talking in the hope of changing the mood.

Leonardo perked up again. "Everything. Everything you could think of. I studied everything. I spent the first few weeks examining your phone, carefully trying it out without breaking it."

"What did you do exactly?" Lisa asked.

"There was a miniature painting of you on the phone."

"You mean a photo?" Sophie said in her know-it-all voice.

"Yes, the photo you took of Lisa last time."

"Were there more photos on it?" Lisa asked.

Sophie shook her head. "No, I had transferred everything onto my laptop at home. Your photo was the only one."

"Yes, but I also took a few of those miniature paintings myself."

"Photos!" shouted Sophie and Lisa in unison.

"Okay, photos," Leonardo apologized. "I took a few photos myself, too. You can do a whole lot of stuff with that phone, did you know that?" Leonardo said, beaming. "After a couple of weeks I managed to figure out how to combine some paint... I mean photos."

"Haha!" Sophie suddenly began laughing hysterically. "You were photoshopping on my phone! You can't be serious? What did you make?"

Leonardo rummaged through his pockets. "Well, I was playing with the phone and messing around with some of the photos on it, when suddenly one of them popped out of the other device!"

Sophie looked at Lisa dumbstruck. "You're joking?" she asked. "Did you really print a photo?"

"Yes," said Leonardo. "Wait..." he continued nodding as he felt around his pockets. "I did. I had Lisa's photo, but I had also taken another picture with a nice background. I discovered I could merge the two photos using your telephone. I tried to insert the background behind Lisa, but before I could finish, a miniature image rolled out of that other device. Ah! Here it is!" He handed Sophie the photo.

"No matter what I tried after that, I was never able to eh... print another one. I'm really sorry if I broke the printing device," he said apologetically. Sophie didn't react, but instead stared silently at the photo.

"I didn't do it right, did I?" Leonardo said. "You see that the horizon on the right is higher than on the left."

Sophie stared silently at the photo with her mouth open. Leonardo had no idea what to make of her reaction. "I wasn't finished, but then the photo just rolled out. If I had had more time, then..."

"No," said Sophie firmly. "It is a beautiful photo. Really!"

"Really?" Leonardo was delighted. "Do you really like it? I wanted to use the photo to make a painting. I think if I carefully copy the photo I can capture Lisa's magical smile in a painting. Wouldn't that be nice?"

Sophie looked at her sister with raised eyebrows and handed her the photo.

When she saw the photo of herself Lisa bit her lower lip. Leonardo had pasted a background of mountains and water behind her image and accidentally printed it. She instantly thought back to the Louvre and what Sophie had said when they were standing there looking at the world's most famous painting.

When she looked at Leonardo Lisa's eyes were shining. "Sophie's right, you made a beautiful photo. It would be supercool if you painted it. Who knows, maybe I'll be famous one day," she winked at her sister as she handed the photo back to Leonardo.

Sophie nudged her sister. "Just as long as you don't get a big head or anything, sis."

Leonardo put the photo back into his pocket and continued his story. "We have to hurry, I already hear people out on the street. We don't have much time left. It's almost dawn, you guys really have to get out of here." Leonardo began pacing nervously back and forth. "Really, my friends from the future, I already hear voices downstairs, you have to hurry!"

Jack and Tom nodded. They unfolded the metal rods and set up the portable planetarium in the middle of the hall.

"So you were able to use my phone?" Sophie said, looking at Leonardo. She had obviously connected all the dots in her head. "You were also able to use the phone to translate my geography book. That's why you know so much about the earth, the stars…"

Leonardo nodded.

"And because you spent two years on that island with all those bones..."

Leonardo nodded again. "Did you know that you saved my life? When I was on Poveglia working with all those bodies, I became sick, really sick. There was a moment when I thought I was actually going to die, but then I took your pills. Without those I would probably have died from the plague or some other gruesome disease."

"And the planetarium?" Sophie asked. "You traveled through time? What did you do? Who did you meet?"

Leonardo looked up at the windows; the orange glow from the morning sun was clearly visible. "You have to go, it's a matter of life or death now, hurry up!" he said in a panic.

"Leonardo!" Sophie sounded desperate. "Tell me!"

Leonardo shook his head. "There's no time left." He looked her straight in the eye and spoke rapidly. "Yes, I was able to use it. Thanks to your phone! I met somebody..." He looked up again and saw that it was getting brighter outside. "Actually, I made a mistake when I used the planetarium, a small mistake. I was on Poveglia and I was looking for Christ. I was hoping he would return to earth five hundred years into the future, in 1976. I wanted to visit him, but I made a spelling mistake." He quickly glanced up again.

"But where did you end up?" Sophie asked.

"At someone's..." he shook his head. "You really have to go now!"

"Sophie, grab a wire... fast!" shouted Lisa. "Leonardo's right, people are coming. If they see us and that painting up on the wall! That can never happen, we have to get out of here."

Still panicking, Leonardo ran to the hallway and came back a few seconds later. "You have to go now! My assistants are coming up the stairs. I'll occupy them for a few minutes, but you really have to go, now!"

They stood around the planetarium while Jack hastily dripped water into the planets.

Leonardo ran around in a circle, kissing each of them firmly on the cheek before running back towards the hallway.

As Jack began counting down Leonardo turned around abruptly. "Sophie!" he shouted from the doorway. "You said you were going to Venice two days from now?"

"Yes!" Sophie shouted, nodding frantically. "Together with Jack!"

"Your backpack!" The words echoed through the hall. "Poveglia isn't far from there. Your backpack is buried three steps from the easternmost point on the island's southern half."

"Poveglia?" Sophie said startled. The thought alone was enough to turn her stomach.

"Make sure you find that backpack," Leonardo shouted. "It's important! Then you'll have all your answers. There is someone who..."

FLASH!

Wednesday, June 25th, afternoon

"How was school today?" Lisa asked as she reclined on her sister's bed. "Did you hear any cool stuff about Venice? Are you excited about going?" She didn't even wait for her sister to respond before continuing. "I would be so psyched, man. I mean, tomorrow!"

"Sshh," Sophie put a finger to her lips and continued reading. "This can't be true!" she muttered in a low voice. She rolled back and forth in the office chair while leaning with her elbows on the desk.

Lisa sat up and listened to her sister.

"Here!" she pointed to the screen. "Loads of information about Poveglia," said Sophie a little nervously, "and it's even worse than I thought. Listen to what it says: Poveglia is a small island off the coast of Venice. A narrow channel divides the island into two separate parts."

"You see," said Lisa, "I told you you'd find your backpack and telephone... Tomorrow you're leaving for Venice. Just go to the island and dig up your backpack." Lisa looked at her sister with a deadpan expression.

"Lisa!" Sophie looked upset. "You have no idea what you're talking about. Listen! It says the island is closed to visitors!"

Lisa shrugged her shoulders. "Maybe you can hire your own boat?"

Annoyed at her sister, Sophie shook her head and continued

reading. "Legend has it that in Roman times the island was used to quarantine thousands of Plague victims. Ugh! The island was used as a Plague dumping ground whenever it threatened Europe. An efficient quarantine station that separated the healthy from the contaminated."

"No way!" Sophie was shocked by the numbers she read. "Apparently more than 160,000 people died on the island!"

Lisa shuddered at the thought, but she was also a little amused that her sister was scared stiff before she even got there.

Sophie turned around silently and stared directly at her sister.

"Is that all?" Lisa asked. "Nothing else? I mean, it's all really horrible, of course, tragic even, but it happened a really long time ago. The island's probably just very peaceful and sunny now."

Sophie shook her head. "Come on Lisa, did you hear a word of what I said? More than 160,000 people died on Poveglia. And I have to go there all on my own to dig up my backpack?"

"Jack's going with you, right? He even boasted about doing it. So there'll be two of you! It'll be exciting, a little boat ride, a bit of island hopping, some backpack digging."

"What about all those bones!?" Sophie yelled.

"So okay, there'll be some bones, that's not ideal. But then again, you will get your phone back. What else does it say?"

Sophie looked at her sister suspiciously. "Why are you so eager for me to continue reading? Do you already know what it says?"

Lisa couldn't suppress a smile and nodded subtly. "Yes, I read some of it last night."

Sophie turned around and continued reading. "In 1922 a

mental hospital was built on the island, where a deranged doctor then proceeded to conduct horrific experiments on his patients. He tortured them terribly and then killed them. This doctor later went mad himself and jumped off the hospital tower. The ghosts of those killed continue to haunt the island today." Sophie gulped a few times and tried to steady her breathing.

"In 1968..." Sophie swallowed again and began reading the sentence anew. "In 1968 the mental hospital was shut down and the island abandoned. No one is allowed to set foot on the island. To this day it is closed to visitors."

Lisa had in the meantime climbed onto the bed and was pretending to be a zombie. She wobbled back and forth across the mattress, gurgling and with her arms stretched out, until she fell back onto the bed laughing hysterically.

Sophie sat silently in her chair.

"Oh, sorry Sophie," Lisa said, "but don't you think it's kinda ironic that you of all people have to go to that island to recover your backpack?"

"Haha, funny... not! How am I supposed to get onto the island?" Sophie said, looking annoyed at her sister. "You always have an answer for everything, so let's hear it. How am I going to recover my backpack and all the other stuff?"

Lisa jumped up from the bed and walked back to her own room with a smile on her face. "I've already thought of that," she shouted from the hallway. "Let me just grab a few printouts you can take with you when you go."

When Lisa came back into the room, Sophie was staring breathlessly at the screen. She dropped the printouts on the desk with a thud. "Last night I did a lot of research and it's true – no boats go to Poveglia. It is officially off limits. And if you don't believe me, Google it yourself."

"And your point?" Sophie responded. "How am I supposed to get to that horror island? I'm not like Leonardo, I don't have an infinite amount of time to build a boat!"

"Who said anything about building a boat?" Lisa pointed at one of the sheets of paper. "This is Venice and that there is Poveglia. It's about two miles, that shouldn't be a problem." Lisa tried her best not to laugh at the terrified look on her sister's face. "What you need to do is…"

Thursday, June 26th, late afternoon

Sophie was sitting at the back of the bus, leaning against the window. Immediately after boarding, Jack had purposely thrown their bags across a few seats and claimed the entire back row for the two of them.

Sophie looked out the window pensively, silently counting the trees racing by, just like she always did. Every time a tree passed, she twitched a toe slightly. It was almost dark. She'd hardly uttered a word since the bus departed several hours ago.

Jack had already read the skateboard magazine he'd brought with him three times and was bored. "What's wrong with you?" he asked. He looked at Sophie and tried in vain to get her attention. "Hello!" He waved his arms, but still no reaction. He kicked Sophie in the knee with the nose of his sneaker, yet still no reaction. In a final desperate attempt to get her attention he pinched her thigh.

"Ow!" Acting on instinct, Sophie punched him and irritably massaged the area of her thigh he had just pinched.

"What?" She looked at him angrily. "What do you want?" she hissed.

Taken aback, Jack moved up a few seats and leaned back against the window. "Sorry, man." He shook his head in astonishment. "I just want to know what's up, that's all. I don't get it. We've done some amazing stuff already... and now we're off to Venice! It's all so awesome, and I just don't understand why you're so angry?"

"I'm not angry. Well okay, I am angry, but not really." Sophie fumbled her words. She grabbed her travel bag, pulled out the sheets of paper, and tossed them at Jack.

"My backpack, remember? And my phone? Well, read these."

Jack picked up the printouts and read them quickly. He held his breath as his eyes darted across the pages.

"Holy moly," he said, "that's some island. It's just as scary as it was in Leonardo's time. Scarier even." He gave her a sympathetic look. "I'm really sorry you lost your things."

"Lost?" Sophie said indignantly.

"Lost, yeah, I mean that they're on that..." He shook his head.

"I haven't lost them, I know where they are. I'm just not looking forward to retrieving them. That island's a nightmare!"

"It sure is!" Jack responded. "And off limits."

"Now do you understand why I'm not all happy-go-lucky? I mean, sure, I'm looking forward to the school trip, but the idea that we have to go there..."

Jack gulped and coughed hard. "*We*? That *we* have to go there?"

Sophie nodded her head and pointed at a map on one of the prints. "Last night, Lisa and I looked it up on the internet and we read that access to the island is strictly sealed off. No boats go there either, so we have to figure out a way to find ourselves a boat. And to make matters worse, I think we'll have to go there at night so no one sees us. That's the only viable option."

"Uh," Jack stammered. "I, uh, I... do you mean that we...

you and I... that we have to go in a boat, in the dark, to that island?"

"Yes, Jack!" Sophie said resolutely. "I need to get my things back, you know that. At Leonardo's you were all macho about it and said you'd go... or are you backing out now?" She stared straight into Jack's eyes, waiting for his reaction.

Jack recalled what he had said while caught up in the moment in the Hall of the Five Hundred. But now that it was actually happening, he would have liked nothing more than to bow out. He quickly weighed up his options, but realized he didn't really have a choice. He couldn't let her go alone in the dead of night.

"Are you nuts?" he did his best to sound brave, "of course we'll dig up your backpack together. I'm not afraid, you know." He sat up straight with his back against the window, chin up, chest out. His legs were stretched out across the seat. Sophie made a quarter turn and sat exactly the same way so that their feet touched in the middle.

"That's a relief, Jack. But I sure hope we don't die in the process."

"At least we have the entire back row to ourselves, so for now let's just relax and enjoy the ride," Jack said, smiling as casually as possible but still looking a bit worried to say the least.

Friday, June 27th, morning

The bus slowed down and pulled into in a large parking lot.

Mr. Hackett, who was sitting up front, grabbed the microphone. It made a low popping sound when he tapped it with his finger in an attempt to get everyone's attention.

The entire class was woken by the dull thumps reverberating around the bus.

"*Buon Giorno*! Good morning! Welcome to Venice!" Hackett's shrill voice blared from the speakers.

As Hackett walked them through the schedule for the day, Jack squinted his eyes and looked out the window. Still tired, he rubbed his eyes and slid over to sit next to Sophie. Before he could even say a word, she held her finger demonstratively to her lips to indicate she was listening to what Hackett was saying. They were first going to transfer to a waterbus that would take them to their hotel. In the afternoon, after lunch, they would visit a museum. After dinner everyone would retire to their own rooms, which they'd be sharing with a classmate.

Sophie divided the schedule up into mini pieces and visually compartmentalized each piece in her head. Tonight would probably be the best time to sneak away and attempt to reach Poveglia. Hopefully, they could slip away unnoticed when everyone went to their rooms. She took a deep breath at the thought of what awaited them.

As if reading her thoughts, Jack patted her reassuringly

on the shoulder. "We'll go get your stuff tonight, it'll be okay. But first..." he excitedly fist-bumped her, "...first Venice. Awesome!"

Hackett's voice was still blaring from the speakers. "For now, I hope you have an amazing school trip, a trip you'll remember for the rest of your lives!" Everyone on the bus started clapping and cheering.

Jack leaned in towards Sophie. "You and I will definitely remember this trip for the rest of our lives," he chuckled.

Hackett marched busily back and forth, checking to make sure all the students were on the boat. Once he was convinced they were, he gave the captain a sign that they were good to go. The engine started with a noisy growl and the boat pulled away slowly. Rolling slightly on the waves, they steered towards Venice.

Sophie listened to the water lapping against the side of the boat. She tried to memorize as many details as possible so that later, in the dark, she'd have a few points of reference. She was looking out over the water together with Jack when Hackett suddenly appeared behind them.

"Extraordinary, isn't it? " he said, taking in the view, too. "There are dozens of islands in the lagoon, of which Venice is the most famous."

Jack nodded without saying anything, but Sophie seized the opportunity to pry some valuable information out of Hackett. "That's Venice over there on the right," she said. "I recognize some of the buildings, but those islands off to the left, which ones are those?" She tried her best to sound as upbeat and friendly as possible.

"That one there," Hackett said, pointing to a large island,

"that is San Clemente, a private island with a hotel and a resort. And that small one nearer to us is La Grazia. It was once a dump, and there used to be a hospital there once for people with contagious diseases."

Sophie felt a shiver run down her spine. La Grazia sounded like another island she would prefer to avoid.

"And that one?" asked Jack, who understood the reason behind Sophie's sudden interest.

Hackett looked at them surprised. "You kids have been very inquisitive lately, and here you are again asking more questions. That's great, this eagerness to learn."

Jack and Sophie nodded in agreement and smiled their biggest smiles, hoping this would help deter Hackett from asking any difficult questions himself.

"You mean that tiny island?" Hackett continued eagerly. "That tiny island to the left behind San Clemente... I've forgotten its name, but it's rather boring. It has a few buildings and a harbor for boats, but there's not much to do there. Once it was a beautiful retreat for wealthy families. Or do you mean that large island to the right of San Clemente? If that's the one you mean, well, that's a relatively new island, it's only been there for about 150 years..."

Sophie was annoyed that she still didn't know which island was Poveglia. She only knew which four weren't. They had just passed three more relatively close islands, and there was one more off in the distance. She guessed it was the last one. Knowing her luck, Poveglia would probably be the farthest one away. "And that island way back there?" she asked. "Which island is that?"

"That one's haunted!" Hackett said, dead serious.

Jack and Sophie held their breaths simultaneously.

"How do you mean?" Sophie asked tensely.

"That's Poveglia, no one would want to go there. In fact, no one is allowed to go there anymore. It's completely off limits. Here's the thing..."

Sophie was no longer listening. Mission accomplished, she now knew which island they had to go to. "Are we nearly there?" she suddenly asked.

Hackett turned around. "Uh...yeah," he said, before going off to give the captain a few last instructions.

"I knew it," Sophie said, shaking her head, "the farthest away! Of course it is! You'd think things would go my way for once," she grumbled. "Jack, remember which island it is." Sophie said, sounding very serious. "It's the farthest island, and the one with the tower you can see from here."

She was taken aback by the sound of her own words. "Oh no, that tower. I bet it's the one the mad doctor threw himself off all those years ago."

Jack was relieved when the boat bumped against a buoy and came to a halt. It broke the tension. After docking, everyone stepped onto the quay. Sophie and Jack were the last to climb out of the boat, and they trundled along at a casual pace behind the rest of the class.

Hackett caught up to Jack and Sophie. He was delighted by the enthusiasm they had both been showing recently. He began a conversation again for no particular reason. "You're not going to believe this, but we had actually reserved a cheap hostel for the class, until last week we got an unexpected phone call..."

"Really? And?" asked Jack, feeling a bit ragged from the boat trip.

"Yes, a phone call!" Hackett said, "From the Hotel Cipriani!

265

Someone has made an anonymous reservation for us and paid for everything!" He looked at them elated.

"What's so special about that?" Sophie asked.

"Hotel Cipriani is the most exclusive hotel in Venice! We were actually planning to stay in a very basic place, but someone – probably one of the students' parents – made an anonymous reservation for the entire class at the most luxurious hotel in town. Isn't that just fantastic?"

"Wow!" whooped Jack. Never in his life had he stepped foot inside a luxury hotel. This was the best news they had heard all day.

"This is our hotel!" Hackett called, running up to the front of the group to herd everyone inside.

"Awesome, isn't it? A super luxurious hotel!" said Jack upbeat. He looked around with an enormous grin on his face, cooing in delight.

Sophie had to admit the announcement was a pleasant surprise. She lifted her right hand to massage the muscle between her neck and shoulder to ease the tension she had been feeling.

"Please form pairs and then give your names to the reception desk. Once you have your key you can go to your hotel room, freshen up, and then we'll meet down here in the lobby at noon." Hackett's eyes were lit up with enthusiasm.

He picked up his bag and, key in hand, was the first to head up to his room.

After all the other students had paired up and collected their keys, Jack and Sophie stepped forward to get theirs. Sophie started using her hands and waving her arms in an attempt to communicate with the receptionist.

"It's okay, I speak several languages, so you can speak your native tongue if that's easier for you," the receptionist told her with a friendly smile.

"Oh, cool!" Sophie said happily before continuing. "Uh, we need a key. Sophie and..."

"Jack," the woman said. "Your name's right here. Yes... yes..." She nodded again as she read the remarks next to their reservation. "Yes... okay," she said quietly to herself before turning back to Sophie and Jack.

"Right now you're standing in the Palazzo Vendramin, which is a separate wing of the Hotel Cipriani. The hotel itself is around the corner. Your teacher and classmates are all sleeping here, but it says here that all the rooms in the Palazzo are full..."

"What?" Jack sounded super disappointed. There was no way he was going to end up sleeping in a hostel.

The friendly receptionist nodded. "No problem. It also says here that two rooms have been booked for you in the actual hotel, in the Hotel Cipriani. That's just a short walk through the courtyard."

"Much better!" Sophie said without meaning to. "So we're the only ones in our class who are sleeping in that wing?"

"That's right. Your classmates have already taken the Palazzo's 16 rooms. Unfortunately, we were two rooms short in this wing, but everything has been taken care of." She gave them both a wink.

"And don't worry, you may be a bit farther away, but you have the best view from your rooms. Can I be of any further service to you?" She waited for them to say something. "Come with me, I'll bring you to your suites." Full of purpose, she walked out from behind the front desk and ushered them towards the exit.

Feeling very chirpy now, Jack and Sophie followed her through the flower-filled hall out into the beautiful courtyard. Jack's eyes nearly popped out of his head as they walked past the Olympic-sized swimming pool.

"This is the only swimming pool in the center of Venice. It's filtered seawater and is heated all year round. If you want to..." The receptionist gestured invitingly towards the pool.

When they got to their floor she stopped and opened one door for Sophie while pointing to another one down the corridor.

"That's yours," she told Jack. "A door inside connects the two rooms. When you open it you have the entire Palladio Suite at your disposal..." She stood away politely from the door and let Jack and Sophie in first.

Jack's mouth fell open in amazement. "I've never seen anything like this... this is awesome!"

Even Sophie looked astounded. She'd never seen so much luxury in one place.

"Oh... by the way, did I mention... the Palladio suit comes with a private boat with its own skipper. He can take you wherever you'd like to go." The woman made it sound like it was nothing out of the ordinary.

"Are we allowed to take the boat out ourselves?" asked Sophie.

The woman shook her head. "The skipper will take you anywhere you like. Lots of movie stars and other famous people stay here. The hotel is famous for its discretion."

"Nine o'clock," Sophie said. "We would like to use the boat at nine o'clock this evening. We'll be done dining with our classmates by then and it won't be completely dark, right Jack?" Jack nodded.

"Is that possible?" Sophie asked boldly.

The woman nodded politely again. "I'll make sure the boat is waiting for you at nine o'clock," she said as she walked over to one of the windows. "Over there," she continued, pointing to a spot on the quay, "that's where you can get the boat."

"Thank you," said Jack and Sophie in unison.

"No thanks necessary. Enjoy your stay in Venice!" She nodded again and silently left the room.

"Sick!" Jack said as he ran around the enormous suite, his sneakers making a funny squeaking sound on the marble floor. The room felt like a glass capsule towering above the water. The floor-to-ceiling windows offered panoramic views of the lagoon.

Sophie walked to the side of the suite with the best view over the water. She closed one eye and looked through the large telescope standing before the window on a tripod. She slowly moved it around until she found what she was looking for and gently adjusted the lens until the image was sharp.

"Poveglia," she said with a little shudder.

"I'm going to take a shower," called Jack as he ran back to the bathroom in his own suite.

"Wow!" he yelled. "Everything's marble! Unbelievable!"

"Really?" cried Sophie, stepping away from the telescope and smiling again. She tried to forget about Poveglia and relaxed her shoulders. She walked to her own bathroom where she found a basket full of bottles filled with shower gel, shampoo, conditioner, body lotion, and bath foam. She filled the bath, sniffed every single item, and dumped two entire bottles of foam into the tub.

The students sat on the waterbus's benches enjoying their sandwiches. The boat traveled at a leisurely pace through the Canal Grande, the long S-shaped canal that runs through the center of Venice.

Hackett stood up as they approached a special bridge. "Guys," he shouted, trying to get everyone's attention. "Pay attention, we're about to pass under the world-famous Rialto Bridge. It was built at the end of the 16th century. And over there, that's the Galleria dell'Accademia, home to the original Leonardo da Vinci sketch *The Vitruvian Man*. I was hoping that after last week's lesson, in which we discussed Leonardo da Vinci, we could go see the sketch, but unfortunately that's not possible. The drawing is extremely fragile and is seldom shown to the public."

Hackett was surprised to hear a few groans of disappointment coming from the back of the boat.

Encouraged by the students' interest in the sketch, Hackett suddenly thought of something. He leaned over to the captain and asked him a question. The man reached into his pocket and handed Hackett a Euro coin. "Have a look at this." Hackett passed around the coin. "On the reverse side of the Italian euro is *The Vitruvian Man*, Leonardo's most famous drawing."

During the cruise, Hackett continued to talk about the interesting locations they were passing – hotels where famous movies had been filmed, the San Marco Square, and various historic buildings. The boat made a wide turn and re-entered the broad canal.

"This is our stop. Let's go, everyone off, and head for the entrance," Hackett commanded the group. He ushered everyone towards the entrance of the Peggy Guggenheim Museum, one of Italy's most important museums of modern art.

The Vitruvian Man by Leonardo da Vinci, painted around 1490, is kept in Gallerie dell'Accademia in Venice and displayed to the public only on very rare occasions. With arms outstretched, the man fills the irreconcilable spaces of a circle and a square.

Once inside, the students were allowed to explore the artworks on their own. Jack and Sophie went into the first gallery.

"Aren't these the things that hang above babies' beds," Jack said mockingly.

Sophie couldn't stop herself from laughing. "Those are mobiles and yes, they're similar to the things you hang over a crib. But these hanging mobiles are world famous. They're by Alexander Calder..." She smiled apologetically. "That's what happens when your father is an art historian."

"Shall I be your guide?" she asked in a posh voice.

Jack had to laugh, but he nodded. "Okay, sure."

Looking around, Sophie didn't recognize most of the art, but there was one work she was familiar with. She walked towards a painting of four large white flowers. She stood up straight and said in an aristocratic tone: "This is by Andy Warhol, maybe you know the name?"

Jack nodded. "That's the guy with the cans of soup, right?"

Sophie smiled. "You see, you recognize it too. Come on, let's get out of here. I don't really know any of the other paintings in here either."

They strolled through the rooms for a while, stopping every now and then at an artwork that caught their attention, until Jack suddenly looked at his watch.

"We've got to go, the boat's about to leave for the hotel. Then we only have time for dinner before..."

Sophie froze. She had briefly forgotten about tonight's mission.

Jack noticed the anxiety on Sophie's face and placed a reassuring hand on the shoulder. "Tonight on the island... don't worry, it'll be okay. There's no such thing as ghosts so there's nothing to worry about!"

Friday, June 27th, evening

There was an amazing selection of desserts after dinner, including Ricotta cheesecake, Tiramisu, Zuppa Inglese, and Panna Cotta. But even though everything looked really delicious, Sophie and Jack were hardly able to eat a bite. When everyone was finished eating, Hackett stood up. He grabbed a glass and tapped his spoon against it. A shrill tone reverberated across the restaurant.

"Boys and girls, it was a really great day. I'm pleased that you were all so attentive and enthusiastic. We've had an amazing dinner, too, but now..." he looked at his watch, "it's just past eight-thirty. Time for everyone to go up to their rooms. So goodnight, sleep well, and I'll see you in the lobby tomorrow morning at eight a.m. sharp!"

A ripple of applause went around the tables, and then everyone stood up and sauntered off to their rooms. Sophie slipped into the hall unnoticed and headed towards the reception desk, where she was happy to see that the friendly receptionist was on duty for the night shift.

"I have what may seem like a strange question," Sophie said. "But is there any chance you have a shovel I could borrow?"

The receptionist looked a bit surprised, but then nodded and disappeared out of sight. A few minutes later she returned with something that looked like a design shovel. The tool was foldable and made from glistening black metal. A normal shovel probably wasn't good enough for a super luxury hotel like this.

"Anything else?"

Sophie shook her head, but couldn't help asking the receptionist: "Aren't you at all curious why I might need a shovel at this time of night? And doesn't it bother you that we're taking the boat out while our teacher and classmates are heading off to bed?" She looked directly into the woman's eyes.

The receptionist shook her head. "Discretion, remember? We don't ask questions here."

"Hmm, discretion," Sophie mumbled as she walked back to Jack with the mini shovel tucked under her arm.

"One thing's for sure, I could never work in this hotel. If someone asked me for a shovel late at night, I'd probably call the cops and tell them that one of my guests was planning to murder and bury someone," she said.

The enormous suite smelled amazing thanks to the scented candles burning in the room. The beds they had jumped about on that morning had been made up again. A gigantic fruit basket and a bowl of candy had been set on the desk at the window.

"This is so awesome!" Jack said softly.

"It's amazing! I wouldn't mind just lying in that soft bed and watching a film, but we have no time to lose. So hurry up!" Sophie said firmly.

They both changed into suitable clothes and hurried down to the quay, getting there just in time. The speedboat arrived at nine o'clock exactly.

The skipper, dressed entirely in black, jumped onto the quay and indicated that he needed to use the restroom. He pointed at the boat. "Me toilet. You wait in boat," he said in broken English with an Italian accent.

"He has to pee," Sophie giggled, as the man ran up to the hotel. "Come on, we'll wait in the boat."

They nervously climbed into the boat. Although it was nearly dark, they could still see the island in the distance. The tower stood out against the light on the horizon.

"I've got a bad feeling about this," Sophie suddenly said. "The last thing I want is someone spying on us while we're on the island." She looked around and mustered all her courage. She had the feeling Lisa would do the same thing. "Jack!" she shouted. "Turn the key and hit the gas!"

Jack looked at her perplexed, but didn't need long to think about it. This would probably be the only time in his entire life that he would get to skipper a speedboat. He fearlessly stepped forward and turned the key with his right hand. The boat's powerful engines roared into life.

"Untie the lines!" he shouted.

Sophie ran to the side of the boat and untied the rope from the bollard and swung it back into the boat.

"Hold tight!" Jack yelled. He turned the wheel to the left and opened the throttle. The propellers on the enormous outboard engines began spinning powerfully. Sophie slammed back into her chair and experienced a moment of déjà vu. It was just like being in Hans's Ferrari. The enormous force pushed her back into her seat as the boat shot out into the lagoon at full speed.

Jack was totally in his element. With his teeth clenched, he held the wheel firmly with both hands to keep it under control. He blinked his eyes in an effort to stop them watering from the force of the biting wind.

The speed with which they flew over the water tilted the bow up dangerously high, causing the boat to smack fiercely against the water. Walls of water splashed up on both sides of the boat each time it slammed against the surface.

Sophie tried to attract Jack's attention, but the deafening roar of the engines drowned out her words.

"Jack!" she yelled. "Jack! Slow down! I don't want to die just yet! And we have to get to the island!"

Jack couldn't hear a thing and simply looked back with an elated look on his face. But when he saw the fear in Sophie's eyes he let up on the throttle, slowing down the boat.

With a loud thud both engines suddenly cut out. For a few seconds their momentum carried them forward until they were left bobbing in the middle of the lagoon.

Sophie looked frantically about. They were completely alone in open water. The nearest island was San Clemente. "Jack, what have you done? Start it up again!"

Jack looked anxiously at the boat's panel and saw a flashing red light. "Please no," he whimpered. "I think the engines have overheated."

Sophie breathed deeply in and out a few times before getting to her feet. "Don't panic," she said to herself. "You haven't even reached Poveglia yet... Don't panic."

"I think we should wait a few minutes before turning on the engines again. It might not be a bad idea to slow down a bit..." said Jack, embarrassed.

Sophie looked at him angrily. "Were you trying to kill me?" She smacked the back of his head.

"We're more than halfway there," Jack tried, cheerfully.

Sophie didn't respond, but instead turned away and stared at the lights in the distance.

"It's beautiful, isn't it? Venice at night?" Jack tried again. "There are not a lot of people who have seen it from this angle."

Sophie grumbled but had to admit the view from the boat was breathtaking. "Just as long as we don't drift further out to sea," she said quietly.

"Drift?" asked Jack, as he looked around. "The island over there is the one with the hotel and resort, that wouldn't be so bad." Jack was doing his best to make sure the mood in the boat didn't deteriorate any further.

"Jack!" Sophie looked at him and shook her head. "That would mean having to swim a few hundred yards, and in the dark! We'd never survive. And don't forget, we have to get to Poveglia!"

Jack tried the ignition again. With a loud roar the engines came back to life.

"You see," he laughed, relieved. "No problem! We're good to go."

"Hmm, you lucked out, that's all!" said Sophie, giving him a knowing look. "Just slow down, okay?"

Jack skillfully piloted the boat slowly towards Poveglia, almost as if he had been doing this all his life. When they got close they circled the island for a quick look.

Poveglia was split in two by a narrow channel. Sophie recognized the ghastly tower from the pictures on the internet. It was dark and they could only make out the silhouettes of buildings, bushes, and trees. It was deathly quiet. No birds, no crickets, nothing.

"Leonardo said we had to go to the southern part." Sophie pointed to a spot where Jack could dock the boat. A shiver ran down her spine as he secured the mooring line to the quay. When the boat came to a stop she clambered ashore.

"Wait," she said. "Check in the boat, there's got to be a flashlight. And don't forget that silly-looking shovel."

Jack rummaged through the compartments until he found a flashlight. He climbed out behind Sophie carrying the flashlight and shovel. "I'm glad Lisa's not here," Jack said. "She'd be doing her best to scare the living daylights out of us."

"That's what you'd think all right," said Sophie. "But she's afraid of the dark. She wouldn't start pulling any pranks around here." She stood still and looked around nervously. "We'd better hurry, we have to go to the farthest point on the eastern side of the island. Brrr," she said, trembling, "everything looks so spooky."

They reached an enormous, rectangular building. Jack and Sophie couldn't find a path around it. It was impossible to go left and the bushes on the right were impenetrable. Reluctantly, they walked towards the entrance of the dilapidated building.

"Guess we have no choice but to go in," Jack said quietly.

The building was covered in scaffolding that looked like it could collapse at any minute, and was surrounded by an iron fence. Jack turned on his flashlight and searched for an opening in the dark. He found a large hole in the fence and, crouching down, they managed to crawl through. Sophie was glad she'd thought of bringing a flashlight because it was pitch dark inside. She suddenly stopped and grabbed hold of Jack's arm.

"What's wrong?" asked Jack.

"That smell! I think I can smell the bodies!"

Jack breathed in deeply trying to figure out what Sophie

meant. "That's not dead bodies you smell. They've decomposed already."

In the dark, Sophie couldn't see that he was shaking his head.

"That's the smell of rotting wood. Mold on wet wood, no big deal, okay?"

"My heart's racing a mile a minute," Sophie whispered. "This place scares the crap out of me."

"I'm carrying a really big shovel," Jack said in a low voice. "I'll whack the first zombie I see."

"Zombies are already dead, but thanks anyway." Sophie grinned nervously.

They carefully stepped over some debris and bits of fence lying here and there on the ground. Jack shone the flashlight all around him after every three steps.

"We have to go right, that's east. We have to go to the right-hand side of the island," Sophie said softly, continually looking around her.

Dong! The sound of a large bell reverberated around the building. Sophie went pale with fear. She put a hand up to her mouth and had to do her best to keep from hyperventilating. "Did you hear that?" she said softly. "I read about that. That's the bell tower. That sound you just heard is the bell!" She grabbed Jack's sleeve.

"It's probably the wind," Jack said dismissively. "When the wind blows up in the tower it makes that thing swing back and forth. That's why you hear the bell." He wanted to turn around and keep walking, but Sophie poked him in the ribs.

"The bell," she said in a high pitch, "the bell was taken down years ago. It's gone! So how come we're hearing it?"

Jack felt a slight shiver run through his body but he did his best to hide it. "Maybe we didn't hear it right," he grunted as he jumped out through a broken window.

Standing at the edge of the woods he kept an eye on Sophie as she climbed through the broken window behind him. "Which way?" he asked. He was just about to try and force his way through some thick bushes when Sophie heard a terrible scream that continued to echo ominously over the entire island. *That must be the sound someone makes when they're being murdered*, Sophie thought.

"Did you hear that? This place is really haunted! Hurry up, I want to get out of here as quickly as possible."

Jack nodded hastily. "Yeah, I definitely heard it! I'm sick of this too! Let's just go and dig up your backpack as quick as we can." Using all his strength, he started swinging the shovel furiously in front of him to cut a path through the thick bushes. Every now and then he used the flashlight to check all around him. They stopped walking when they reached the other side of the woods. A vast expanse of hilly grass stretched out before them.

Sophie stood next to Jack and gulped. "This must be one of the mass graves." She took the flashlight from Jack and walked up to the edge of the island. When she reached the outermost corner on the eastern side, she turned around and took three steps back. "It should be here! My backpack should be buried right here." She composed herself, grabbed the shovel, and began digging frantically.

A few minutes later she hopped back out of the hole, covered in sweat, and handed Jack the shovel. Sophie shone the light on him as he dug out big scoops of dirt until he suddenly stopped. "Is that...?" he muttered. "Are those skeletons?"

He tossed the shovel aside and dropped to his knees,

carefully sifting through the loose dirt with his hands.

"On no, ugh!" Sophie screamed.

Jack lifted up a skull. The lower jaw was missing and there were two teeth sticking out of the upper jaw.

"So, we're in the right place," Sophie whispered, "but please, get rid of that head."

She picked up the shovel and psyched herself up again. "Don't give up, Sophie, you're almost there, don't give up, just dig. They're only bones… They're only bones, they can't hurt you." She continued to dig frantically, even as the skulls and bones flew all around her.

"Yes!" she screamed when she saw a piece of canvas sticking out of the dirt. She threw Jack the shovel and began tugging on the cloth. Using her hands, she dug up the rest of the dirt until her backpack came loose. Smiling, she pulled it out using one of the shoulder straps and then remained on her knees for a while trying to catch her breath.

"And now, let's get out of here, fast!" Jack said.

They quickly shoveled the dirt, skulls, and bones back into the hole. With the backpack hanging over Sophie's shoulder, they ran as fast as they could back along the same route. They were laughing uncontrollably, mostly from anxiety. They leaped into the boat, gasping for air.

"Hurry up, loosen the line!" Jack said as he inserted the key in the ignition and turned. "What are we going to say to the skipper when we get back? He won't be happy!"

"We'll make something up. What matters is that I've got my backpack back!" Sophie threw her hands in the air in delight.

"Too-da-loo Poveglia!" she shouted, as Jack opened the throttle. "One thing's for sure," Sophie screamed above the roar of the engines. "The next time we have to go to a haunted island, it's Tom and Lisa's turn!"

Jack threw the door open and they tumbled into the suite roaring with laughter.

"Did you see the skipper's face?" Sophie cried. "I didn't understand a word he said, but he was nearly foaming at the mouth!"

"I think he called us spoiled rich kids," said Jack, who secretly relished being called that for once in his life.

Sophie laughed hysterically. "We're lucky he waited for us on the quay and didn't call the police. I think he was afraid he might lose his job at the hotel. He should never have left us alone with the boat, of course."

She walked to the bathroom and scrubbed her hands thoroughly. "You should wash your hands, too! And bring the backpack with you."

Jack followed her into the bathroom carrying the backpack. "It's almost crumbling to pieces. Look, the material is rotting. I wonder if everything's still in there." He brushed the dirt off the backpack above the sink and then handed it to Sophie.

For a split second she saw her backpack buried again under the ground amongst all the bones. Startled, she let it fall to the ground.

"Gross," she said, "That's not sand, that's corpse dust!"

She picked up the backpack again between her thumb and finger and wiped it clean with a hotel washcloth. She nervously opened it up and peered inside. "I wonder how environment-unfriendly the plastic coating on the inside is, because it's still completely intact. That can't be good!"

One by one she carefully removed each item from her bag. "My geography book..." Sophie had to laugh when she put the heavily thumbed-through book down next to the sink. "Look, the little printer... and the boxes of pills... empty."

She reached into her bag again. Empty. "Where's my phone?" she cried in desperation. She anxiously turned the backpack upside down and shook it. With a soft thud a thin black piece of plastic fell onto the floor. She shook her bag frantically. "Jack! Where is my phone?"

Jack shook his head in surprise. "How should I know?"

"And what's that?" Sophie picked the black piece of plastic up off the floor and held it in front of her face. "There's a hole in the middle you can look through! But what on earth is it?" She bent the piece of plastic slightly, but stopped when she realized she might break it."

"Do you think this is why Leonardo told us it was important we recover the backpack?"

Jack put his hand next to the square piece of plastic. "It's about five inches long. Let me see." He took the piece of plastic from Sophie's hand and looked at it closely. "It doesn't weigh a thing!" he said as he studied it.

"What does that say?" said Sophie, taking it from Jack's hand again and turning it over. There was something written on a dirty white sticker on the back, but it was difficult to read. Sophie went to the desk by the window and turned on the reading lamp. Using the light, they both tried to figure out what it said.

"I think it's in English," said Sophie.

Jack nodded. "I think so, too."

"I think it says…" Sophie stammered, "I think it says 'Secret Scouts'…"

Monday, June 30th, late afternoon

Lisa was lying on her sister's bed with her legs up against the wall. "Wow!" she said upside down. "That's such a cool story. And how awesome is that – racing across the water in a speedboat! And then that island, oh man, Jack! Super cool! Did you really have a skull in your hands?"

Jack sat on the bed with his back against the wall, just like Tom. He shrugged his shoulders casually as if what he had done was the most normal thing in the world, but his smile was full of pride.

Lisa turned over and sat restlessly on the edge of the bed. "Guys," she said, "we've had two really cool weeks!"

Sophie spun around in her chair and nodded. "That's for sure. And how cool is it that we got to hang out with Leonardo? That we actually met him twice!" Sophie winked at her sister. "Mona!" she added. "How bizarre is that?" Sophie shook her head laughing as she spoke to her sister.

"I'm curious what our next adventure will be," Lisa said. "We're going to use that planetarium again, right?" She looked inquiringly at the others.

"Come on Lisa, it's never enough for you, is it?" Sophie said. "Take it easy. We've just been to Renaissance Florence twice, and Jack and I are just back from Venice! We shouldn't be too reckless with that thing."

Tom was lost in his own thoughts. "Did you guys see the

ermine just now?" he asked. "When we walked past, Prattle was standing at the window with the creature in her arms acting as if nothing had happened."

"I'm glad the ermine can't talk like that eagle in Florence," Lisa laughed. She threw her sister a look. "Too bad about your phone, that really sucks," she said casually. "And that weird piece of plastic, what do you think it is?"

"It looks like it belongs to another device," Jack said.

Sophie shrugged her shoulders as if to disagree. "I don't know, I don't know what it is, but seriously..." she looked intently at her sister. "It totally sucks that my phone is really gone."

"Here," Lisa tossed her sister her phone, "It's my fault you lost your phone. Keep it, I'll be getting one from Mom and Dad next year."

Sophie plucked the cellphone out of the air with one hand. She gave her sister a look of gratitude. "Share it?" asked Sophie. "We can both use it."

Lisa dismissed her offer nonchalantly. "Don't worry about it, I'll let you know if I ever need it. I'm more interested in finding out what that is?" She pointed to the square piece of plastic lying on the desk.

"Me too," Sophie muttered. "Me too. And by the way," she said, a little nervously, "that book! Our book! We're not going to give it away, right?"

Jack looked at her, confused. In his head he had already deposited the money into his bank account. "Why not?" he asked. "Thirty-one million... we'll be stinking rich!"

"Sure," Lisa nodded, "but then everyone will know everything, including about the planetarium and time travel. If we sell it, we'll never get to travel through time again. There's no way they'll ever let us use the planetarium."

Sophie shook her head. "I agree with Lisa. We can sell the book whenever we want, if we want to."

"I agree," Tom said. "What would we do with all that money anyway? We probably wouldn't even be able to touch it until we're eighteen… and I think all of this is just so awesome!"

Jack nodded his head. The prospect of buying a scooter didn't really excite him anymore. Calcio, on the other hand, was something he'd remember for the rest of his life. "Yeah!" said Jack. "Deal! We'll keep the book a secret for the time being while we explore the future!" He stood up and walked to the middle of the room where he held out his right hand. "Let's vote. I'm for time travel and against selling the book."

Sophie stood up and laid her hand on top of his. "Me too!"

Tom and Lisa followed suit. They stood in a circle for a few seconds with their hands stacked on top of each other.

Lisa had a huge smile on her face. "I'm game for anything, but for our next trip I want to go somewhere else…"

Three months later

Monday, October 6th, afternoon

Sophie raced up to her room.

"Wait up," Lisa yelled. "Tell me!"

Sophie sat down at her desk. "I figured it out!" she screamed.

"You figured what out?" asked Lisa, who was standing behind her now, gasping for breath.

Sophie shook her head to tell Lisa she was too busy to answer her. She began typing furiously on her laptop.

"We couldn't figure out what that thing was, could we? Do you remember, Lisa?" Sophie opened a drawer and took out the piece of black plastic she had found in her backpack.

"Today there was this guy at school who had a computer book with a picture of this exact same thing in it," Sophie said as the search results flashed up on the screen. "Look! Is this it?" she suddenly asked, pointing at the screen.

Lisa leaned in closer. "Yes! That's it!" she cried out. "Exactly the same!" She squinted her eyes. "But what is it?"

Sophie read the Wikipedia page out loud. "A floppy disk is a storage medium for computer software."

"A floppy disk?" Lisa said perplexed. "I think I've heard of that before. A storage medium? What's that supposed to mean?"

Sophie continued reading. "A storage medium..." Her eyes darted across the screen. "A storage medium... a floppy disk is just some kind of USB stick, something you can store data on, only from like... way back. It says they were used up until the 1990s!"

"I bet there's a message on that floppy disk!" Lisa said excitedly.

"We need a computer with a floppy drive," said Sophie. "A really old computer, and I think I know where we can find one." She transferred the information from her laptop onto her telephone and, feeling full of confidence, got up to go. "You coming? We're off to the library. We can pick up Jack and Tom on our way."

Jack and Tom were amazed by what the girls told them and immediately went with them to the library. They walked down through the town as fast as they could, passing terraces filled with people enjoying the autumn sun.

"Now what?" Jack asked, out of breath, as they entered the building.

"Over there," Sophie pointed to a green door down a long corridor. "There are really old computers in the room behind that door. I remember seeing them when I was in there once."

"What were you doing in there?" Jacked asked surprised.

"Nothing," Sophie shrugged her shoulders. "The door happened to be open one time I was here, that's all. And I took a peep. I was just... curious."

"You know what she's like," Lisa joked.

They walked down the corridor as inconspicuously as possible. Every now and then they stopped and pretended to flip through a few books. They slowly made their way to the door and, when they were convinced no one was looking, quickly sneaked into the room.

"Ugh," said Sophie, "it still smells really stuffy in here."

"I don't think anyone ever uses this room." Jack looked around and ran his fingers over the old computer screens.

"Yuck!" he said, as he flicked a ball of dust off his hand.

"That one, up there," said Sophie. She showed them the picture on her phone.

Jack climbed up the shelving unit and carefully lifted the beige computer off the shelf.

"Hand it to me," said Tom, who took the machine and set it down on the ground in the corner. He unraveled the cord and plugged it in.

"What about this? I think this is part of it as well," Jack said, holding an oblong box with a slot in it.

"Great, I think that's where the floppy disk goes!" Sophie said excitedly. "Hand it down, I'll see if it works." She sat on the ground next to the computer, connected the thick gray cord to the oblong box, and turned the machine on. It began to rattle.

"Hmm," Sophie sighed. "Does that sound normal to you? It's taking forever to boot!" She held the floppy disk impatiently next to the narrow slot.

Lisa paced restlessly back and forth. "What do you think we'll find on it?" she asked. "I bet it's a message from Leonardo. Maybe something about the planetarium... or about that book... or the telephone."

Peep peeeeeeep! The computer finally burst into life.

"Wow," said Sophie. "It actually works." She quickly slid the disk into the opening. The computer immediately began to rattle loudly. "Oh no, not this again," Sophie scowled, crossing her arms in frustration.

Nervous but excited, the others stood behind her joking about the computer's speed.

"Sshh," said Sophie when the screen began to flicker. "Something's about to happen."

Jack, Tom, and Lisa dropped to their knees and sat next to

Sophie. Slowly but surely, the computer began to play a video.

"That's Leonardo!" Tom yelled when a man appeared on the screen.

"Hello my friends!" he began. "As you can see, I did it!"

"We can understand him," Sophie said. "I can hear my phone."

Leonardo was standing in a dark room with what looked like two desks in the background. A strange man with a straggly beard and an old-fashioned haircut was standing next to him. The unknown man had a huge grin on his face. He held Sophie's telephone in the air so they could hear the translation.

"However, I don't want to talk about me right now," said Leonardo. "I met someone who really wants to meet you, too."

The man moved closer to Leonardo and seemed to be staring at them through the screen. He began talking enthusiastically. "You must be the Secret Scouts Leonardo told me about! You crazy guys!" He shouted into the camera. "You have to come visit me, really! Come as quickly as you can! Come to one, one, one, six, one…!"

The door behind Tom flew open. "What are you doing in here?" asked a grumpy-looking library assistant.

Sophie quickly turned off the computer and pulled the floppy disk out of the slot. She slid it into her pocket and stood up.

"Nothing," the four of them said in unison. They all looked at each other and then slipped by the man at the door and took off running.

Thank you

We are grateful to and extremely happy with our enthusiastic test readers from U.S. schools:

Sierra Elementary School, Rocklin, CA
Brett Shirhall, Cynthia Brown
Scott, Liam, Lauren, Alex, Jack, Kai, Sydney, Aidan, Natalie, Sophia, Jaret, Alyssa, Ana, Allie, Anna, Callie, Annie, Ashley, Adam, Yousef, Brooke, Brad, Daisy, Syrus, Wade, Andrew, Mona, Riley and Joey

British International School of New York, New York, NY
Shehla Gouse
Hailey, Taya, Ava, Lindsay, Tess, Jason, Grace, Emi and Sophie

Huntington Seacliff Elementary School, Huntington Beach, CA
Monique Huibregtse, Michelle Twogood
Isabel, Jack and Lauren

Ainsworth Elementary School, Portland, OR
Diane Goff
Lise, Jack, Ella, Henry, Annika, Indi, and Trotter

Salem Middle School, Apex, NC
Michael Manholt and his sixth grade students

More than 50 people and companies put a lot of time and energy into creating the most awesome book trailer in the world. We are honored to have had the opportunity to work with these extremely talented people.

Production company - JUNGLE (junglecreate.com) / Executive producers - Dennis Kind and Wendel Kind / Producer - Dennis Arnoldus & Ronald Bavelaar / Director - Erik Eijgenstein / Director of Photography - Goof de Koning / Focus Puller - Tom Duiker / 2nd ass. & drone operator - Mark Modder / Editor - Marc Mookhoek / Sound Design - Morrison Bramervaer & Christoph Mühl / 'Sophie' - Isabel van de Meent / 'Lisa' - Jolijn Coerts / 'Jack' - Olivier Guffens / 'Tom' - Sebastiaan de Boer / 'Leonardo da Vinci' - Mark van Eeuwen / Gaffer - Glenn Bruintjes / Best Boy - Aaron Homma / Light ass. - Manouk Moreau & Ruben Soekhan / Sound - René Wolf / Photography - Shannon Cornelis & Gail Meijer / Set Dressing - Eva van de Ven & Hugo Braat / Set Dressing ass. - Romee Nederhand & Annick Nieuwenhuis / Styling - Christina Isadora Sofia & Elle Raangs / Hair & Make-up - Madelon Prinsen / Acting coach - Laurie Reijs / VFX producer - Stefan Beekhuijzen / VFX artist - Matthijs Slijkhuis & René Berendsen & Danny Torrelli / VFX Art Director - Jesse Hovestreijdt / Colorist - Fernando Rodrigues / DI Producer - Fleur Stikkelorum / Crane Operator - Ruben Ordeman / Equestrian - Debbie & Wendy van Weert / Horse - Deux / Voice over studio - Jordy Stokvis / Male voice over - Andrew Steingold / Production - Vicky Simons & Robert Bulthuis & Esther de Jong.

And special thanks to Tim Koldenhof Producties (Casting), Simon John & International School Hilversum (Casting), Teylers Museum (Filming location), Het Licht (Lighting), Vintage, Art & Design (Furniture), Collezione Apocrifa da Vinci (Codex), Remco Mastwijk (MD Filmmore), and Hans Jonker (Support).

Watch the official

Secret Scouts book trailer

www.SecretScouts.com

Credits

ISBN: 9789082875607 (Hardcover)
ISBN: 9789082875614 (ePub)

JUV001010
JUV016100
JUV064000
JUV037000

Translated by: John Weich
Edited by: Danny Guinan
Cover design: Dennis Kind and Wendel Kind and Teo van Gerwen
Design Logo Secret Scouts: Smel, www.smel.net
Cover photo: Shannon Cornelis
Layout: Coco Bookmedia
Secretscouts.com: Remco Borsato

www.secretscouts.com
www.facebook.com/secretscouts
www.instagram.com/secretscoutsofficial
www.twitter.com/secretscouts

© 2018 Dennis Kind and Wendel Kind
Published by Mokum Media, The Netherlands

Part 2: in stores fall 2019

Secret Scouts and The Missing President

After narrowly surviving their adventure with Leonardo da Vinci, Tom, Lisa, Sophie and Jack receive a mysterious message from a world-famous genius. Spurred on by his enthusiasm, they decide to visit him in his garage in 1976, where he tells them about 2217, a machine from the future.

When they return to their own time they are shocked to learn that the past has changed. President Obama has been completely erased from history! In a frantic search for answers they find a mind-blowing clue in a five-hundred-year-old painting in Amsterdam's Rijksmuseum!

Determined to set history straight and find the president, the friends travel to the German city of Aachen in the 16th century, where they are witness to the event of the decade: the coronation of Charles V. Making their way through the crowded city they experience at first hand how danger can lurk around every corner.

Finding the young Obama in the Middle Ages is one thing, getting out alive is another thing altogether. Not to mention their search for the 2217 that compels them to fly a hot air balloon all by themselves to the dangerous islands off the coast of California known as 'The Devil's Teeth'.